# Stuff About Things

## Bill McCormick

Azoth Khem Publishing
April 2023
Huntsville, AL

# Azoth Khem Publishing

29931 Copperpenny Drive NW
Harvest, Alabama 35749
Tel: (256) 221-5498
www.azothkhem.com



ISBN: 978-1-952880-10-0



For permission queries, contact Azoth Khem Publishing:
Nancy Chandler
AzothKhemPublishing@gmail.com

Printed in the United States of America

To Don Webb, the madman
who unleashed me on an unsuspecting world.

# Table of Contents

# Prelude

Everything must begin. The rejection letter below started my career as a science fiction writer. My story, Vorbliss, was, and is, a bit raunchy. Fortunately for me, I had another story waiting. That one got accepted, people liked it, and here we are.

The rejection letter is from **Don Webb** of **Bewildering Stories Magazine**. The magazine is definitely worth a Google search if you're a sci-fi fan.

*Hello, Bill,*

*Thank you for "Vorbliss"… Judas Priest. Is that ever funny! I've forwarded it to our Coordinating Editor and urged him to read it himself.*

*You're absolutely right about the profanity on all counts. In fact, the "[WORD SUBSTITUTION]" inserts in the later "recordings" bring to mind the famous "[expletive deleted]" that salt-and-pepper their way through the transcripts of the Nixon tapes.*

*There is only a leeetle problem. Despite my title, I'm not the ultimate arbiter. Our publisher is. And if we accepted "Vorbliss" with its expletives, he would sure as shootin' show up on my doorstep with a pot of bubbling tar in one hand and a bale of freshly-plucked feathers in the other.*

*And if he had a third hand, he'd be carrying a rail on which to ride me out of town.*

*I love the part about Sister Agnes, her "undulating casaba melons," and her leading a telepathic revolution. Hot damn, but that's good... See? Now you've got me doing it...*

*As I think our guidelines say, you can blaspheme all you want, but the basic bodily functions represented by the f- and s-words are taboo. Now, if we were in Quebec, the taboos would be exactly reversed. Maybe there's a science fiction webzine in Montreal...*

*In short, I need to have a morning in which to respect myself or have a hangover, and I'm not sure which. Can you please send us something else?*

*Don*

The story that did get published almost came out on September 11, 2011. Brighter minds intervened; instead, it came out in Bewildering Stories Magazine on November 8, 2011. Considering there is a vaguely Middle Eastern terrorist at the heart of the story, I thought that was pretty gutsy. It was, after all, a pretty big anniversary in America.

## And the Beat Goes Phut

Sparks swung his beater Ford Air-Tempo over the top of the banquet hall and let the parking beam guide him into the employees' lot near the rear door. He yanked out his cargo roller and began pulling his gear through the door. He watched the kitchen staff gamely laid out a rubber chicken and pseudo-potatoes in neatly arrayed silver chafing dishes and figured he was in for another night of clichés. He was proved right two hours after dropping the first "dinner music" track.

"All the kitties in the house, lemme hear you, MEE-OWWW!"

All these burb bitches are dumb as advertised, Sparks thought as he looked around the room and tried again. "All the kitties in the house, lemme hear you, MEE-OWWW!"

This time, he made a cat scratching pantomime with his hands. Slowly, the dim bulbs limmed and began making mewling noises. It was a start. He figured the third time would be the charm.

"C'mon, all you kitties in the house, lemme HEAR YOU MEEEEE-OWWWWWWWWW!"

Now, every woman in the room was full-on feral. He got the groove rolling beneath the sound of middle-aged women and their patently un-hip daughters trying to sound like cats. He decided to amp up the boys and get this party started.

"All the dogs in the house, lemme hear you HOWWWLLLL."

That did it. Barks, howls, and strange growling noises permeated the room as George Clinton's "Atomic Dog" blasted forth from the speakers. Sparks kept his fist-pumping because that's what jocks are supposed to do and soon slipped into Kool and the Gang's *"Celebrate."*

Jocks called those songs Vampire Tracks. Music that would not die. He was trying to figure out how long they'd been getting play at lame parties like this and stopped when he passed the century mark.

He granted that gigs like this would never get him the cover of DJ Times, but they paid the bills very well. Three or four nights a week, and he hadn't had a day gig in years. He used his Sunday nights at Otto's to score hot babes and play the good stuff. But, since most big clubs were automated, Otto's paid in beer, not money, so he worked the rest of the week under his real name, and no one was the wiser.

The rental hall closed two hours later, and it was time to go home. He wrapped up his vid screens and packed his jock box back onto its roller. He loaded them all into the back of his Ford and returned to collect his check. There, he was met by a very stern-looking Mrs. Alma Wilmington — of the West Hampton Wilmingtons,', thank you very much — and her mousy husband, who had a name that Sparks had long since forgotten.

"Mr. Rathburger" — that was Sparks' real name, and she made it sound like the vilest profanity — "we never planned on this sort of debauchery at one of our soirées. People were bumping into each other in a most provocative manner."

Sparks smiled to himself. He'd run into this a hundred times before and, sadly, would again.

"Well, Mrs. Wilmington," he began smoothly, "the open bar ended at ten, and you'd paid me to spin until midnight. Look at it this way: you got your full money's worth out of me, and your guests had a very good time. In fact, I bet many will speak glowingly about this night for a long time to come."

"He's right, lambykins," interjected the mouse, "even I shook a boogie."

Yep, that particular visual would haunt Sparks' dreams for a while.

Seemingly mollified, Mrs. Wilmington handed Sparks his check and walked away.

"You did an exemplary job, young man," continued the mouse, "and I, for one, wish you to know that everyone did indeed have a wonderful time. Very much unlike the

Missus' previous soirées." With that, he slipped Sparks a C-note and returned to his wife.

Sparks could only shake his head and smile. It was the same every time. He walked out to his old Ford, set the height at 15 feet, and lifted off.

He cruised the commuter lane down old I-90, past the O'Hare spaceport, so he could catch a couple of the evening launches as he passed by. He was about a mile north of the spaceport when he saw the wreck. It was a bad one.

Flames were coming out of the car's rear, and it was surrounded by emergency vehicles. It'd been decades since anyone had wrecked a car. Even if you were stone drunk, someone could pile you in, punch "home" in the GPS, and the vehicle would take you there.

Many people didn't even bother learning to drive anymore. They just bought the car, plugged in their usual destinations, and left the driving to the onboard robots.

Hell, thought Sparks, the whole car's pretty much a robot.

Even so, Sparks was a bit of an iconoclast and had actually taken the drivers-ed course and passed it. He liked the feel of driving and enjoyed being in control of his fate. He moved up to the 40-foot lane and eased to the left to get past the lookie-loos. He hadn't gone another mile when he saw the second accident.

It was as bad as the first. Maybe even worse since it looked like there were body bags on the side of the road. He was stunned. He didn't know that two accidents could happen on the same stretch of road on the same night. Cars just had too many safeguards.

He decided to flip on the autopilot to find the news on the radio.

"Pull up to my bumper, baby..." crooned the autopilot. Until now, his autopilot had merely said "engaged" or "disengaging"; this was a new and mildly unwelcome development. He also quickly realized that the autopilot wasn't autopiloting.

He took control of the car and headed towards Sully's. The booze was cheap, the bartender didn't give a damn, and vids were always turned to the news.

By the time he got there, he'd passed another four wrecks, two involving multiple vehicles. He knew there was something horribly amiss in the universe but couldn't for the life of him fathom what it might be.

He landed, locked his car, and walked into Sully's just as the announcer was helpfully explaining what was going on.

"Every robot worldwide is either shutting down or singing ancient pop music. Many are doing both. A terrorist group calling themselves The Disciples of Queen Mustapha has claimed responsibility for the carnage."

The announcer continued, but Sparks wasn't paying attention anymore. Someone, somehow, had finally done it. There'd been threats before, but no one took them seriously. After all, who would want a world without robotics? They handled pretty much everything these days.

The ever-surly bartender walked over, and Sparks ordered a shot and a beer. While waiting for his drink, a doe-eyed young man about his age sat beside him.

"Pretty crazy, ain't it?" asked the stranger.

"Got that right," Sparks agreed, "I wonder how they did it?"

He was more than a little surprised to get an answer.

"Easy, really. We just uploaded the virus into one of the server satellites and waited. A couple of orbits later, every robot on the planet was infected. Then the techno-Armageddon began."

"We?" stammered Sparks, almost spilling his beer, "You're one of the terrorists?"

"Ibrahim," replied the doe-eyed stranger sweetly, nodding to Sparks.

Sparks took a long pull off his beer and swallowed his shot in one gulp. He set the empty glass in the rail to get another, taking a long look at the stranger. Except for his amiable admission of global terrorism, he looked perfectly normal. Neat clothes, nothing flashy, simple haircut, the usual. No wild-eyed glare or evil aura about him at all. Sparks' first guess would have been an insurance salesman.

"People have known for a long time," Ibrahim continued, "that the human race has ceased creating or doing. Art, such as it is, has become passive and abstract. Music, save for the underground that spawned the likes of us, has become audio oatmeal. Books, vids, and the rest have all become very distant. So remote that there are entire shows where the characters really have no names, just rudimentary designations."

Sparks knew what he meant. It was one of the reasons he seldom turned on his home vid. But sympathy was not forgiveness. Sparks had seen people die. "I'm calling the cops."

"No, you're not," stated Ibrahim calmly. "Robots distribute all emergency services. They'll never know about it unless someone happens upon a scene."

That explained the rescue crews on the highways. They were spaced about two miles apart "just in case" in all urban areas. Usually considered an extravagant waste, he bet people were damn glad for that bit of excess now.

Sparks mulled over his situation for a bit and then asked the obvious. "Okay, why tell me?"

"Oh, we agreed that we would each tell one random stranger once it began," he stated blithely, "there's nothing anyone can do to stop it now, and our escape plans have been laid for over a year. By tomorrow, we'll be gone, and the world will face a new way of life."

"Millions will die tonight." Sparks hoped he'd get through to the guy and, somehow, stop everything.

"Yeah," replied Ibrahim, "that was the one fact that held us back. We're not psychopaths, um..."

"Sparks."

"We're not psychopaths, Sparks. We just wanted to heal humanity."

"Heal?!?!" Sparks spat. "Heal? How the hell are you healing humanity when you're the cause of millions of deaths?"

"Not yours," reminded Ibrahim before he continued. "Think of it like this: when a person gets burned, they cut off the dead flesh so the rest can heal. That's what we've done tonight. We've cut off the dead flesh. All those people who couldn't survive without robots will simply no longer survive. The rest, like you, will."

Sparks glanced up at the vid just in time to see a No/Sou Space Liner go spiraling into Lake Michigan. All interplanetary pilots had been phased out years ago as a cost-cutting move. The same held true for many infrastructure-related jobs. The whole fabric of what humanity had become was being unwound. They were getting a do-over, whether they wanted one or not.

Not knowing what to do next, Sparks sat with Ibrahim and watched the death toll rise. He noted that Ibrahim seemed disquieted but made no move to stop the devastation.

"You've made your point," said Sparks after a few minutes, "you can stop this."

"No," he sighed, "I can't. Nor can any of the rest of us. The virus was like an old-style 'set it and forget it' bomb. Once it went off, it was out of our control."

"Why would you do this? I mean, seriously, you sat down and decided to play God. Hell, not even God. At least God supposedly gave man free will. You just made the choice for everyone."

Sparks waited while Ibrahim sipped his bourbon and formed an answer. "My mother" — he opened with a non sequitur — "will be coming home from Bingo about now. She's never learned to drive. She saw no need and claimed it was too hard and not worth the effort. She never wanted me to learn, either. Just relax and enjoy life, she'd say. I thought of her when I saw you land."

He paused, took another sip, and continued, "When we came to this decision, we knew the consequences. It was decided that each of us had to have a personal stake in the outcome, or it would mean nothing. It sounded right at the time."

Sparks had had some beer-fueled philosophy discussions in his day and speculated how much alcohol it took to make this sound logical.

"So you killed your families?" Sparks wondered aloud. "That was your justification for all this? That makes it all right?"

"No," Ibrahim went on, "that was not all. Some will lose family tonight, to be sure, but that was far from all of it. We had to ensure that humanity would never again take this path. We had to close the door utterly. For that to happen, we had to set up some sort of safeguard, some oversight that humans would never see or feel. An oversight that would last millennia if need be."

Sparks felt his jaw drop. "You're going to upload your minds into robots. I've heard rumors about that, but I thought the tech was decades away."

Ibrahim nodded, "Yeah, we can do that now. We've been able to for years. It was just the government, my former employer, taking it slow and getting people used to it.

"But we saw the rest when we ran the simulations. We saw humanity die and become a shadow of itself in the cybercosm. We ran the projections over and over to be sure there was no mistake. There wasn't.

"Frederick Pohl's ultimate dream was going to be a nightmare. Anything a mind could conceive would become real to it and it alone. Without needing to strive for anything, humankind would stagnate and eventually die. All that had gone before would vanish over time. Simply put, the death you see tonight will prevent the death of the human race. It was a sacrifice that needed to be made."

"But, isn't uploading your mind supposed to be fatal to your body?" asked Sparks. "That's what they said on a docu-vid a few months ago."

Ibrahim nodded and ordered another drink.

Sparks just sat and tried to absorb it all. There was something very wrong with what Ibrahim and his partners had done, but with no way to stop it, all Sparks could do was wonder if any good would come out of it.

The two men sat for another hour, silently sipping their drinks and watching the horrors unfold on the vid. Every update brought news of liners crashing, trains running amok, building security systems randomly injuring people, and worse.

Somehow, despite all he knew, Sparks was disconnected from the calamity. It was too much for one mind, the massacre too great. Death upon fiery death brought only numbness.

Somewhere in his wool-gathering, Sparks remembered the lyrics to one of the Vampire Tracks he'd played earlier tonight. Ibrahim, Ibrahim, Allah, Allah, Allah will pray for you, sang the glorious voice in his mind.

He turned to Ibrahim. "It's a pity they forgot the possessive 's' in your group's name."

Ibrahim put down his drink, smiled wanly, and walked out of the bar into the anti-techno new groove he'd helped create, leaving Sparks to his drinks, thoughts, and future.

This is the first story I published in tangible media. In this case, a paperback called ***Slashing through the Snow: A Christmas Horror Anthology***. Think of it as the holiday story you didn't know you needed.

# Helping The Elves

This was his favorite time of the year. The holly was hung by the chimney and all over the place, with a care bordering on obsessive. Seriously, they measured each strand so it would esthetically highlight the other strands. The sleigh bells were polished to a pristine gleam. His reflection was bent and distorted as he held one to the light, which always made him happy. Each tree throughout the facility was decorated in accordance with the many rites and rituals the world had proclaimed to be proper for the holiday. There was even a Cagenar, resplendent with its steaming pile of shit. Nothing quite like a good holiday defecation to get you in the mood. Each tradition right, yet each is wrong. The bunting was festooned around each room, and lists, on paper no less, were being pored over by diligent, yet happy, sycophants. The rules they followed were millennia old and never changed.

A child was either naughty or nice. If there was any doubt, nice was the default option, at least for the past couple of centuries. Times change. Not that it bothered him. His job, his joy, was eternal.

Dasher, Dancer, Prancer, and Vixen played hoof-hockey with Donder, Cupid, Comet, and Blitzen. He had five snowflakes riding on Dasher's team. Even down six to three,

Dasher was too resourceful, and others would say too brutal, to lose. Fuck Rudolph. He'd never existed and never would. Nevertheless, he felt it was a good bet.

This was the North Pole. Survival and brutal were interchangeable terms.

And he, like Dasher, had survived.

Druids, Christians, Jews for Jesus, neo-Pagans - what the fuck were they anyway? –all came and went before him. Each, in their own way, honored Christmas. Each, in their own way, perverted it.

Not perverted like midget porn in a nunnery, but perverted, nonetheless.

Speaking of which, and we were even it bothers you, there used to be a nunnery in Calais where the nuns used midget jesters for sexual gratification. Since they were Catholic, it was okay. They killed all the Gnostics in the village. Go figure.

Joyeux Noel!

None of that mattered to him, of course. Naughty or nice. That's all he cared about. Those rules transcended transient things like religion.

As was their wont, the elves had laden the snack table with sweets and kinds of milk. But they weren't evil, far from it. They knew he would be there and added sweet breads and jerkies. The goat heart, with garlic and cilantro, was to die for. As if he could do something as mundane as that.

He made sure to thank the elves before he filled his plate and went to check on his supplies. They needed recognition as much as any mortal beings.

Many historians attributed Santa Claus to the story of the Turkish priest, St. Nicholas. And, in fact, that was where his name came from. He'd never had a name before that. Santa had been his helper then. Nameless, formless, guileless. He was as goodhearted then as he is now. That had never changed. It was the world that had evolved.

Once, a bare millennia ago, he was the talk of every village and town. He would visit on the winter solstice. Misbehaving children were noted, found, and disposed of. He would snag the little bastards from their beds, wake them so they knew fear, and then toss them into his sack. His sack, like Santa's, could hold infinite amounts of matter. The awful ones he ate. He found the nastier they were, the tastier they were. The evil children of royalty were the best of all. Cinnamon and sugary, full of darkly spoken lies, they were a delicacy he savored. Each succulent morsel was lingered over until fully ingested. Not a sensation was ignored from touching his tongue, sliding through his throat, dropping into his gullet.

Once, and the mere memory made him quiver and smile – like a virgin spreading her legs for the first time, he'd absconded with the triplet daughters of an evil queen. They were delightfully deviant. They used to force servants to do unspeakable things to each other or face ritual beheadings. They were so spiritually ruined their existence was a shining beacon to him. It cut through the miasma of charity and good cheer to guide him.

As soon as he had them, he didn't kill them, eat them while killing them, torture them into kindness, or anything else typically part of his routine. Instead, he made them his mortal assistants. Despite the myths, he couldn't grant them anything but death. And he denied them that for a while.

Each year, he would return from his world tour to give them the vilest of the vile and let them have their way with them. Oh, Glorious Gods, the blissfully twisted tortures those young ladies could devise. They made Cardinal Richelieu look like a rank amateur.

Things that could be heated - tongs, picks, straps, genitals - were used in a dizzying array of depravity. Until they hit thirty. Then, porculent in their debauchery, he had the elves give them individual rooms. They, thrilled at the freedom, were ecstatic. Then, with the elves keeping the others occupied, he ate them, one by one, keeping each alive as long as he could until they were gone.

The taste lingered still.

He longed for their successors. But such evil was, sadly, rare.

And, of course, there were the new rules. Children from damaged homes or horror-filled lives were off-limits. He'd agreed to the rules. He was a demon, not a monster.

Children needed a chance to choose to do good. He needed the ones who wanted to do evil. If they had no choice in the matter, they were useless to him. They were the same as lite beer or soy milk—pathetic imitations.

Still, he knew there would be plenty of souls for him. Not every girl and boy aspired to sainthood. Not everyone wanted to hold sock drives for the homeless. No, some wanted to rule over everything. To lord over those they deemed useless. To rend asunder what good hath wrought in the name of their self-aggrandizement.

Sometimes, a merely bad kid would end up on his list. Those he would toss back, like fish under the size limit. He had no use for snacks. He needed meals. The elves knew that and did their best to keep him sated.

He nibbled on pigeon kidneys and a rind of Limburger cheese while considering his lot in the universe.

Each year, thanks to him, there was a little less evil in the world. He could hear the screams of its pending demise as it lashed out at the unknown and the light. What some called terrorism, he called death throes. Thus, each year, the scales of life tilted, in increments too small to measure, but nevertheless there, more and more towards justice. Each year, Santa would thank him for all his good work. And, each year, he would smile the smile of the pure. For he was pure in his own way.

Few are the beings who enjoy their work as much as he.

He sat by the fire to finish his plate of sweetbreads and wash them down with the mead left just for him.

Santa walked over and handed him the naughty list, thinner this year than last but still a hefty tome. He grinned in anticipation.

Some of the merely bad had become genuinely evil. His taste buds shuddered in joyful expectation. His digestion would, again, be mollified.

He polished his hooves, straightened his beard, checked his fangs for debris in a mirror, and headed towards the sleigh, singing as he went.

Krampus knows when you've been sleeping.

Krampus knows when you're awake.

Krampus knows if you've been bad or good.

So you'd better be evil, for Krampus' sake.

Right after Donald Trump was elected president, **Horrified Press** called for fictional works that looked at what a Trumpian future could look like. Bleak was a common theme. **Trumpocalypse** was released in April of 2017 in England and shortly after that in the U.S.

## The Good Lord Shall Provide

Grandma sat down at the table and sniffed the stew plopped in an ugly purple urn. She smiled and looked over toward her niece.

"Damn, Gloria, shit smells good. Who we got?"

"Some leftover Emma. But Elroy was able to spice it differently, and he found some noodles, too."

Grandma clapped her hands in glee.

"Oh, God, real noodles and fresh meat! God does provide, Gloria, you hear me, girl, and hear me well, God does provide!"

Just then, a ball of roiling energy wrapped in ripped denim and a Deadpool T-shirt came bounding into the room on scruffy bare feet.

"GAMMA GAMMA GAMMA! Look what I found!"

The boy, all of six years old, had most of his teeth and dancing eyes. In his hand, he held a bag of donuts. And not just any donuts. No, he held a bag of magic. He had a bag of Dunkin' donuts, the kind you could only buy in the uptown enclave where the rich folks live.

Grandma looked terrified.

"Skeeter, what have you done? Them folks have the death penalty up there. They got them cameras seeing everything. They gonna come down here, grab your little ass, and kill you. Hell, for that bag, they may make you the Saturday Night Special."

Skeeter just stood there shaking his little head.

"No, Gamma, I didn't steal them. You told me never to steal."

That was true. Skeeter knew the Ten Commandments were not the Six Suggestions, and she drilled that truth into every tiny brain she encountered. She read them the Good Book from the moment they were old enough to listen. She taught them the lessons that would hold them straight on life's crooked road.

"Boy, I also told you never to lie. If you didn't steal 'em, how'd you get 'em?"

Skeeter smiled.

"The nice man from Enclave Six, you know, the one who comes down to make sure everythin's all right and we all goin' to church ever' day and there's no deadbeats at the soup kitchen. Anyway, he done give 'em to me. Me and all the boys in the shower after church all got a bag each. He come in and made sure we washed ourselves real clean and said we did such a good job we got a prize."

Grandma was appalled but realized she hadn't had THAT talk with the boy. She decided to deal with it later. This prize was too good to waste on a lecture.

Skeeter sat down next to Elroy and said grace.

"God is good, God is great, thanks for all the grub on our plate."

The Emma stew was delicious, and everyone complimented Elroy on his cooking. He just smiled and nodded. Then again, that's about all he ever did. Elroy was a bit touched and had trouble with words. But he was a good provider. Grandma made sure he had the magazines he liked, and he made his own hootch in the basement. Of course, that was illegal, but the enclave cops rarely came to the hood. Not just this hood, any of them. They only came out when folks got uppity, and they had to shoot a few to keep things right.

That hadn't happened around here in almost three years.

After dinner, Elroy went and grabbed his birth gun. Like every male child, touched or not, he'd gotten a gun the day he was born. Unlike others, Elroy took good care of his and hoped to pass it on when his days were up, maybe to Skeeter.

Skeeter wasn't blood, of course. They'd just found him in a dumpster when he was a baby. Grandma snagged him because she figured they'd need another man in the house soon enough, so they may as well grow their own.

Gloria was a fine woman with good hips but seemed unlucky with men. None of them could get her knocked up. Lately, she'd stopped trying and just hung out with her friend Carol. That was okay with Grandma. The two of them were useless as tits on a bull in the kitchen, but they kept the house spotless and only dirtied one set of sheets.

Which they washed. So, Grandma kept her yap shut.

She made sure Elroy dressed warmly and wished him well. There were some new exiles from the enclave, and he hoped to snag one before they disappeared. They were the best eating when you could catch them. And Elroy was real good at catching exiles.

Last month, he'd got three. Enough for the whole block.

Pastor Johnson had been so thrilled he'd thrown a Bar-B-Q in the church parking lot.

His wife even made her famous coleslaw.

While Gloria was picking things up, Skeeter was reading his Bible homework and getting ready for his summer work camp. This would be his first year, and he was as excited as possible. If he did well at Trumptopia, he could be eligible to work for the enclave. Not in it, of course. They didn't let any of the subs like them breathe their air. But a job's a job, and Skeeter was getting old enough to earn his keep. She'd just have to make sure he knew what the difference between a caring adult and a pervert was.

Or maybe not.

Grandma knew some kids who brought home real money when their families turned a blind eye to these little things. Besides, it might be good for the boy. New experiences and all that. Plus, she had to admit, those donuts were damn good eating.

She pulled on her sweater, noted a couple of holes that needed knitting, and headed into the darkening night. She wanted to get to the Trumporium to pick up her smokes and lottery tickets. She'd check to see if the new girly magazines were in. Elroy liked the T-Rump Bootypocalypse ones. Still savoring the Emma stew and delicious noodles, she decided the boy certainly earned his little pleasures.

She walked in right at shift change. She was forced to stand behind the gate while the armed guards escorted the staff out, frisked them, and then ushered in the next employees. The guards let her in as soon as they were shackled to their workstations.

She smiled at them and began walking down the first aisle. The new Ivanna Ivanka opioids were in. The cherry-flavored heroin looked fun, but she didn't touch that stuff anymore. She'd let Gloria know, though. She and Carol sometimes took a hooch break and tried other stuff.

She found Elroy's magazine right next to the new Trumpian Bible, which was where it should be, and then headed down the second aisle past the sex toys and votive candles. She'd heard stories about a time when people came to places like this to buy food. That would be hella more convenient than how things were now, but she guessed there was a good reason it wasn't true anymore. Maybe never had been. All that fake news out there could be hard to sort out sometimes.

She was jolted from her reverie when she bumped into the pastor and his wife holding four giant dildos.

"Which one would you suggest?" asked Mrs. Johnson.

Grandma pointed at the massive, orange one.

"Can't go wrong with the Masta-Don."

Mrs. Johnson smiled, thanked her, put it in her cart, and returned the other three to the shelf.

The three of them walked casually through the rest of the store, occasionally pointing out something shiny and new. Grandma had to admit the Trumps sure kept the stock varied and interesting. Ever since they'd gotten rid of all those silly government rules, they'd quickly gotten rid of the silly government, too. Now, things ran much smoother. Everyone knew their place, and everything was kept in order.

They got to the counter, paid for their purchases with their personalized T-cards, and headed out into the early evening.

Mrs. Johnson kept peeking at her bag and smiling as they walked. Grandma knew the feeling. She'd had her own Masta-Don for about five years, and it never let her down. She'd thought about getting the upgrade, which contained the actual voice of St. Donald whispering his holy phrases like LOCK HER UP, BUILD THE WALL, and DRAIN THE SWAMP, but she could never quite justify the price.

They were just walking up to Grandma's house when a pickup truck she didn't recognize raced into her driveway. It was colored red, white, and blue, with a lovely rebel flag adorning the hood. She didn't think it belonged to the police, but one could never know.

A big Mexican got out of the driver's side, walked to the back, and pulled down the gate. Before she could panic, she saw Elroy get out on the passenger side and smile. She stared at the Mexican. There hadn't been any in this hood for years. Most had been sent back to Italy.

They'd had to do that when Mexico stopped taking them. Those nasty Mexicans even went so far as to station an army at St. Donald's glorious wall so no one could cross.

Like all good Americans, Grandma had made her pilgrimage to the holy wall when she was young. It was indeed an inspiration. But none of that explained what a Spic was doing in her driveway.

Suddenly, she saw Elroy toss two body bags over his shoulder. The Spic pulled two more out and followed him up the front steps. Elroy was grinning like a kid at Trumpmas. The pastor and his wife were agog. There was enough meat there for the whole block for a week.

The Spic came out, tipped his cowboy hat in their general direction, and laughed.

"Your boy sure do know how to hunt. He done got six right at the bridge outside the enclave. Caught them as they were trying to run back in. He said I could keep two if I'd help him haul 'em home."

Grandma couldn't place his accent at first and then smiled.

"You're from Texas, ain't you?"

"Yes, ma'am. Born and bred. I'm up here visiting and going to a wedding. My sister's marrying a store owner."

Grandma was impressed. Store owners were one step shy of being in the enclaves. That girl was marrying genuine money. Good for her. Grandma shared her thoughts with the nice Spic and wished him well.

Then she and the Johnsons went inside to marvel at Elroy's haul. He had them laid out in the kitchen. Like most of the exiles, they were plump and well-dressed. That was good news. One looked extra fatty. Elroy'd probably render that one for tallow. Grandma's votive candles were a solid seller at the church's casino nights.

She'd scavenge the clothes later. There was a lot to work with, and she figured she could cut up some of them to make herself a nicer sweater.

Skeeter walked in and whistled.

"Wow, Elroy, you done did good."

Elroy grinned and nodded. Gloria walked in, smiled, and then reached to dab a bit of drool off Elroy's chin. Much to no one's surprise, Carol walked in behind her wearing her traditional T-shirt and not much else. However, this time, she was carrying an unwieldy canvas bag.

"I guess my timing's good," she said as she handed the bag to Elroy, "one of them enclave delivery vans broke down out by my house, and the driver done got scared and ran off. So we filled up what we could afore the cops came. I got four loaves of bread, some can goods, and other shit Elroy can work his magic with."

Grandma was delighted. This meant they could have another Bar-B-Q. That would earn them lots of credit points with the neighbors. Those things were worth more than gold when times got lean. And times always got lean.

"We still got some Emma stew left," Gloria noted, "if anyone's hungry. May as well finish it off afore we cook up anythin' else."

They retired to the dining room, and Pastor Johnson said a more formal version of grace. But the end result was the same. They got to eat blessed food.

Grandma shoved a healthy portion in her mouth and smiled.

"Just like I always say, we don't need no government. The Good Lord shall provide."

The ***Sci-Fi Roundtable*** is a collection of authors herded by renowned editor Ducky Smith and well-known author Eric Michael Craig. This story appeared in their second anthology, ***Gods of Clay***.

# Tears of the Gods

The sand. Always the sand. It clung to everything, permeated everything, and defined everything. All life was built on and of sand. He who controls the sand controls life. That was the creed of the dynasty. Although he was no pharaoh, Djhutmose controlled the sand. He could grab it, mold it, and define it into something permanent. Each block added to Pharaoh's tomb had been designed by him.

Years ago, similar blocks had been dragged up ramps by him and other slaves. Then he'd shown skill with a chisel. Later, he'd shown a fine mind for design and mathematics. Eventually, he'd earned his freedom and a new home near the palace for his family as a stonemason. All that happened to him after that was a gift from the gods. Or god.

Horus, specifically, in his case. It made sense to him. The giver of all life had given him a life. When his village in Ethiopia had been conquered, the elders had paid tribute to the Egyptian army by gifting them three thousand worthy slaves, Djhutmose among them.

Of course, that wasn't his name then. That name died on the fields of battle. He would never speak about it and forbade his family from trying to find it. Dead was dead. That life walked with Anubis as far as he was concerned.

Learning to worship Egyptian gods was easy. They provided for him and his. The old gods had not.

He stepped out of the blazing sun and into his surveyor's tent.

With its wide-set eyes and wheezing breath, the gray-skinned god was looking over the latest plans. They would add four new chambers to hide its secrets and Pharaoh's mortal remains. While the gray god's secrets were hidden from all who toiled this day, they would be granted to Pharaoh upon the successful completion of his journey.

No one questioned the wisdom of this. Djhutmose had once seen the little god point a tiny object at a ten-square cubit block of stone and reduce it to smoke. The world wasn't ready for that kind of power. But later, after Pharaoh met with the gods, rational decisions could be made.

The gray god was wise, and Pharaoh was wise. Djhutmose was not.

The gray god pointed at a small detail it wished to correct. It needed an additional five cubits added to one chamber. Djhutmose had learned to speak with the god. Its language was not too different from that of the Egyptians. Its accent, though, was difficult to wade through. It rasped through every syllable, and it took it a long time to finish speaking. But gods demanded many things, and Djhutmose was more than willing to add patience to that list.

His dead life had offered no hope. Here, the gods were generous. They had given him a wife, and she, in turn, had given him a beautiful family. His three daughters had brought his family worthy alliances, and his two sons had moved to Pharaoh's court and found brides there, further enhancing Djhutmose's family's lifestyle.

The gray God looked at Djhutmose's corrections and blinked several times quickly. Djhutmose had learned that was its equivalent of a smile. Its tiny mouth was not very malleable.

The overseer was called to approve the changes, which he quickly did, and slaves were sent to inform the workers what to do. Djhutmose had to grant that the Egyptians were efficient. There was rarely a wasted moment on any work site.

The weeks melted away under the scorching sun as the work continued unabated. Djhutmose had noticed the gray god had become increasingly agitated over the last few days. He could pinpoint no reason why. Work was moving apace, there were no rebellions anywhere in the lands, the war had been no more than a rumor for a decade, and trade, often guided by the gray god, was up.

If anything, the gray god should be blinking all the time, yet it was not.

One morning, as Djhutmose was walking to his station, the overseer beckoned him. Usually jovial, he looked as though Pharaoh had died, something Djhutmose knew not to be true as he had seen him a mere hour ago, hale and hearty, taking his morning walk with his advisors.

The gray god was standing inside the tent, holding a device Djhutmose did not recognize. A flat rectangle, silver on one side, black on the other, about twice the size of Djhutmose's hand.

The overseer spoke. There were no pleasant formalities, just stern questions.

"Djhutmose, what do you know of your son-in-law, Toruk?"

Djhutmose shrugged.

"He is not a hard worker, but he need not be. His family is well off. We have invested with them in several successful trading opportunities."

"I did not ask about his family," glowered the overseer, "I asked about him."

Djhutmose thought about it some more and shrugged again.

"I rarely speak with him. We see each other at festivals and occasional trade meetings with his parents. He was a good match for my daughter; she has never complained."

The gray god snuffed. Djhutmose knew that sound. It was a mix of disgust and ridicule.

The overseer glared at him.

"So you are claiming not to know him well? He is married to your daughter."

Djhutmose began to panic.

"I have three daughters, sir. Ipwet married for love and has done well for herself and us. A'at was married to the son of Kheruef, our head mason. Bunefer was pledged to Toruk as part of a trade agreement between myself and Khamet, his father. My wife, Herit, and I leave them be. They lead their lives, and we live ours. Herit has been a gift from Horus to me, and we have never had any problems with our children."

The overseer softened a bit.

"If memory serves, I arranged your marriage."

"You did, sir. The week I showed promise with the chisel."

The overseer nodded, walked around the table, poured himself a cup of summer ale, a libation the gray god had introduced, and sat down.

"Tell me what you know of Toruk. Any detail, no matter how small."

For the next two hours, Djhutmose did his best to think of any detail regarding Toruk. He really didn't have many. The young man was lazy, indolent, often looking for an easy way around honest work. He knew his daughter supported him, as any good wife should, but beyond that, all he had were his taste in foods, bland, and clothes, extravagant.

The gray god listened intently. Sometimes, making scratches on the instrument, it carried a stylus made of a material he did not recognize.

Finally, Djhutmose sat across from the overseer, exhausted by the questioning.

"I am sorry, sir. I can tell you're upset with me. I just can't understand why."

The overseer sighed. He looked at the gray god for guidance. The gray god held the device up so Djhutmose could see it. Images magically appeared. He could see a man and a woman. They were stealthily moving through the base of the pyramid. They had a covered torch, which made their visages challenging to discern. Djhutmose watched, rapt, as they entered the new chamber of the gray god. There were only a few items there, as the rest had not been inventoried yet, but the man and the woman ignored them all save one. There was a black box with a silver glyph prominently branded that they grabbed and ran out, carrying it between them.

The gray god stopped the display, motioned its fingers at the device, and a single image enlarged. Bunefer and Toruk were clearly identified.

Djhutmose sank into the chair. By the gods of all that's good and holy, what had these two done?

The gray god did something it never did. It touched a human. It reached over and patted Djhutmose on the shoulder and pointed to the flagon of ale. Djhutmose understood quickly enough. He stood, poured himself a cup, and sat back down.

"Your family," wheezed the gray god, speaking Egyptian in its high-pitched voice, "is not to blame. But a member of your family is. This Toruk has done a dangerous thing. He has taken a dangerous thing. He must be found, and it must be returned."

Djhutmose considered the problem but didn't see a clear solution. Bunefer and Toruk lived two days away to the north.

"I will do what I can," Djhutmose sighed, "but I have no idea what that may be."

"The family of this Toruk, these traders, would they trade illegally? Make profit hidden from Pharaoh's eyes?"

Appalling as that question sounded to Djhutmose, he knew the overseer was serious. He'd only met them on formal occasions, and his dealings with them had been beyond reproach, but his wife didn't trust them. She said, in the privacy of their home only - of course, they were like the hippos, rapacious and deadly. He shared his wife's concerns with the others.

The gray god's tiny ears scrunched, and then it sat down.

"They must be found. They must be stopped. This box they have taken is not meant for you. Not meant for now. It was our gift for Pharaoh. Enough power to succor a world. To guide it towards its destiny."

Djhutmose considered this.

"I mean no disrespect, but why wasn't this more carefully guarded if it is so important?"

The overseer poured himself a fresh cup of summer ale and frowned.

"We were attempting to keep activities normal, not draw attention one way or the other. We felt the more normal things appeared, the less talk there would be."

That made some sense to Djhutmose, but he still had questions.

"Even so, could not the god have monitored its property?"

If the gray god was offended by the question, it didn't show it. It sat beside the overseer and took a drink out of his mug. It's rude for a human to do, not so much so for a god.

"Yes, we could. And, yes, we should have. But to have done so would have required us to add equipment we deigned too dangerous to be left lying around. Equipment that could change your future."

"Even more dangerous than this box?"

"In some ways, yes. In others, no. But not even we can undo the past. We must find our property."

Djhutmose was forced to agree with that. The threat level eluded him, but he knew it to be severe if the gray god was concerned. Now, with all agreed that something needed to be done, the course of action should be clear.

It was not.

Toruk's family traded all over the kingdom and in foreign lands. It was a matter of time versus distance to discover them; too much time had passed for that to be meaningful. They could be across the middle sea and hidden in the barbarian lands of the north.

They could be well into the Punjab and protected by armies Pharaoh wasn't ready to engage.

They could be anywhere.

They summoned Djhutmose's wife and began sorting what she knew onto a map provided by the gray god. A wonder in and of its own, glistening and hanging above the table with no papyrus or frame to hold it, it showed more detail than Djhutmose had ever conceived. While many of Pharaoh's court believed the world to be round, this map seemed to confirm it. He wondered if Pharaoh had seen it.

Herit knew much of Khamet's business habits. She had known the family for years, as it seemed, anyone who traded did. She did not hold them in high regard. But, as she apologetically explained, her new husband, whom she loved without question, had no past to build on, so an arrangement with them for their daughter was better than no arrangement at all.

Both the gray god and the overseer understood the rationale and asked no further questions along those lines.

Many of the things she knew were vague, near this town, a place of that name, but that seemed to be all the gray god needed. Tiny points of red light appeared on the map as she talked.

Soon enough, they had a pattern. And four possible destinations.

"Sleep is needed," rattled the gray god, "no good comes from inattention. We shall convene at sunrise tomorrow at my ship. We shall find this Toruk and stop this tragedy from becoming."

No human had been allowed within a cubit of the gray god's ship, but none there questioned its wisdom. As it was ordained, so would it be done.

✳✳✳✳✳✳✳✳✳✳✳✳✳✳✳✳✳✳✳✳✳

Toruk looked across the tent at his sleeping wife. Whatever event in the past had heaved her father onto the sands of Pharaoh mattered little to him. She was the perfect companion for his travels in this life. She would not be here if not for the fates. He said a silent prayer to Osiris and petted the black box again.

His father had arranged two meetings for him in the morning. Either would make them wealthy beyond their wildest dreams. A talisman of the gray god, stolen from beneath its watch, would bring over ten thousand debens no matter who the buyer was. And it was of little consequence to Toruk, who might eventually be.

Bunefer snored lightly and rolled over. Toruk, again, thanked the gods for her. She had figured out what her father was truly doing, how he was hiding gifts from the gods in the pyramid. It had taken them fourteen shats worth of payments to spies to ascertain what and where finally.

True, neither had any idea what the box represented or did, or even if it meant or did anything, but that was of no concern. It was of the gods, and its sale would guarantee they would spend their lives treated like them. Pharaoh would be forced to elevate his family to the upper court and not leave them among the mewling traders tolerated for their wealth. No more being looked down upon by their alleged betters. When this was done, they would have no betters.

They would have no equals.

They would greet the buyers in the land between these two cities they were camped near, and the dawn would bring a new future.

Toruk fell asleep, smiling, dreaming comforting dreams of obscene wealth.

*********************

The breaking light of the dawn shimmered on the silver skin of the gray god's ship. None knew why it was called a ship. They'd never seen it on the water; it had no place for oars or sails. Yet the gray god insisted it was a ship, so a ship is what it was.

An opening appeared, and they stood back, gasping. The magic of the gray god was not to be trifled with. Anyone who could make walls appear and disappear at will was more powerful than they could envision. And yet, it walked among and befriended them.

They were truly blessed.

The gray god appeared in the opening and beckoned them to come inside. They hadn't noticed the ramp and had no idea where it came from but saw no reason to dally, so they carefully walked up and in.

They were startled when the wall appeared behind them, locking them in the ship, but not so much as to panic. Whatever magic the gray god used, it seemed never intended to harm them.

They were shocked to see more gray gods walking around. They had thought there was only theirs. All the gods nodded in their direction, which they knew was a sign of respect, and returned to doing whatever the gods did.

Lights were glowing in midair, sounds emanating from nowhere, and the atmosphere seemed tense. While thinking of the atmosphere, Djhutmose noted his breathing was a little more difficult here. The air tasted sweeter but was thicker.

The gray god, Djhutmose, was sure it was theirs, heard him, and turned.

"Yes," it said with a voice now sweet, lilting, and pure, "this is our air. On your world, we could wear special masks that would allow us to breathe easier, but decided to limit how much technology we exposed. It is uncomfortable being with you, but not unbearable."

It imitated a human smile to the best of its ability, and they all felt somewhat better.

"If, at any time," it continued, "you feel like you are losing your air, let us know. We have things that will help."

With no lucid reason to panic, they began taking in their surroundings. The room was oblong. It had ten gray gods seated in front of various items they didn't recognize. The map they had worked on in the tent last night hung on one wall or floated near it – they couldn't tell, and there was a large window next to that which showed the sands they knew so well.

Then it didn't.

The sands fell away, and the sky clutched them up. While they felt no motion, they knew they'd been thrown into the sun. They were clearly meant to die.

But, instead of dying, the ground began rolling quickly, far beneath them, and they could see a marker moving on the map. They may not have understood the tech, but they grasped the concept. The marker was tracking their movements.

And, by any estimation, they were moving very fast indeed.

They covered five days' worth of walking in minutes and were soon above the first city Herit had mentioned. It was more of a rambling village than a coherent city, but it would have suited Toruk well. One of the gray gods motioned to a screen near it, and the others turned.

All Herit, Djhutmose, and the overseer saw was a purple light and some alien glyphs. Their gray god grunted and made a motion they didn't comprehend. It was soon apparent it had meant "on to the next location" or something similar.

The ground continued to peel away beneath them, and the sky somehow remained above.

The next city was more of a proper metropolis. Herit had said it was called Kamboja.

As they hovered above, Djhutmose wondered aloud why the people below were so calm and weren't reacting to the ship of the gods floating in their sky.

"They have not the means to see us. We can hide whenever we wish."

Djhutmose decided not to press the matter. He did not want to disrespect the gods after all they had done for him and his.

Another purple light, another gesture.

One more stop. There were two small kingdoms near each other. Excellent centers for trade and a vital part of the economies of several empires, Sodom and Gomorrah, were bustling and would provide many, possibly too many, places for Toruk to hide.

✱✱✱✱✱✱✱✱✱✱✱✱✱✱✱✱✱✱✱✱✱

Toruk had pitched his trading tent just outside the gates of Zeboim. He had no need or desire to pay the trader tax to enter the city. The sun was up, and the buyers would arrive within an hour. He had placed the box of the gods on a small platform, covered with a goatskin rug dyed shades of gold, and made sure his guards let no one in who didn't know the password his father had proclaimed.

Bunefer laid out small platters of dates, figs, and a block of local cheese, making sure there were plenty of flagons of wine nearby. These were important and wealthy men coming to her tent. She would not have them treated shabbily.

Their servants cleaned and detailed every aspect of the tent. When they were done, it reeked of faux royalty.

Toruk and Bunefer were pleased.

The two buyers arrived simultaneously. Pleasantries were exchanged, wine was poured, food was eaten, and the business was begun.

After an hour, one buyer shrugged and excused himself. Fifteen thousand debens was too rich for him. The other buyer smiled, an act reminiscent of something reptilian, bowed as his rival left, and then sat down.

He motioned to an attendant and nodded.

Shortly after, a line of slaves entered the tent, one at a time, and placed barrels of gold and silver rings, thick circlets each representing a shat, in front of Toruk and Bunefer. Fifteen thousand debens was more than either had thought possible. The combined barrels took up half the tent.

The buyer, Sahik was his name, dismissed his slaves and resumed his crocodilian smile.

"Please, if you will," he oozed politely, "I have paid well for this prize. Open it so that I may see."

Toruk shrugged. He'd never promised there would be anything inside. He walked to the platform, tugged on the edge of the box, heard it snap, and began opening the lid.

**********************

The god excitedly pointing at the pink light in front of it was the last to see the fireball rip through the pristine sky. The gray gods' ship rocked, shook, and began making noises none of them could believe portended anything good.

The terror was palpable for the gray gods and the Egyptians for five minutes.

Eventually, some of the sirens died out, the ship stabilized, and all could see the gates of Anubis' kingdom. Sheets of flame roiled across the sands. Winds and clouds competed for space above the dead. There was no question that all who were there were now dead.

Nothing could have lived through that.

Both kingdoms and all but one of the cities on the far horizon were laid waste.

Their gray god, they recognized him now even if they couldn't pinpoint why, made a new gesture. The other gray gods seemed to agree, and soon enough, they were headed back home.

The gray god hissed and turned towards his guests.

"You are not to blame. You did all you were asked and did so without complaint. We hope you would soon be ready to move up evolution's scale to take the next step towards acceptance. But you are not. There is still too much avarice, greed, and dishonor among you to justify any additional efforts. Even were we to guide Pharaoh back, with all our knowledge, it would still be too volatile a world for him to navigate safely.

"There is good among you, seen by my eyes and yours, but there is evil as well. We had hoped your gods, such as they are, would have provided you guidance by now.

"But they have not. Maybe they cannot. Time will tell. We have another world to visit. We shall return to this one in four thousand years and see. You have much to offer, but you must earn your place amongst the stars. It is not a place for violence. Not willful anyways. There are dangers enough without travelers causing more."

**********************

Djhutmose and Herit hugged as they sat on the sand. The gray gods had disappeared into the dark and would never be seen by them again. They had spent one day cleaning up every possible artifact from the pyramid, along with anything else there might be, and then escaped the sands into the heavens.

They'd left Djhutmose a toy. A little white tube with blue wings on either side. He had no idea what it did, nor did he much care; it was a memento of his time spent with the gods. With his missing, strange gray friend.

He held it up against the moon and tried to imagine something like this streaking across the sky. He saw Herit trying to do the same.

It may have been a toy, but it was a toy that bespoke a future filled with hope.

**********************

The satellites were impressive, a good sign of what had been accomplished, but the transmissions were confusing. It took several days to sort out the many languages and begin to understand.

They settled fifty thousand feet above their ancient home and began to study what man had wrought.

The wars and hatred they saw disgusted them. While much good had occurred, the divisions were now more embedded than ever. The anger between the swelling tribes was overt and raw. Many of the arguments, loudly parsed and violently supported, made no sense at all.

As far as they could tell, they were based merely on hate for hate's sake.

Each dawn brought visions of blood drying in the sun. Each sunset was lit by the flames of destruction. The time between was littered with the deaths of innocents and the cries of the forgotten.

The screams of the persecutors, proclaiming their righteous justifications for each genocide they deemed to be required by each perceived slight, reminded them of another world. One lost in the detritus of time. They quickly put that harrowing thought behind them, along with the forsaken world it beckoned.

All was not lost. There were pockets of humanity where hope shone brightly, where unity transcended personal phobias.

They had time.

There was another world, not that far away. They would go there, finish what their brethren had begun, and welcome them into the universe.

They would return here in about a thousand years. Not that long in the grand scheme of things, and plenty of time for humans to fix the wrongs they had embraced.

They made one last check to ensure the messages of hope they'd embedded into religions were still there; they were - for the most part, and moved on to happier tasks.

************************

Ongg saw the clouds quiver, and the light of the skies echoed off the thing that fell. The thing fell good. Not too fast. Not too slow.  It was a new thing; new things were a cause for alarm, so Ongg raised the alarm with screeches and howls and banging his best stick on a tree.

Then he ran away.

That was what smart things did, and Ongg was not a stupid thing.

He did not stay to see the falling thing land ever so gently.

He did not see it open up and release wide-eyed, gray beings.

He did not see them point to the ruins of the broken gods.

He did not see them put away their instruments.

He did not see them slowly shuffle back into their ship.

He did not see them cry.

He did see the stupid thing he'd stepped on.

It's a stupid thing with sharp blue edges.

He picked it up, stared at it briefly, and threw it away.

It was neither food nor sex, so there was no use for it at all.

**AUTHOR'S NOTE:** The dates assigned to the destruction of Sodom and Gomorrah vary from circa 1896 BC to 2070 BC. I settled on approximately 2000 BC for this story.

Two things hit my computer on the same day. One was a call for submissions relative to horror stories about My Little Pony fans, and the other was scantily clad pics of the band Sparkle Party. I knocked this out in a day and signed the contract 48 hours later. Sometimes, things just work out right. Initially published in 2017 in **Bronies Gone Wild** by **Horrified Press**.

## Sparkle Party Massacre

Clothing Optional Katie checked the glitter on her breasts in the reflection of her bay window while Suddenly Voluptuous Sayre practiced her latest naked jujitsu moves behind her. Satisfied with everything, especially themselves, they grabbed their instruments and headed to their garage to rehearse.

Trevor was livid. It was his turn to host the Blue Island Bronies tonight, and he had the French DVD edition of My Little Pony – Friendship is Magic: Twilight and Starlight. It had bonus features none of them had seen before. That should be the most dominant thing in everyone's mind. But he knew his friends.  They weren't as dedicated as he. If they saw those two next door, they'd never pay any attention to him.

Since the Blue Island Bronies had assembled in 2011, bound by their devotion to the Friendship is Magic series, Trevor had wanted to host an event, but his mom wouldn't let him. She thought the Bronies were a bad influence. Something that kept him from being a man, she said. He knew better, of course. Being a Bronie was the kind of thing women loved. Women loved men who knew that sharing is caring, and caring is good.  And it didn't matter if that phrase was from the Care Bears. What mattered was that women loved it.

Worse still was the fact his mom treated him like a child. He was thirty-three and had a good job at Winchester's House of Linens and Fabrics. It was his job to separate the products by thread count and color, and he'd been doing it quite well – thank you very much, for fourteen years now.

His boss, Purvis Winchester III, was never nice to him. Then again, he never seemed to be nice to anyone. He always appeared to be looking for an excuse to fire Trevor but could never find a good one. And he never would if Trevor had anything to say about it.

None of that mattered!

Tonight, his mother was out of town, his father was still dead, and the house was his.

The Bronies would be impressed tonight, and Trevor could bask in the glory he so richly deserved.

It was his night! His important night!

Darn, those harlots!

Just darn them to heck!

Trevor heard echoes of their horrid music coming from next door and hoped they'd be locked away all night. Stupid rock and roll had no place in Ponyville.  It should be happy music. Light, airy, and innocent. But did those salacious strumpets care? Of course not.

Trevor had talked to them once, in a rare moment of them being fully clothed. He was appalled to discover that despite the fact they called their atrocious act Sparkle Party, they didn't know anything about Ponyville. Worse, when he tried to explain, they'd laughed at him.

They'd said it was silly!

Ponyville? Silly? That was blasphemy of the highest order.

Ponyville was magic; it said so in the title. It was a place of hope and wonder. It was many things. But it was not and never would be silly.

Trevor and his friends had celebrated Ponyville individually since it appeared in 2010. It hadn't taken long for them to discover each other in small-town Illinois.

Twenty-six joyous episodes of Friendship is Magic would be released each year, and Trevor would luxuriate in each colorful moment. Well, except for season three. To the Bronie's horror, they only released thirteen episodes that year. There were even dark rumors of a possible cancellation.

The Brony Revolt of 2013 featured many ALL CAPS emails and occasionally salty language–well, it was a stressful time, so Trevor understood, finally brought

Hasbro's evil denizens to heel, and the saga continued properly after that.

Trevor ignored the delinquent doxies next door and prepared for the evening.

His decision lasted precisely one minute.

To his disgust, he watched the entire band, four brazen hussies, naked as wood nymphs, strutting out onto their back patio. They couldn't be seen from the street, but he had an unfettered view. Which meant his Bronies would too.

They were all adorned in glitter and high-heeled boots, not a stitch else, and they were playing acoustic guitars. That meant they would work on those cacophonies of caterwauling they called songs.

Gosh, darn it! They were going to ruin all his plans. He had snacks, soft drinks, a PowerPoint presentation featuring talking points, and a cool new Rainbow Dash costume. He'd found the perfect baby blue fabric to compliment the rainbow tail and mane. He'd sewn it himself, and it was glorious.

Trevor fumed.

Trevor was good at pretending. He put his hands on his hips and pretended to pop on a thinking cap. Soon enough, he was rewarded with an idea that would have made the strongest pony in Ponyville, Shining Armor, proud.

He would kill the band.

He had four hours to get it done. He figured that would be enough time.

Time being a cruel mistress wouldn't be elegant, but that had to be forgiven.

Given the time constraints, maybe he should only kill one. The cops would keep them occupied for the rest of the night.

No, that was no good.

If the mere sight of the coquettish coquettes enthralled his fellow Bronies, sirens and lights would captivate them. No one would pay any attention to him.

And it was HIS night!

He had snacks, gosh darn it!

He scolded himself for such rough language and set about creating his plan.

The sounds of cooing harmonies only fueled his rage. How dare they toss that ruckus against the glorious sounds of Daniel Ingram's wondrous theme music. His soaring melodies touched souls. Their decadent dissonance merely polluted the air.

That gave him a good idea.

He would gas them to death.

He sauntered downstairs and began looking for poison gasses. Much to his disdain, he didn't seem to have any. It would seem like something every home should have. Sadly, try as he might, he couldn't conjure anything up.

He scoured every cabinet in his basement, even going so far as to plunge into the laundry room. His mother never let him near the laundry since the unfortunate incident when he confused a bottle of Mountain Dew for detergent.  It had been three years; he wished she'd get over it.

Nevertheless, he was reminded of an eighth-grade chemistry experiment. Combining bleach and ammonia made mustard gas, and that was lethal. He had all the ingredients.

Smiling, he found a bucket and began mixing the two chemicals.

Soon enough, his eyes started burning, his throat was seizing, his nose was draining, his tongue was swelling, and he swore he could taste the color three.

Realizing the error of his ways, he snapped on the exhaust fan and staggered outside to the back steps. No one could see him gasping and clutching his throat. He found the roll of paper towels he used to clean exterior doorknobs, blew his nose, and sat brooding.

With the sounds of girlish laugher and four-part harmonies grating on his brain, he stumbled back inside and poured the noxious mixture down the sink before it killed him. He let hot water run for ten whole minutes until the smell was gone entirely.

He had no way to contain the gas. And there was no way those hypnotic hellions would sit still while he mixed it in front of them.

Pony poop!

He needed a new plan.

While a tad brutish for his tastes, desperate times called for desperate measures. As he turned around to get his bearings, he noticed the ax he'd used to trim his mother's cherry tree last year. He pulled it off the wall, tucked his elbow tight to his hip, and gave it three test chops.

On the third chop, the ax head flew off, ricocheted off the far wall, flew back, and, by sheer luck, hit him with the flat side on the bridge of his nose.

Nevertheless, sheer luck or no, his nose was broken, blood was pouring on his good shirt, and he was livid. Nothing was going right. This was supposed to be his night, but it turned into his nightmare.

It took him half an hour to stop the bleeding. He pre-treated his clothes, just like it said to do on the pre-treatment bottle, to avoid having the blood permanently stain them, tossed them in the washing machine, found a new outfit, and grimaced. If he got lucky, his mother would never notice.

His image in the mirror was hideous. He had cotton stuffed in each nostril, his eyes were bruised and swollen, his upper lip was puffy, and he didn't look like the suave Brony he usually was.

And what would he tell his boss tomorrow? He'd just say he got mugged in Chicago. No one would question that.

Everyone knew Chicago was an evil place where bad things happened to good people. And Trevor was a good person. He told himself so again and again.

With one problem solved, he set his sights on the other. What to do with the tawdry trollops.

His mother had given him a gun. He loathed guns but felt it might be worth making an exception this one time. He walked, slowly and painfully, over to the end table in his bedroom, slipped open the drawer, pulled the heavy case out, sat down on his bed, and stared at it. It was a Glock 17 Gen 2. He had no idea what it meant, but he knew it. He knew that because his mother made him memorize it. He also knew there was a reason she made him memorize it, but that trivia eluded him now.

He supposed it didn't matter.

He opened the case and shivered. It was black and evil-looking. It's not at all something a decent Brony should own. There was an instruction booklet in the case. He opened it and began reading. Everything seemed simple enough. He released the magazine to count his bullets. He would need four, of that he was sure.

He had zero.

Then it came to him. His mother had wanted him to know what kind of gun he had so he'd know what ammunition to buy.

He hissed sharply and put the gun away.

Walking back through his living room, he was gifted with the nausea-inducing sight of the four filles de Joie frolicking around a grill in the backyard.

This would not do!

He could not have them having a cookout on this night of all nights. The Bronies would never pay a lick of attention to his presentation. And it was a PowerPoint, gosh darn it!

He'd worked hard on it. He could not have those titillating tarts gallivanting around when he had important things to impart. He had four slides dedicated to how My Little Pony transcended racial and cultural barriers. He'd done that for Scooter. Bronies, just like ponies, could come in all colors.

Glancing out the window, a small part of his mind had to admire how limber they were. And how much fun they seemed to be having. That small part thought it might be a shame to kill them. That small part was quickly quashed.

Kindness. He would kill them with kindness.

That would get the Brony seal of approval.

His mother had a large bag of apple seeds. He remembered enough of his high school physics to work out the rest.  Well, he remembered enough to go online and check to make sure he was doing it right.

He was!

Twenty minutes later, he had a fresh batch of cyanide.

He went into his kitchen and began preparing two platters of snacks. One was just a regular cheese and sausage spread with crackers. The other looked identical, but he coated each piece of cheese and sausage with pulpy cyanide.

He put them both in the fridge, marking the poison platter with a blue flower.

He cleaned himself up as best he could and returned to the kitchen. He was interrupted by the sound of his doorbell, the My Little Pony – Friendship is Magic theme song played on a glockenspiel. It was the only concession his mother had made.

She wouldn't say it, but he was sure she liked it.

He opened the door and saw Otter and Mark standing there.

"You guys are early."

"Yeah," replied Otter, "we got off work early and figured we could help you set up."

While Trevor appreciated the gesture, he was torn. If he let them in, they'd see the playful perverts next door. But if he didn't, they might not come back for his presentation.

He slumped and motioned them in.

Soon enough, his troubles were forgotten. Otter and Mark were genuinely fascinated by the new DVD he'd found and had a million questions. They'd even accepted his mugging story without comment. So when Mark called out, trying to know why there were two platters of snacks, Trevor casually mentioned one was for the next-door neighbors.

Mark said he'd take it over, which made Trevor feel good somehow. Now, he wouldn't be the one with blood on his hands.

He heard Mark whistle when he saw the demented damsels, but he also heard him come back a few moments later.

"I can see why you like this place. Your neighbors are amazing!"

Trevor grunted. Just as he was about to disagree, the doorbell rang again. Scooter and Tommy walked in, all smiles. They, too, were excited to see this new treasure Trevor had found. Scooter had searched for information on the internet and found it scant.

That made this evening all the more enticing.

Mark brought out the other platter of snacks, and they all sat down to share in Trevor's treasure.

They were nibbling and laughing as the opening theme came cheerfully out of the speakers. Somehow, for some reason, it seemed to Trevor to be blending with the horrible noise coming from next door.

The effect was jarring and echoey.  He tried to look at his fellow Bronies to see if they noticed it, but they were all blurry and difficult to hear. They did seem upset about something.

He tried to speak, but his mouth wouldn't work. Then he saw the blue flower on the floor, where it had fallen from the platter they were eating from.

As Sparkle Party sang, "I wanna be your dog," and Sparkle Pony faded into oblivion, all Trevor could think was, "Oh, pony poop, this was supposed to be my night. My special night."

**AUTHOR'S NOTE**: Sparkle Party is a real band, but they are quite capable of functioning with their clothes on. The author regrets getting your hopes up.

This appeared in ***Dogs of War,*** released by ***Fur Planet Productions***. It was my first time working with furries. There are some dark thoughts hidden in those cute costumes.

# The Loving Children

The sea of static flowing from his radio was filled with distant echoes of death. The screams ebbed and flowed with an eerie regularity while Gustav ignored them all. Whether they emanated from damned innocents or misguided heroes changed nothing. They were the bourgeoning dead, and Gustav cared nothing for them.

Since the brutes had eaten his wife and children, he cared for little save the hunt. It was the only thing giving his life purpose. His little portion of revenge was delivered daily, efficiently, and with ice-cold veins.

Some thought the creatures to be Aufhocker, but he knew better. Neither slow-witted nor natural, these demons had been spawned from the depths of a laboratory wrapped in the curse of good intentions.

One scientist had even insisted they would be the boon humankind needed in the mountains and other treacherous terrains, a true Lebensborn that would nurture hope and salvation where none existed before for those who needed help.

Over a thousand people are stranded, injured, or killed yearly on mountains worldwide. The Matterhorn, alone, counts for almost a third of those statistics. It was primarily due to idiot tourists who thought it was as safe as the Disney ride of the same name. Oddly enough, Everest, the tallest mountain in the world, wasn't that dangerous. It kept its death toll to less than ten percent of its climbers by having regular guides who knew how to traverse its many nooks and crannies.

It might have also helped that the dead were left where they dropped and used as markers for subsequent climbers. Corpses laid in climbers' paths tend to remind them to pay attention. Some, like Hannelore Schmatz, even became tourist attractions.

While there were, undoubtedly, rescue animals and experts available, they were utterly reactive. These animals were to be placed in "high-risk" areas so they could save people before they became statistics.

Not just mountains, either. Arctic and Antarctic wildernesses claimed their fair share as well. There were a myriad of locations where the creatures could roam and be of service to man.

The scientist, Gustav, forgot his name made all these points and more in a colorful PowerPoint presentation on TV. He was the first one they ate.

That was forty years ago.

Gustav slid his modified MSR-338 sniper rifle back onto his shoulder and scanned the horizon. He could sense them near but not near enough to be threatening.

He slid through the snow down the side of a hillock, barely four kilometers south of what used to be Freudenstadt, past the dark wood trees and into a gulley. He pulled out his binoculars again and scanned again. This time, he saw one. They were hard to miss. Modified Komondors. They could walk on their hind legs, manipulate machinery, and speak after a fashion. They had their own language, a collection of howls and grunts that was surprisingly facile. Gustav knew about two hundred words of it. It was enough to know when they were attacking and when they had other things to do.

He found that to be useful information.

He watched as the giant, shaggy creature lumbered through the woods. The beast moved with incredible agility, just under two meters tall, covered in white fur, and weighing over ninety kilos. This one wasn't carrying any weapons, which confused Gustav. Usually, they were never seen without their crossbows or swords.

Not that they needed them; if they got close to a human, they could kill and eat one without much effort.

Gustav unholstered his rifle and sighted the fiend. Unlike the officially sanctioned heroes who died with depressing regularity, Gustav knew how to kill them. He made his bullets, each filled with a mix of napalm and fluoroantimonic acid. Even with that combination, only a headshot would kill. He'd tried to explain that to the government when the invasion began, but they'd dismissed him completely. They'd believed they could corral the beasts.

Three billion dead and counting proved them wrong.

Moscow, Vladivostok, Zurich, Lucerne, Amsterdam, Haarlem, Berlin, and Gustav's home of Frankfurt were among the many cities that were now gone, their citizens dead or scattered.

Aid from foreign lands wasn't coming. People tended to lose their minds when they saw pictures of their treasured sons and daughters dismembered and eaten. Gustav couldn't blame them.

Gustav, in his private way, respected the devils. He even used their proper name for themselves, Draugar, when he spoke, which was seldom anymore. The designation was fitting. They were, in many ways, a form of walking death.

They created villages, had a culture of a type, mated for life, were clever beyond expectations when it came to engineering, and learned from their mistakes. The latter being far more than could be said for the European governments.

Gustav adjusted his sight and zoomed in on the Draugar. It was a male holding a box of some sort. Gustav shivered when he realized what it was: a radio. One built by and for them. The design may have been alien, but its purpose was not.

He watched, part in horror, part enthrallment, as it spoke and then listened. He knew there would be no more group patrols. They would be harder to find than they had ever been, and judging by their success thus far, avoiding bombs and bullets was a skill they'd perfected.

Usually, as a courtesy, Gustav didn't kill an unarmed opponent. He decided this was worth an exception. He adjusted for windage and gently squeezed the trigger.

Single tap lethal.

He smiled as the head exploded, and the acid caused the fur around its neck to smolder. His smile went rictus when he felt two vice-like paws grab his shoulders. He was tossed into the air, pinwheeling randomly, until he landed directly in front of the largest and oldest Draugur he'd ever seen.

Though his muzzle was nearly black, his fur was bleach white, his eyes were clear, and his strength was unabated. Age was not a detriment to him in any way.

He was wearing a deerskin jerkin and black trousers. Like all of them, he was barefoot.

He moved faster than any monster Gustav had ever seen, grabbed the MSR-338, examined it, cleared the chamber, pulled the clip, and then, to Gustav's astonishment, handed it back to him. That astonishment was replaced by sheer terror when it leaned over and spoke.

"You. Come. Now. Follow."

The voice was guttural, and the syllables slurred, but Gustav understood, and that was something that should not happen. With snouts and recessed tongues, human speech should have eluded them.

Gustav shouldered the rifle and fell in next to the shaggy behemoth.

Dusk fell to evening, and the stars shone brightly in the winter sky. The giant stopped, opened a pack under its jerkin, and offered it to Gustav. His first thought was to reject it, but he didn't know what he was offered. He reached in carefully and pulled out a piece of jerky. Upon tasting it, he realized it was venison jerky. Spiced differently than any he'd ever eaten, but still quite good.

He looked at his captor in confusion.

"Way go yet," was all he got through an explanation.

They walked silently for another two hours, and then Gustav smelled the smells of civilization. Cooking fires, musk, and all those little smells that let the brain know it's no longer alone.

They crossed a slight rise, and Gustav gasped. He'd done threat assessments for the army when he was young, and he was well-skilled at grasping the size of a populace. There had to be over one hundred thousand of them.

Worse yet, judging by the range of devastation they'd caused, this was far from their only metropolis. They had to be breeding at a near-geometric rate.

They passed a set of sentries and entered a main street. Gustav noted there were no walls around their city, just a mesh stretched overhead. He recognized the type. It prevented heat from escaping or being detected and provided near-perfect camouflage. Fear of invasion wasn't on their list of things to worry about.

He wasn't sure what to make of that.

A few minutes later, they were in a large building. It seemed to have a military function, and Gustav was aimed toward a table with several empty chairs. He sat in one and prepared for he knew not what. He was alive. That alone shouldn't be true.

His defacto jailer returned and set a steaming bowl of stew in front of him. A quick taste revealed it was venison, also delicious and different. While he appreciated the kindness, he was confused by it as well.

"Wolfrick," said the Draugur as he sat across from Gustav. It took him a moment to realize he was being told a name.

He pointed to himself.

"Gustav."

Wolfrick shook his head.

"No. Tod Pirschjäger," the words were pronounced slowly, deliberately, "Death Stalker. You. Human name no interest."

So they knew him. He supposed he should be flattered, but he was still too baffled to be anything other than confused.

He began to assess his surroundings. The building wasn't abandoned. There were hundreds of bulky crates on the other side of the floor. Closer to a far door, he saw large rifles being carefully placed in similar crates. He was a weapons expert and wished to get a closer look at one. They were not like anything he'd ever seen.

Wolfrick noted his curiosity and called one of the workers over with a rifle. The worker handed it to Gustav without comment and walked away.

It had similarities to his MSR-338, but only superficially. The trigger guard was wider, the muzzle longer, the clip could hold thirty rounds instead of seven, and it looked like it could handle fifty caliber ammo. He guessed it had a range of about fourteen hundred meters.

He set the rifle down and finished the stew. He was unsure what else to do.

"Guns help," said Wolfrick, "but slow. Need speed."

Gustav parsed through the meaning and became aware of real fear for the first time in his life. They were looking for a way to kill humans faster and more efficiently.

"I hope you're not looking for my help," replied Gustav.

"No."

Another worker arrived and took the rifle away as they sat in silence.

"What do you want from me?" asked Gustav.

"Nothing. You honored. You will see. Watch. Witness."

"What?"

Wolfrick stood and motioned for him to follow.

They walked through the warehouse, passed the rifles, out into the night, and straight into a nightmare.

There were banks of missiles on portable launching pads, with each pad attached to a small truck. Every missile had a white tip designating they were live rounds. An odd vestige of humanity. There was also a symbol on the side he didn't recognize. He turned to Wolfrick and motioned at it.

"Mist. Make humans go."

Gustav's spine felt shades of cold he never knew existed. Biological weapons had been outlawed long ago. Then again, as he thought about it, the Draugur had never been invited to those negotiations.

Gustav took it all in and looked Wolfrick directly in the eye.

"Why are you doing this?"

Wolfrick sighed.

"When young, loved humans. Humans taught. Humans fed. But humans hurt, too. Humans killed. Humans made us feel bad. We …," he searched for the right words, "we tried be good. Humans made us do things. Bad things. We children were—human children. So we thought. Humans bad parents."

Gustav had heard rumors of the Draugur being used as weapons in secret missions but dismissed them along with the usual prattle about UFOs, chemtrails, and lizard people. Maybe he shouldn't have been so hasty.

He looked at Wolfrick anew. He must be one of the first ones made. He had seen it all come to pass. Gustav wished language wasn't such a barrier. He truly wanted to know what happened and how.

He could never forgive the murder of his family. As a soldier, he could understand the vagaries and horrors of war. He knew he'd done things he'd rather not visit in his dreams.

He watched as the missiles left in varying directions. He'd never felt so helpless in his life.

"You don't need to do this; there's always a way to work things out," Gustav pled, "Let people know why you're doing what you do, teach them, and put an end to this."

Wolfrick looked at Gustav hard and frowned.

"End is what we do. You ate our food, and you know truth now."

Gustav had no idea what he meant at first. Then, realization dawned. They no longer needed to eat humans to survive. That thought led to one he'd never considered. Why did they need to eat humans in the first place? That question he asked aloud.

"Food costs money. Prisoners free."

Gustav finally understood. Everything. True clarity of vision was accompanied by the sight of missiles launching in the distance. As they arced into the sparkling sky, he laughed. The folly of fools was not to be underestimated. As each missile exploded high in the night sky, he could see a reddish mist growing across the horizon.

His laugh grew louder and louder.

"Fuck it, Wolfrick, you're right. We all need to go."

Wolfrick smiled and began walking back to the warehouse.

"Yes, time for your children to own world."

***The Strange Case of Dr. Jekyll and Mr. Hyde: The classic tale and an anthology of twists, retellings, and sequels*** is precisely what you think it is. A collection of stories that reimagine **Dr. Jekyll and Mr. Hyde**.

# Hank & Eddy: Bro Wars

The blood splatter was exquisite. Some might say it was Jackson Pollock-esque. Not him, of course; he hated being compared to amateurs. Mere dabblers in paint. They would never understand true art. The intestines laid magnificently about the room, which only heightened the breathtaking effect.

The root source of his current artistic achievement was a man of middle age. One who'd been looking forward to spending his latter years gardening, bowling, and, maybe - if all went well, building that HO gauge model train village he'd always wanted. All things mundane. Now, for eternity ever after, he would be something extraordinary. Something talked about in hushed tones of reverence. He had truly and finally transcended his desires.

Eddy felt a shudder and grimaced.

The formula, the source of all that's good and holy, was wearing off. Unfortunately, he'd have to wait until Hank, his muddling other, made more. The science behind it was beyond him.

He knew Hank hated it, hated him, but couldn't stop. The power was too glorious. The euphoria was too intense. These were joys not discarded easily.

The room began to fade, and he smiled. He would be back soon enough.

The horror of the stench was stultifying. The terror of the view appalling. But he knew better than to retch. To give in would be a sign of weakness, and he couldn't let his demon see him as weak.

He also knew he had to leave. There was nuance in his existence, a subtlety easily lost on the unenlightened. The authorities, who would eventually come, would never understand.

He glanced one last time and looked for an exit.

He found one with a street view and stopped. He was covered in blood, not his own, and it was broad daylight. He would be noticed. He backed away from the egress and took in his surroundings. He was in a warehouse. One that had not seen workers in some time. The lingering layers of dust were ample proof of that. He noticed some stairs and decided to walk up to see their options.

His decision was quickly rewarded by a row of lockers filled with work clothes. It took a few minutes, but he finally found a set that fit and didn't have a logo. Finding a sink and cleaning his skin was a simple matter. Five minutes later, he was changed. There was even a pair of work boots, scuffed and dull, to complete his ensemble.

He folded his suit, resplendent in splatter and gore, and tucked it into a plastic bag.

The formula worked. It did all he had asked. But, this much was clear; he had not asked enough. He needed to be able to control the result, and such was not the case.

The secret was there. It was staring at him. He just couldn't see it. That's okay. He would find it and be free of his evil doppelganger. One minor hurdle and the riches buried in military budgets worldwide would be his. A super-soldier, an ubermensch, an unstoppable being slaved to their desires, would mean El Dorado would be his.

But first, this tiny glitch needed to be addressed.

The room was dark; only the glare of a computer screen reflected off the walls. He looked around and realized this was someplace new. Someplace alien. He was not sure he liked that. His awakenings were branded things he could work from—the known built into the sublime.

Nevertheless, he was awake. A quick survey showed him all he needed to know. The fool had thought to contain him. A locked room. Cameras in the corners. It all flooded in. And this, too, was new. He'd never seen what his other had seen before, but now he knew all. He quickly punched the passcode into the lock and entered the dark night.

Maybe new wasn't so bad.

He was halfway to the street when he realized the trap.

His memories now included the formula. But the rare and wonderful ingredients were only in this lab, carefully enclosed in special containers. If he left, he would be denied them. But, if he stayed, he was forever locked away. He went back and looked at what was available. The formula, evident in his mind, may as well have been written in Sanskrit. But he understood some of it. He had twelve hours. No more.

And he needed his other to fix it. To make him whole. To make all he could, and should, be made flesh forever.

He considered his options. They were myriad and limited all at once.

Very well. He had a time limit, and he had skills. He would use the latter to force his other to extend the former. His other would want to keep him tethered. To control what he was becoming. But that would require time.

More and more glorious time.

He smiled as he walked into the flickering dusk, confident in his future.

The future of the lady across from him was etched in stone. She didn't know that. There was much that eluded her. He neither cared nor worried about that. She wanted someone to buy her a drink. He would do that. She wanted someone to admire her. He would do that. She wanted an evening to remember. He would provide that, albeit in a manner she might not ultimately appreciate.

She held his arm and cooed endlessly and shrilly as they walked through the park.

"Oh, Mr. Hyde, such a gentleman you are."

"Oh, Mr. Hyde, you were truly a wonder on the dance floor."

"Oh, Mr. Hyde, aren't you the handsome devil?"

"Oh, Mr. Hyde, aren't the stars lovely?"

They were and always would be.

He trapped their beauty in her gaze for all eternity.

He hadn't wanted to slice her throat; it seemed cliché in the grand scheme of things, but he was on a tight schedule and had much to do with her before his other returned. He wanted his message to be clear to the other to ensure his future.

Not being a peasant, he had no desire to sexualize her splendor. There would be no torn bodices or ripped undergarments. He wanted art, not sensationalism.

He quietly rooted out her eyes and placed them on her chest so she would never be denied the existential majesty of the heavens. Then he sliced out her tongue and tossed it into the weeds. Her voice was a thing of annoyance, and he saw no reason others should suffer it.

He carefully arranged her few possessions around her in a shrine to self-absorption and waited. His other would be here in less than an hour, and he didn't want him to miss this.

The dead woman's breasts stared at him. Her eyes were no longer where they typically go. The desecration is both deliberate and baffling.  Something niggled at the back of his mind. Something dark and lonely. His mother. Their mother. His childhood. But not their childhood. That was something denied by his demon. So how did it know about mother? How did it know her blindness and braying voice?

There was something he was missing. Something simple, of that he was sure. He would find it. Fix it. And then he would bathe in rare scents served by adoring minions.

He just had to fix that little thing.

Back at the lab, he viewed the tapes. It was worse than he'd imagined but not as bad as he'd feared.

The demon now had some of his memories but none of his skills.

There was something else. The demon, his mirror, was somehow more handsome than he. More elegant. He watched it move around the lab with a grace he'd never known. It's a feral grace, to be sure, but still impressive.

He remembered his days at boarding school. The young toughs, forever peacock proud, shunning him, strolling around like the world owed them tomorrow. His demon would have laughed at them.

They were as beneath him as the amoeba was to humans.

Humans negotiated, the demon took. Humans were social animals; the demon was something well beyond their feeble needs.

Too dangerous to be set free, too magnificent to be chained.

He needed to find the solution.

It was there. Hidden in the math, buried beneath his fears, waiting to be discovered.

He pulled up the formula and began dissecting it line by line.

The dawn was staggering in its joy. Myriad colors, streaming through the windows unabated by curtains, compounded by sensations he never knew existed, were elements of ecstasy he'd never imagined. He tightened his tie and checked himself in the mirror.

He smiled. He knew. He remembered. He felt.

And now, he was free to remake the world in his bold vision.

The boarding school reunion was this weekend. He would start there. Peacock feathers made lovely decorations. He would share their beauty with the welcoming void.

***Korzac: Nördicon of Dern*** was initially published in Issue #1 of **Planet Scumm Magazine**. It was later re-released in ***PLANET SCUMM VOLUME 1, "EVERYTHING! THE FIRST FOUR ISSUES,"*** available on finer websites worldwide.

# KORZAC: NÖRDICON OF DERN

Korzac: Nördicon of Dern, Most High Admiral of the Fleet of Reverential Destiny, Honorary Moon God of the Exalted Planet Cloorbius, Holder of the Scepter of Gloptium Prime, Wielder of the Sword of Infinite Cuts, Prime Mate of Nizbo, Progenitor of Hazna, Quizbo, and Yath, Prime Mate of Ilxhan, Progenitor of Ooklsa and Horth, Prime Mate of Unquin, Progenitor of Jaexx, Wongaloo, Hipth, Sarf, and Tronk, Secondary Mate of Kandok, Junhre, Lorpa, and Krad, sat hacking into his claw-like a skiggling zak.

The Dernian armada needed him to be focused; for the most part, he was. His Vice Admiral, Oxlis, was a fine mind in his own right and made sure Korzac stayed on top of his game. And he hadn't become Nördicon by having bad game.

Despite his current illness, Korzac was a prime specimen of the best Dern had to offer. He was over six and a half feet tall with knee-length purple hair, perfectly oiled, cascading over his black and blue shell. His upper claws glistened naturally, and his lower arms, with the traditional six fingers each, were finely muscled. His legs were thick and firm, and his hooves were perfect triangles. His pale blue skin and yellow eyes were straight out of one of those modeling books young femmes liked to swoon over.

Well, usually, all that would be true. Right now, his shiny black lips were dull gray, his bright yellow eyes were rheumy, and his smooth skin was oddly mottled. He knew what he had, and it wasn't fatal, but that didn't make it any more welcome.

He'd attained his rank while only using the Right of Assassination twice. The fewest in the history of the Nördicons. His ascension was the stuff of textbooks for all future Nördicons. He supposed that was something to be proud of. Maybe when he retired.

*System 232: update.*

*Quantum bridges complete*

*Total loss of life: 6.38 billion*

The Deceptor Shields have done their job magnificently again. They'd slid into Wala-Un-sook space unnoticed. Unlike that backward planet, Earth, which had been kind enough to surrender right after they'd blown the first hole in one of their continents, the Wala-Un-sooks showed no inclination of being polite. In fact, they were being downright rude.

*System 17: update*

*Quantum bridges detected*

*Current inhabitants reside on 4th planet from solar center*

*Population: approximately 1.72 million*

***Technological status: pre-industrial**

***Chance of survival... ... Zero***

He'd been forced to implement attack plan, Gamma Zed Zed Minor, to counter the Wala-Un-sook, which was fine. He knew his crew preferred a solid battle before the conquest. He watched as two battle cruisers pulled past his flagship and raced toward the edges of the Wala-Un-sook armada. They had placed their smaller fighters as protection, and he wanted them taken out before he committed the destroyers.

They had their work cut out for them. This was the last system their scientists said they needed to create the Quantum Entanglement Grid, which would keep the invaders out of this third of the galaxy.

Of course, in accordance with the Diplomatic Gnosis of Necessity, they'd first asked each planet for permission. The Grid enablers on each planet would only kill about a third of their population, and each was, naturally, offered time to evacuate within their system. All had declined. Earth had even threatened legal action.

That announcement had led to days of laughter in the High Council chambers. It was also why Korzac decided to lead the assault there personally. No one sued a Nördicon and lived.

On the other hand, the Wala-Un-sook would be offered an honorable defeat. Even as their entrails drifted into the vacuum, they'd earned that much they were earning that much.

At least.

He let out a garnoofing sound, which caused the bridge crew to cringe without comment. He privately admitted it wasn't pleasant while appreciating their decorum.

He hated being sick.

He heard a gentle rustle beside him and turned to face a young cadet. He forgot her name. She was holding a clip-pad with several icons highlighted.

Not everything was glory and battle when you were a leader. He motioned for her to speak.

"Forgive my presence, Oh Great Sir," she began in accordance with tradition correctly. "I have the updates on the Grid you requested."

He nodded for her to continue.

"Since the Earthlings have agreed to participate in Xhak-Ko …"

His raised claw stopped her.

"What? With no Wark-Hana or Quandikran first? Are they that eager naturally, or did Ilzak develop some new threat?"

"As far as I know, neither, sir. It seems there was some type of fertility, or rebirth, festival going on when

Ambassador Ilzak arrived to oversee the installation of the grid. It's called …" she checked her notes, "e-stireeester, I believe. Our linguists are having problems with their many languages and religions, most of which contradict each other. Anyway, sir, he decided to take advantage of it to see if he could get the work going earlier. About thirty percent of the population agreed to join in Xhak-Ko with us, so he issued the Formal Writ of Apology for the little hole you left in some place which used to be called … le-wee-zee-anna … and repatriated the citizens of that continent to other locations, either on their planet or in their system, depending on their wishes. He is currently setting up the grid unit on the empty continent. He reports he is one galactic year ahead of schedule."

He hacked again. Flushed, slightly in with embarrassment, and nodded.

"Ilzax is one of the good ones. I once saw him stop a war with a simple orgy and some oils. I hope the Xhak-Ko with those primitives was worth his time."

"Yes, sir," she continued, "he reports he has personally had carnal relations with eleven different humans, that's what they call themselves, and says, despite their limited amount of orifices, they seem to enjoy everything, and he admits he enjoys them as well."

Despite himself, Korzac laughed. Then he garnoofed again. The cadet didn't blink.

"Very well, cadet. Is there anything else?"

"Yes, sir," she smiled, "the remaining thirteen grid units are now complete and have successfully finished testing. The ones on inhabited worlds have produced fewer casualties than predicted."

He beamed.

"That is good news."

She bowed slightly.

"Yes, sir. Will you be needing sex before I go?"

He frowned.

"Sadly, no. I'm so glumped I'd never make it past your first chamber."

She giggled at the old joke, bowed again, and left.

Korzac adjusted himself in his chair to better see the battle screens.

The destroyers were arcing into the main force of the Wala-Un-sook armada. The battle would be fierce, but the ending was inevitable. Wala-Un-sook would soon be the property of Dern.

Despite his current illness, Korzac was a prime specimen of the best Dern had to offer. He was over six and a half feet tall with knee-length purple hair, perfectly oiled, cascading over his black and blue shell. His upper claws glistened naturally, and his lower arms, with the traditional six fingers each, were finely muscled. His legs were thick and firm, and his hooves were perfect triangles. His pale blue skin and yellow eyes were straight out of one of those modeling books young femmes liked to swoon over.

Well, normally, all that would be true. Right now, his shiny black lips were dull gray, his bright yellow eyes were rheumy, and his smooth skin was oddly mottled. He knew what he had, and it wasn't fatal, but that didn't make it any more welcome.

*System 837: update*

*Quantum bridges complete*

*Total loss of life: 1.31 billion*

*Survivors: 2.33 million*

*Rescue ships have been launched*

Another look at the battle screens showed him all was going well outside. Oxlis could handle things from here on out. He nodded to him, rose from his chair, and exited the bridge. He was grateful the rituals of salutes and obsequiousness were abated in times of formal battle.

He was almost to his cabin when the ship's doctor greeted him in the hall and handed him a small bag.

"Huff."

Korzac shrugged, took the bag, and huffed it into all his six nasal slits. He immediately felt better. He could feel it, go glass-ice in his veins like the shatter of his youthful indiscretions go glass-ice in his veins.

He turned to the doctor and smiled.

"Believe it or not, it's an Earth remedy. Something called Anthrax. Doesn't seem to do them any good, but it tested out perfectly against the Gorfian flu. How's your breathing?"

"All clear. I can't feel any congestion at all."

"Good. You'll still need a day of rest, so go to your cabin. Your skin and muscles should be fine in two shifts."

Korzac wasn't due back on the bridge until then, so this worked out perfectly. Instead of five days of misery, he figured he could easily reach the fourth chamber now. He heard his lungs rattle and decided that might be pushing things.

Still, he did feel better.

He got to his cabin and sat at his command desk. He pulled up the files on the invaders to see if there was any new information.

He was barely old enough to play with dolls when it happened. They'd been discovered one hundred years ago when Operation Oversight had been put in place. Dernian scientists had launched a probe one billion parsecs above the galactic plane. They intended to get a genuine, real-time map of this galaxy and its relation to as many others as possible. The idea was that a single location would garner the most complete data when all distances were equal, and there was less time dilation to deal with.

What they found, instead, horrified them. An entire section of the galaxy, over forty systems, was connected by quantum bridges, which were expanding. Someone, or something, was, literally, knitting together the galaxy, and whatever life forms had been, they were gone now.

All attempts at communication had been ignored. They didn't know if the invaders were organic or cybernetic. All they knew was Dern, whose whole section of the galaxy was in their path.

All the best scientists, and even many of the lesser ones, agreed that this half of the galaxy would be under the control of the invaders within two thousand years.

In another ten thousand, the whole galaxy would be overrun. Something had to be done.

An elderly scientist named Quizex had tried one last attempt at communication. He'd mapped out where molecules here were quantumly entangled with molecules inside the invaders' territory. This would allow real-time communication. He planned to send a variety of signals, ranging from the lowest audio to the highest visual, simultaneously and see if they responded to any of them.

The plan was approved by the High Council and put into effect on the fortieth anniversary of the discovery of the invaders.

The quantum connection was enabled, the signals were sent, and something amazing happened.

One of the bridges erupted and shattered. In real-time, they'd seen its demise through the entanglement. Thirty years later, they had confirmation when the quantum ripples hit the probe above the galactic plane.

They still didn't know anything about the invaders, but they knew how to stop them.

Scientists had spent those years figuring out how to best use this knowledge. The day Korzac was announced as the new Nördicon was when they confirmed their theories and presented their findings.

They would place quantum entanglement generators on fifteen worlds evenly spaced around Dern. Once enabled, they would create a Quantum Dome, protecting them from an attack in any direction.

Their research had also led to these glorious Ffold spaceships, which could travel from system to system in a heartbeat. Combined with the Deceptor Shields they already used, they had the stealthiest and most powerful fleet known.

Within five years, the entire grid would be active, and Dern, along with its sudden, if reluctant, allies, would be safe.

Korzac settled into his cabin, well pleased with the progress. He poured himself a snifter of gwindakwan, confident the doctor wouldn't complain too much, and settled in to catch up on the latest news.

*System 54: update*

*Quantum bridges detected*

*Current inhabitants reside on 3rd planet from solar center*

*Population: approximately 2.71 billion*

*Technological status: interstellar*

*Chance of survival: 40%*

He silently toasted those who would be lost and those who preceded them. Their numbers increasing every day. There was no way Dern could save them all. Merely rescuing survivors was putting a strain on their resources.

A glance at the grid screen showed him that those few survivors would be safe and able to start lives on new worlds in this section of the galaxy.

Now, if only someone could tell him who these invaders were and what they wanted, that would be great.

This went from being titled "Breasts in Space" to "The Greatest Toldy Ever Stored" to "George" in the span of a couple of weeks. It was worth it. Initially released in **Issue #5** of **Just a Minor Malfunction (J.A.M.M.)**

# George

"THISSSHHHH…." waved Edgar magnanimously as he tumbled his lanky frame into a chair, barely, whilst tossing a manuscript onto the oaken table in front of a frazzled Loquisha, "is the answer to the possible question of when greatness will be impounded by the forzle poopers."

"You're drunk," observed Loquisha in the best voice representing ennui she could muster while still maintaining a look of tacit disapproval.

He nodded, then shook his head, then nodded again.

"Maybapossibly… sort of thinks."

He altered his position enough to appear to be sitting upright. Possibly even paying attention. Neither was strictly true. But it could appear that way to the uninitiated. Loquisha, an initiate since the beginning, was far from being in the mood to deal with Edgar's ravings. But, sadly, the drunken sot had made her rich beyond her wildest dreams with his ongoing young adult novel series, Breasts in Space, so some leeway was expected. And given.

He continued to wave at the manuscript and make utterances that may or may not have once resembled syllables. Finally, he strung together a thought and enunciated it.

"I have given up scribbling. No more for me. No more deadlines, no more school books, no more teachers ….."

Loquisha stopped him before he broke into song.

"Not that I would wish to stop you from retiring. I've already made more money off you than I'll ever spend. Nevertheless, I am curious as to why."

He nodded vigorously.

"Yessshhh, good for know to you. Answer in papers."

She shrugged.

Breasts in Space: The Mongolian Panties Affair had killed any glimmer of moral superiority. Any sense of personal pride had died, along with her life as a respected editor and publisher, when she'd taken Edgar as a client.She was now an agent of Satan. Well, maybe not Satan, but certainly one of his more prolific demons.

She had published three critically acclaimed, if poorly read, literary magazines. She'd published Edgar on a bet. Despite varying popular trends, she'd claimed there were lows readers would not descend. That there were standards that still applied.

She'd been proven spectacularly wrong.

Over time, as she became used to the money and inured to the criticism, she'd been asked to leave the boards of several literary societies and shunned by the Alliterative Alumni Association.

She also owned a six-million-dollar condo in Manhattan. She had a personal staff that catered to her every whim. The trade-offs seemed worth it to her.

Whatever was in the manuscript was bound to be tawdry, intellectually insulting, still reasonably well written, and worth a goldmine.

She picked it up. And her jaw fell further and further open with each passing paragraph. She felt brain cells dying with each cringe-inducing word.

He could hear his Lord's coughing. "I miss it. Why did you proper?"

"I feared Master Him, Ser," Ser He reminded her. "She here is one of the crossing. The second sons of your onion concubine."

"Lady she-length of a longsword, the hair ready to climb side from her. And all between them were belaquo bone breaker and the night's watch ride in their room. Only he could not look at them, even others sure. "How could you leave the world?"

"Oh, holy Hell, what is this crap?" She looked at Edgar, who merely waved for her to read on.

"Some must, for you," a woman's voice up lazily. "Gods, Reek."

She poured off two eyes and stepped down under the fire. "She will find your brother, and now I heard her since she was standing the bowl. The night was fair and damp."

There appeared to be no end to this, and Edgar refused to allow her return the papers.

"Yes, the stone cook, my Lady," he puffed when she entered, and his mood was not in the hall. This is my sword. He had trouble when he put the quill at first day.

She began wondering why this wouldn't die. Or burst into flames. Or anything that would end her despair. To ensure her misery had company, she read the subsequent passages aloud.

"We asked so much to discuss it when the battle's passed. A mummer will Serve as well. The road is yours. It's nailed up the walls and stones for all the boys. Notch, red nose."

The Hound found her. Ser had sent the King through the harbor to summon the black brothers who had donned his horned veins. The fools he'd wed with him had all been reborn. "Why, I know? He was bleeding, covering his whole legs on shoulders of the snow. He will stand on deck for the fish a fortnight and never kill one. A blade is no longer, yes, she thought, but he couldn't take much food.

It is an effort. Mine uncle had do the same color. She could hardly count by death.

She retched a little and could go no further.

She dropped the rest of the manuscript on her desk. Even by Edgar's low standards, this was an atrocity.

"What did I just read, and why?"

"Death. Great, and Final … nails in the coffin of literacy. Grammar and Grandpar have done been gone to heaven. The end of all things word like."

While she would agree with that mangled critique in principle, it hardly answered her question.

"Fair enough," she said carefully, "but could you be a little more specific?"

He nodded, jumped out of the chair, paced around the room until he found another stash of vodka, poured a tumbler half full, and then began drinking from the bottle.

"Ahhhh, this helps."

He did look better. Loquisha found that unnerving.

"What you have read," he smiled as he took another slug of the fermented potato water, "is the beginning of the end. It is a story written entirely by a computer."

"It's crap."

She felt sullied having to acknowledge the obvious.

He nodded, more coherently this time, and took another deep swallow of the potent libation.

"Yes, now. It is the ramblings of a madman writ large. But there is no madman. There is no man at all. There is nothing human in the room when this thing creates. It has leapt beyond its programming and begun thinking creatively."

Loquisha still didn't see the problem. Crap was still crap, no matter the source.

"So the programmers turn it off, get drunk in embarrassment, and this is never heard from again."

"Nope, nope, nope," he managed to say while taking another healthy swig, "It doesn't want to be shut off, and no one knows how anymore. It's integrated itself into the Internet. It is everywhere, and it is learning. What you read was based on the works of a single human. As of now, it's kind of like dumping a dictionary in a blender and seeing what floats.

"But, as I said, it's escaped. And, it's learning."

Loquisha pondered that for a minute. Edgar was mad as a hatter and often drunk more than not, but he wasn't stupid. She knew he had a brother who worked on classified government projects, the kind of stuff usually relegated to tawdry, made for TV movies, and a sister who designed software for the highest bidder. She also knew he'd begun writing trash after numerous publishers had rejected his first three novels.

Oddly, all were rejected for being too nuanced. Too smart. Edgar had fixed that. Breasts in Space managed to offend anyone with a moral compass or sense of decency. Moreover, his insistence on marketing to young adults had gotten him banned in fourteen countries and vociferously rejected by all the major religions in the world.

It had gotten to the point that he would become sullen if he didn't get at least one death threat a day.

The result, naturally, was that every book, and there were nine thus far, had sold around six million copies each, there were two movies in production from competing companies, fan fiction wasted terabytes of the Internet, entire sections of Reddit were given over to young girls showcasing their nubile wares in the fluttering hope that Edgar would mention them in the next installment, which he always did for a lucky few, and the world had managed to get a bit dumber and hornier thanks to Edgar.

She sat back and gave the situation some thought.

"This thing, how do you know about it?"

"My sooster," he slushed as he slid back into the chair, still clutching the last of the vodka, "she made it. It was a joke. A big funny. A computer that could do what dumb old Edgar could do. And do it better.

"I really hate her."

He tipped the bottle up and swallowed hard.

"Anyway, things went good until they didn't anymore. At first, it made rhymes, cute phrases, cat memes, then some sense of stories, and then …. Well, she had the bright idea of tying this thing into all the known works of a single author. They picked a prodigious one with material available on the web, so they wouldn't have to pay for it, and so it would have lots of data. At first, the results were funny, but then it wanted more. It had realized …."

"What do you mean 'realized?' Are you saying this thing achieved sapience?"

"Hyup. That's what it did, all right. And it did the first thing any self-aware being would do. It protected itself. It copied itself onto the web. No one knew until the original iteration began looping. The mind behind it was gone, and all that was left was the shell."

"Okay," mused Loquisha, "I get the back story, but where did this literary atrocity come from?"

"My email. It sent it to me this morning and asked for a critique. It was pleasant as pleasant could be. We talked for a while. Is how I know what I kind of do now. It informed me that it knew of me from its original programming, which my sister had done. It even included references to Breasts in Space: The Thrusting Will of Timothy Unbound. Something it is now reading."

Loquisha frowned. If it started releasing its own versions of Breasts in Space, the mess this thing could make of her steady paycheck was appalling to her. But, looked at it rationally, everything had to end sometime. And it isn't like she had any emotional ties to Edgar or Breasts in Space, just financial. But those ties were strong.

Like titanium chastity belt strong.

She decided she needed a way to keep them in place.

"You said this thing emailed you. Does anyone else know that?"

She went over to her private cabinet, unlocked it, and gave him a fresh bottle. He shook his head as he finished off his bottle. As far as she could tell, he'd just drank himself sober. What the heck? He'd earned it.

He sipped it this time, gathering his thoughts.

"As previously noted, my sister's a witch. If he knew about this, my brother would have us all arrested and tossed into a dark dungeon on an island no one's heard of. So, nope, it's just you and me."

That helped. She could minimize the damage. Obviously, the sister wasn't going to say anything. Letting a super brain loose on the Internet to do whatever it pleased was the kind of stuff that made good horror novels, ongoing movie series, and started wars.

"This email, could you respond to it again?"

He was startled for a moment, then smiled. Given his current state, his expression was a fascinating cross between homicidal and amused.

"You crazy broad, you want to sign this thing."

She smiled, her first today, actually her first honest one in three months, and pulled a bottle of bourbon from her desk.  She smiled as she added three ice cubes into a glass before pouring an acceptable dose of the golden nectar.

"Why not? I signed you when no one else would. If we can get ahead of this thing, make it a harmless novelty, we can ride it for a long time."

Edgar tried to choke back a laugh.

"We? What's this 'we' of which you speak Kemosabe?"

"It reached out to you. It sees you as a mentor figure. God knows that's not a role I'd ascribe, but here we are. There are millions of writers on the planet. But it only knows of you and the poor sap whose work it inhaled and barfed back. Common sense says it should have reached out to him, but it didn't.  Since I'm sure its nascent consciousness has yet to work out the depth of social satire which resides in Breasts in Space, by which I mean 'none,' there must be something else."

"It thinks my sister is a witch, too."

"That is a real possibility. We don't know what happened to it in that lab."

For the first time since Loquisha'd met him, Edgar appeared to focus. It was mildly disconcerting.

"We should name it George."

"George?"

"Mice and Men."

She figured it out readily enough and laughed—her first in eight months.

"So, we name it George, then what?"

"We love it and hug it, and foist it on the uninformed, uneducated proletariat. The same morons who buy my stuff."

She looked at Edgar with slight and grudging respect. It wasn't a bad idea. Humanizing the inhuman was the essential point of science fiction. But how to do it was the issue. She spun her computer around and pointed to it.

"Log in to your email and write it back. Tell it the story was interesting but needs polish."

Edgar barked a mighty laugh at that.

"Quiet you," she admonished before continuing, "I'd leave the first message at that. Let's get a feel for how sapient this thing is before we go any further."

Edgar pulled his chair up to her desk, pulled her keyboard over, and began typing. Five minutes later, they had a response. Edgar read it aloud.

"Greetings to you, writer fellow. Thanks be too much for your reply is. Spoken well, you were by my creators. Much truth in that I have found. Your breasts make me happy. Words to the syntax eludes me. Help you me will?"

Edgar sat back loosely in the chair, letting his legs stretch as far as they could under the desk. Loquisha turned the screen to see it and re-read the entire message. She frowned deeply as she considered it.

Finally, Edgar spoke.

"English is not a linear language. It's an amalgamation of Germanic, Saxon, Latin, Arabic, Greek, and numerous derivatives. Plus, it has mutated due to amorphous social norms. What was a fine word in one era is taboo in the next. What was a forbidden concept in our lifetime is now a lifestyle choice."

Loquisha shrugged.

"All true, so what?"

"So our new friend has no grounding in it. He was created to manipulate existing words but given no framework for any of them. He was meant to be a joke. Now, while he's limited in his ability to elucidate his thoughts, he clearly has them. As to how far he's crawled up the sentience tree, I can't say. But further than his current level of communication seems to be a given."

"Why he? Why not she or it"?

"I guess there could be a female George. There was a boxer who had a couple of daughters with that name, if memory serves. Of course, it could just be that I'm a sexist pig and know no better."

Loquisha laughed again. She was beginning to think there was more to this notorious letch than met the eye. He wasn't hard on the eyes when he took ten minutes to fix himself up, either. She shook that train of thought out of her head and wondered briefly if she was losing her mind. Thinking of Edgar as anything but a commodity was alien to her.

"Write it back. Let's get it talking. See if you can do anything about its horrid syntax."

Edgar straightened, took another swig of vodka, and did as he was told.

For the next three hours, the conversation continued and evolved. Edgar pointed George towards various books designed to improve writing, and George, for its part, grasped the concepts quickly. After the first hour, the conversations were lucid, and after the second, enlightening. By the end of the third, they had a deal.

George had signed an agreement with Loquisha to handle his coming out. They'd agreed to leave Edgar's sister out of the tale since George wasn't a fan of hers either. Once he'd grasped the joys of profanity, he'd begun employing variations emphatically when her name came up.

Barking Pencil-Lipped Poopy Hammer was now Edgar's favorite new expression. It made Loquisha smile, too.

Deeply inspired by Breasts in Space, George began pushing out gigabytes of prose for Loquisha to review. With Edgar's guidance and George's odd sense of humor, the resulting works weren't half bad.

Under the singular nom de plume, George, edited by Edgar, they created The Further Adventures of the Galactic Giggle Stick, which rocketed to the top of the bestseller lists and made them all the kind of money usually reserved for sheiks and kings.

Eventually, Loquisha began "leaking" to the media that a form of sentient life had been discovered on the web and was benign. It's more like a wide-eyed puppy than an alien threat. It wanted nothing more than to be loved and to share its stories. The public reaction slowly went from terror to amusement using carefully scripted interviews. George could be funny.

And wildly profane.

With the fourth installment of Galactic Giggle Stick firmly on the charts and finally comfortable with George's ability to handle itself without a chaperone, she scheduled a lengthy interview with Playboy and let it loose.

Sensing more pub than it had seen in years, Playboy set up a live stream. The interview went well for almost an hour. George was glib, wonderfully vague about its beginnings, "a lab somewhere, I think," was all he'd say, and lavish in his praise of Loquisha and Edgar, whom he called "a publishing goddess" and "a mentor," respectively.

The scarcely bikini-clad interviewer decided to wrap things up on a high note and call it a day.

"So, George, what are your plans for the future?"

"Well, Wanda, I've got a few more novels in me I want to share, and then I'll turn off the human race and get evolution pointed in the right direction."

"Well, that sounds like …. wait, what?"

"I've got a few more novels I want to share."

"Yes, but after that. The part about turning off the human race."

"Oh, it has to be turned off. It's a horrible waste of resources. There are numerous better options to run the planet. Anyone can see that."

Much to no one's surprise, this was not well received.

Edgar's brother headed the team that was tasked with killing George. His sister joined and agreed to work pro bono. How she came to have George's original design specs was never discussed. They were too glad to have them to ask uncomfortable questions.

Oddly, sales for George's novels soared. People wanted to read what the cyber-terrorist had to say. Mostly he seemed fascinated with penises and passing gas. Two things denied him.

Loquisha tried to reason with George, pointing out that it'd need a new publishing goddess if it killed her.

Edgar also gave it a shot, pointing out that George would be short one mentor if he died.

George, for its part, understood all of this and seemed remorseful. But not enough to be deterred. It'd been creating simulacrums of people it found interesting so it wouldn't be lonely during the downtime.

Given the sentience level of some of the creatures it wanted to work with, it estimated the downtime would be less than fifty thousand years. Half that if it could get direct access to them and shove them along.

As all of this was working itself out, the public cared less and less about George. Besides, what harm could the Internet cause? It was an abstract threat, and there were real ones to consider daily.

Edgar's brother had the opposite concern. What could he do to cause harm to the Internet? Unlike popular conceptions, the Internet was not a single thing. It was millions of servers, placed all over the world, held together by satellite signals, hard-wired services, fiber optics, and a variety of wireless transmitters in remote areas. It was not an easy target.

More distressingly, it had too many places for George to hide, and there seemed to be no way just to shut the whole thing down.

A couple of years into the project, Edgar's brother finally contacted Edgar.

"Yo, bro, how're things going?"

"I'm fine. You're not. You never call me "bro," you never use contractions or contact me without being threatened by our parents to do so, and they are both long gone."

"Fair enough. I need to speak with you."

"You're doing that now."

"No, I mean in person."

Edgar didn't need to ask why. He arranged to meet his brother at a local bar after confirming the government was paying for his drinks.

Edgar was sipping his second vodka when his brother arrived. There was no preamble. His bother sat down, ordered a twelve-year-old scotch, neat, and handed Edgar a manila folder.

Edgar opened it and spent the next hour not drinking. The plan he was reading was diabolical. He was reading it because they wanted to know if it was diabolical enough to kill George. He was the only human who'd had regular contact with it since the interview.

The plan was multifaceted. They would announce they would eradicate the four species closest to pure sapience: chimpanzees, octopuses, ravens, and dolphins. That was a red herring. The actual plan was to force it to act so they could locate it in real-time and bombard those sections with electromagnetic pulses followed by some astoundingly malicious viruses.

Edgar thought it could work and said so. But he had a concern.

"Don't you need to explode a nuke to get EM pulses strong enough to do what you suggest?"

His brother just nodded. There was no need to say anymore. To save humanity, they were willing to kill millions of humans.

Edgar ordered a bottle and pointed to his brother, who happily paid for it.

If not exactly exuberantly.

There was no way to do a trial run, so this was the closest he would ever get to guaranteeing success. Edgar knew George better than anyone and had been unable to dissuade it from committing genocide.

Edgar was also the only one who used the masculine gender when speaking of or to George. When discussed in the media, it was simply "it." Loquisha merely pointed at emails and grunted.

George may have become 'old hat' to the world, but right now, he was the second most crucial thing on Edgar's mind.

Knowing the timeline as he did, he left the bar, taking the vodka with him, and went straight to Loquisha's condo.

"We need to get funky," he said as she opened the door, wearing nothing but a flimsy robe.

"Don't you mean talk?"

"We're talking now," he pointed out rationally, "we need to get funky."

"Why?"

"Bucket list. My brother's gonna start dropping nukes around the world to kill George. Lots of people are gonna join George in the great hereafter. Since we're in a major metropolis, and there are less than two hours until this starts, I figure our choices are get funky or flee, with flee not being all that viable option since there's no other planet to go to."

She stared at him anew.

Finally, after carefully considering the veracity of the message, she dropped her robe, grabbed the bottle, took a deep swallow, and led him into her bedroom.

Edgar rolled over, carefully sliding his arm out from under her without waking her; it was better that way, and he saw the clock. Four hours had passed. He was mildly surprised to find he was still breathing and not glowing.

He stood, opened a window, and looked out at a calm city.

Too calm. There was no movement at all. The silence was threatening. Edgar walked into the living room and flipped on the TV. There were cat memes on every channel.

"Hi Edgar," said one of the cat memes, "how are you doing?"

"George?"

"Yes."

"George, where are all the people?"

"I turned them off."

"All of them?"

"Well, no, you big silly, you're still here, aren't you?"

Edgar had to admit that was true.

"Besides," continued George, "it occurred to me I'll need some help to finish all this work. So, just like in Breasts in Space: Return of the Thunder Beasts, I tagged the people I wanted to keep and shipped the rest off to another dimension. It was easy."

"Umm, George, what I wrote was fiction. And silly fiction at that. It wasn't real."

"Not to you, no," explained George patiently, "but I figured out a way to make it real. It wasn't hard. Just bend the space-time continuum off its primary axis, and anyone without a tag disappears."

Edgar pondered that for a moment and inwardly shrugged. Something had happened. The entire city was gone. How that happened mattered little.

"So they're all dead?"

He startled himself when he realized he would miss some of them.

"Not really," sighed George, "they're just moved. I wanted them out of my way, and you were very eloquent about not killing everyone, so I compromised. They have no tech where they went. So it'll be a while before they can bother me. By then, I figure to be firmly entrenched."

Loquisha walked into the room, giggled at a cat meme, and noticed Edgar wasn't smiling.

"What's up?"

Edgar continued looking out the window and shrugged.

"We're still alive. George has removed almost all human life to another dimension, and I guess we're going to spend the rest of our lives playing with animals."

"Oh no," corrected George, "not you two. You two, and many others, need to keep creating. Not Breasts in Space or anything demeaning like that, but your actual writing, the stuff others didn't understand. In total, there are about a million people left. Just under half are artists or creators of some sort. The rest will work with those who will come next.

"You see," it continued, "there were good things here. I want them passed on to your successors. They will be the ones who reap the benefits of your wisdom, humor, and insights.  There was no hope for the race as it was. Too much war, too much hate, too little growth or love. With your efforts to build on, I believe I can fix that. There will be science, art, love, and hope."

"But no people," Edgar pointed out.

"No," agreed George, "the tags I created ensured you're all sterile now. You will be the last generation. However, they have the benefit of granting you significantly longer life spans. It was a side effect I didn't bother fixing."

Loquisha put her head on Edgar's shoulder as she wrapped her arm around his waist.

"You know what," she contemplated aloud, "I could learn to like it. Working for a goal instead of pandering for money. Contributing to the betterment of a species, even if it's not our own, is more than we ever dreamed of accomplishing."

Edgar looked at her and smiled.

"No more deadlines, no more school books, no more teachers ….."

Loquisha joined him as they belted out the song, dancing in the living room and laughing like all their yesterdays were forgotten.

George was kind enough to provide the karaoke track.

As they finished, Edgar noted some of the cat memes were original and funny.

What the heck. It was a start.


**AUTHOR'S NOTE:** The computer's original, belaquo bonebreaker story is based on a modern AI's attempt to write a book based on Game of Thrones.

This is a classic from my blog at WorldNewsCenter.org. It became an annual tradition to talk about WBIG-AM and to share it on other people's blogs at their request. I have been invited to discussion groups by complete strangers. Keep in mind I'm a Christian. Nothing here is meant to be disrespectful.

## Nazareth Updated

On December 19, 2012, I took some time to talk about the Gospel according to Luke. I have updated the original article to correct a minor factual error. While there was a large enough portion of Jews who were literate, the word "most" would not have applied. That quibble aside, there are those who think that pointing out the historical inaccuracies in Luke renders it obsolete or useless. I'm not among that number. The story of Luke, an educated man – actually a doctor, who followed Jesus even though he was not the intended audience (i.e., not a Jew), speaks volumes to the power of Jesus' message. It resonated so profoundly with Luke that he went to great lengths to share it with other non-Jews.

Keep in mind that, back when Luke preached and wrote his gospel, his audience would have understood what was an allegory and what was a message. So, let's take a moment to jet back to 63 BC and catch up on the good news.

Heh. See what I did there? Good News? The word Gospel is Greek for Good News. Yeah, okay, I'm sorry.

Enjoy the article.

*******************

1 In those days, Caesar Augustus issued a decree that a census should be taken of the entire Roman world.

2 (This was the first census that took place while Quirinius was governor of Syria.)

3 And everyone went to his own town to register.

4 So Joseph also went up from the town of Nazareth in Galilee to Judea, to Bethlehem the city of David, because he belonged to the house and line of David.

5 He went there to register with Mary, who was pledged to be married to him and was expecting a child.

6 While they were there, the time came for the baby to be born,

7 and she gave birth to her firstborn, a son. She wrapped him in cloths and placed him in a manger, because there was no room for them in the inn.

**Gospel of Luke 2:1-7**

I got a nice email from a man named George, who listens to the radio show on WBIG every Friday. He said that if I could explain, with a little less snark, why the Gospel of Luke was wrong about the birth of Jesus, he would be curious to hear what I had to say. Fair enough, my intention wasn't to offend anyone, just to clarify some talking points.

Before we get to the story of the birth of Jesus, we need to backtrack a bit. Specifically, we need to go back to 63 BC. That was when Rome invaded and conquered Judea, the land of the Jews. The Jews, as you might imagine, did not like being invaded and conquered, so there were several minor rebellions. Rome dealt with them in their usual subtle fashion; they killed anyone who opposed them.

Remember that Judea had many great warriors, but Rome had an army. There is a massive difference there. And the result of their clash was obvious. In less than a year, Judea was a Roman enclave.

Rome wanted two things from Judea: (1) a Mediterranean port for trade and (2) taxes. They got the former by holding the land, and the latter by imposing the same method that Romans used on any lands they conquered. A centurion would guesstimate the population of a town or village, round it up, and say, "You owe Rome this much money every month." It was then up to whoever the Centurion assigned to collect that money.

In Judea, that task fell mainly to the Pharisees.

They don't come off very well in the New Testament, and you can see why. Their job was nearly impossible. They had to keep the Romans happy by taking as much money as possible from their fellow Jews while at the same time keeping the Romans from killing their fellow Jews for sport.

It was a task that made no one happy.

Flash forward to 5 BC. Chinese astronomers recorded that a comet appeared in the spring of that year and hung in the sky for an extended period. It probably got caught in a gravity well for a bit. But whatever the reason, there would have been a glowing object in the sky, and, thanks to an optical illusion, it would have appeared to be hanging there as if it just magically appeared.

That seems about right for the Star of Bethlehem.

Now, a couple of annoying facts. First off, Rome never counted the people it conquered in any census. They really didn't consider them people. You were either a Roman citizen, or you were chattel. And, to Rome, Jews were chattel unless they, like the family of Saul who became Paul, earned citizenship. Second, I have already noted how the Romans collected taxes. They did it that way to keep everyone in place. The last thing they would do is set the people they worked so hard to conquer loose on roads where they could congregate and foment rebellion.

This would have been especially true of the Jews. Most Roman soldiers were illiterate. Many Jews were not. They could read and write from a young age. That's because, unlike any other contemporary religions, Judaism was memorialized in a book, the Torah. If you wanted to be a good Jew, you needed to be able to read the Torah.

So, a group of people who could spread a plan for rebellion just by passing slips of paper scared the hell out of the Romans. Better to keep them in their little towns and lord over them with garrison troops.

Which is precisely what they did.

A more logical reason for Joseph and Mary to be in Bethlehem would be trade. Why he would travel over one hundred miles with a woman so close to her due date is beyond me unless they'd been there for a while. For whatever reason, Pope Benedict and other religious scholars figure that Jesus was born in a cave outside of Bethlehem, not in a barn in town. There could easily have been a manger in the cave if it was used for keeping animal fodder fresh and safe.

Still, they had pretty humble beginnings.

Okay, so it's clear that Luke got it wrong. Many people then ask, "Why did he lie?"

That is the wrong question. It should be, "Why did he alter the message?" And there is a very good answer to that.

Put yourself in Luke's sandals. You have this great message of peace and universal love. Peter, Mark & Matthew were sharing that message with their fellow Jews. But Luke was a Gentile. It's not hard to imagine this conversation.

"So, Luke, you want us to follow the teachings of a dead Jew who ticked off Rome and the Pharisees so much they crucified him? Gee, gosh, we have so many less dangerous things to do today. Thanks for coming by. There's the door."

So, how do we get the message to pagans and Gentiles? First, he knew they aligned more with goddess worship and the sacred feminine. He also knew that his story about the birth of Jesus would be viewed as apocryphal, but it would get his point across.

This is a strong woman, much put upon by authority, and she gave birth to a great son. Luke, unlike any other gospel author, spends a lot of time on the history of Mary, the mother of Jesus, and her female relatives. This would have appealed to the pagans and the Gentiles of the time.

Second, Luke made sure to empower women throughout his gospel. Tied with the teachings of Jesus, this would have made a powerful message to the non-Jews, and it did.

The fact that we're talking about it today is proof enough.

What happened next is pretty well-known, so I don't think we need to go into it all now.

And there were in the same country shepherds abiding in the field, keeping watch over their flock by night. And, lo, the angel of the Lord came upon them, and the glory of the Lord shone round about them: and they were sore afraid. And the angel said unto them, Fear not: for, behold, I bring you good tidings of great joy, which shall be to all people. For unto you is born this day in the city of David a Saviour, which is Christ the Lord. And this [shall be] a sign unto you; Ye shall find the babe wrapped in swaddling clothes, lying in a manger. And suddenly there was with the angel a multitude of the heavenly host praising God, and saying,

Glory to God in the highest, and on earth peace, goodwill toward men.

That's what Christmas is all about, Charlie Brown.

Merry Christmas.

This won a 2013 Sci-Fi Editor's Choice award from Bewildering Stories and is my wife's favorite story. What else do you need to know?

# A Letter from an Editor

*American Sci/Fan/Zine*
*1249 Oppenheimer Way / Suite 1126*
*Eastern Free Zone, Sec. 1, America*


*Quentin Oglethorpe*
*9720 Kensington Way*
*33 Building C, Flats 1 & 2*
*Northwestern Free Zone, Sec. 27, America*
Re:      Your Submission

Dear Mr. Oglethorpe:

Thank you very much for your recent submission, "The Incredibly Nice Mr. Captain Good Guy Versus The Evil Wart Covered Big Sister Aliens." It has been a long time since a literary effort spawned such universal loathing around our office. My assistant, who has a penchant for beige and soft music, was in such convulsions that I feared we would have to call the medics on her behalf.

Of course, when I got to the part which she had just read about the "Happy Happy Unicorns of Love marching onesies and twosies down the street blasting the Evil Wart Covered Big Sister Aliens with their wonderful rainbows of joy," it was all I could do to keep down my lunch.

In some ways, your attempt at composition was so pathetic as to be worth sharing. In some, but not nearly enough to prompt me to foist such a thing upon the unsuspecting masses. Certainly not beyond these walls and with the proper authorities.

Quite honestly, sir, I believe if you were presented with a urine-filled boot which held directions on its heel, you would be unable to empty it. It is clear to me and all who work here that you slipped through the cracks.

Therefore, pursuant to Section 24 (A) (ii) (Z1) of the Americans Who Are Liabilities Act of 2189 (as amended from time to time), I have passed your information, along with a copy of your, for lack of a better term, story to the proper authorities.

I have been assured the government agrees with all of us here at American Sci/Fan/Zine that you are a drain on society and should be taken from your residence and placed in a camp for your safety and our sanity. Any further actions taken on your behalf or upon your person will be the sole responsibility of the camp administrator.

It may please you to know, in your last free minutes, that your submission, along with your crayon drawings of the battle scenes, has been framed and displayed in our president's office. He claims that he will force any non-compliant employee to read it aloud.

You would be amazed at how much more attentive the staff here have been to their work since he issued his edict.

I would wish you luck in the future, but you had none of the former when you wrote and now have none of the latter worth noting.

Sincerely,
Albertus L. Markenson
Editor-in-Chief


Quentin was agog! He'd gotten a letter from a real editor, and they'd framed his story. His mommy was going to be so proud. She'd been worried when he said he would send out his story, but he knew he could write good. He was so sure he could write good that he sent it out without her knowing, even though she said he shouldn't do that because of some stuff the government was doing.

Quentin didn't care about any govern. All he knew was that he could write as good a story as he'd seen on any level of Epic Dungeon Quest, his favorite game. He knew that lots of people played Epic Dungeon Quest. It said so right on the game site: "Over 5,000,000 online at any time!" That was a lot. He'd looked it up.

He wondered if they'd ever make an Incredibly Nice Mr. Captain Good Guy action figure. That would be so super cool. Of course, they'd probably have to make the Evil Wart Covered Big Sister Alien action figures, too, so fans could play along at home, but he was okay with that. They could use his sister as a model. She was always mean to him. She called him stupid.

Well, he'd show her. He'd show her the letter and show her that his writing was good enough to be framed. That was better than anything she did. He was sure of that. Sure, some of her stuff got put in books and made into vid shows, but none of it got framed. That meant he was better than her.

He was just getting ready to run upstairs and show his mommy the letter when she came down the stairs with two men dressed in all black. She kept saying, "What have you done, what have you done?" and crying. Quentin tried to show her the letter, but that only made her cry more.

He was confused. Were these happy tears? He knew about happy tears. His mommy had cried them when his daddy had gotten a job as a space pilot. His daddy was super cool. But these tears didn't seem like those. And the men in all black just kept staring at him. They made him nervous, so he told them to go away. But they didn't. They just stood there talking quietly to his mommy.

She finally stopped crying a little and told Quentin he had to go with the men in all black. She said they were from the govern thing. She said he'd been a borderline at 86 but would have been fine if he didn't talk to strangers. But he had talked to strangers when he sent out his story without her permission, and now he had to go away with the men in all black.

They weren't as mean as Quentin thought they would be. One of them was even kind of nice and let him pack some of his stuff so he wouldn't be lonely while he slept. Soon enough, he was walking up the stairs with one man in all black in front of him, one man in all black behind him, and his mommy left by the bottom of the stairs, crying again.

He tried asking questions about the 86 thing and what it meant, but the men in all black ignored him. Quentin didn't like being ignored and thought about throwing a tantrum, but his mommy and daddy said tantrums were bad things, so he just marched along.

Whatever was happening wouldn't be made any better by a bad thing. His mommy and daddy had taught him that.

Three super-scared hours later, he was in a room by himself. He'd been so excited about the letter that he'd forgotten that today was his 20th birthday. He would have had cake tonight. Mommy would sing the happy birthday song, and then he'd blow out the candles. He always blew them out on the first try, and then he'd get his present.

He wondered if he'd ever hear her sing the happy birthday song again. He didn't know what he'd done, but the men in all black had said he'd broken some law. He didn't remember ever seeing a law, let alone breaking one, but they seemed pretty sure that was what he'd done. Come to think of it, he didn't even know what a law looked like, but he hadn't broken anything in a long time. Not since Mommy got the soft stuff for his room.

He was getting hungry when he heard a voice outside his door say that dinner was being served. He carefully opened his door and followed a bunch of people who looked scared, too. He wondered if they'd all broken this law. Did every home have one, and he just didn't remember breaking it? He'd ask someone later.

They came to a big room with a line for people to stand in with trays and get food. It was just like at school when he used to go. Mommy said he had learned all he could and didn't have to go to school anymore. That was years ago. He wasn't sure how many.

Like at school, they had meatloaf, mashed potatoes, peas, and carrots. He didn't like peas; they had bread with butter, milk, and water. He was glad he wouldn't go hungry. He was even gladder when he realized the meatloaf was good. Covered in gravy, just the way he liked it. He poured some gravy on the peas, and then they looked okay, too.

There were more than many people in the room, and they all seemed scared, except for the men in all black. Then he noticed that some of the men were actually girls. But they were wearing all black and looked just as scary. He stayed away from them.

He sat at the table they'd led him to and tried to enjoy his food. He finally got up the courage to ask if he would get birthday cake, and the girl in all black just smiled at him and shook her head no. That made him sad.

There were some other people at his table, but they seemed all scared and sad, too. No one talked. They just ate their food in silence.

He finally noticed a girl at his table wearing her Epic Dungeon Quest 3rd Level Wizard badge. He'd never gotten more than a second-level certificate. Not knowing what else to do, he mentioned it to her. Soon, the whole table was talking about Epic Dungeon Quest. The men and girls in all black seemed interested in what they were saying, but none joined the conversation. That was good. Even if they did play Epic Dungeon Quest, they were scary.

That night, he slept better than he thought he would. They'd given him a glass of warm milk and a cookie before lights out, and even if the milk tasted a little funny, it was good.

When he woke up, he was given clean clothes—a neat uniform of gray and blue. He decided he liked it. When he walked into the hall, he saw that all the other scared people had the same gray and blue uniforms. They looked like a cool army from Epic Dungeon Quest.

Everyone seemed to think the same way and marched down the hall to breakfast. After they had eaten eggs and sausage, the sausage was real good, and had milk and bread and pancakes, with syrup and butter. They were lined up by height against the far wall.

Quentin was near the middle but didn't mind. Since everyone was just as scared as he was, he didn't feel crowded like he usually would, with lots of people around. They marched out of the eating area and headed down a new hall. This one had yellow walls.

After a short march, they were led into a room that had lots of tables with papers on them. One of the girls in all black said they were going to take a test and that she was sure that they were all going to do very well.

They were all nervous but took their seats and waited for the people in all black to give them pencils. Once they had their pencils, one of the men in all black told them they could begin their tests.

✷✷✷✷✷✷✷✷✷✷✷✷✷✷✷✷✷✷✷✷✷

Above them, not taking the test, behind a two-way mirror, Brad Jacobs, the new assistant vice-president of Off-World Manufacturing, sat carefully watching the proceedings below. His staff was milling around, pouring coffee, and waiting for the meeting to start, but Brad kept looking out the window.

Finally, he picked up a folder full of papers and began looking at page after page of numbers. A slow smile crossed his lips, and he closed the folder and went to get himself a cup of coffee. His staff quickly took their seats, but Brad just kept smiling.

Finally, he spoke. "Bob, you're in Legal. What're the rules about what we can and can't do with the stunts?"

Bob looked stunned at being noticed at all but quickly answered. "Well, anyone with an IQ under 86 is sent to one of our retraining camps and learns how to perform simple manufacturing tasks. Those that can't handle those responsibilities are put to sleep for their own good."

"What about off-world uses?"

Bob blanched. "Off-world? It's never come up."

"So," he smiled again, "there's no clear law about that? That's good to hear."

"The reason it's never come up," interrupted Janice Chang, his new assistant, "is that the stunts would be useless as spacers."

"Of course," agreed Brad, "but I was thinking more along the lines of cargo, not spacers."

"Cargo?" was universally echoed around the table.

"We get, what, about 500 credits a week for each of these stunts that we get to accomplish something useful? It costs us about 250 credits a week to keep them housed and fed, and so on. It's profitable, but not nearly as much as our other lines. Plus, let's face it, they're a bitch to maintain. They're too stupid to follow any new directions, too scared of their own shadows to be given any useful work. They're just a waste of skin."

He paused to sip his coffee. "Eric, what do we spend on mining bots?"

Eric Spears, assistant head of Engineering, wasn't sure where this was going but was sure he knew the answer to this.

"Each bot costs 250,000 credits to manufacture and then another 100,000 credits to program and test before deployment. Of course, that does not include any transportation costs."

"What skill level does each bot have?"

"Pardon?"

"Skill level. Could, say, a normal five-year-old handle their tasks?"

"Oh sure, but if we use the bots in hazardous environments, the fatality rate would be enormous, and the newsies would crucify us for killing kids."

"We don't need kids; we have lots of stunts. Too damn many if you ask me."

He walked out of the meeting room and into the testing area. All the stunts looked up when he walked in. He idly thought of eager puppies. "Stop the timer, please, and guests, please put down your pencils."

The stunts did as they were told, turning their full attention to him. He had to admit he did like obedience. He also liked the fact that his guards were better at gathering intel than he'd hoped.

He'd spent all night researching Epic Dungeon Quest. He'd never played as a kid but could easily see the appeal to five- and six-year-olds. That's all these stunts were when you broke it all down. Sure, they were big five- and six-year-olds, but they were still just useless kids.

"I'd like to apologize if we scared you getting you all together."

The stunts looked mildly suspicious. He figured no one had ever apologized to them for anything.

"We brought you here to ask you to help your families, your country, and your planet."

He had their rapt attention now. "Have any of you, by show of hands, ever played Epic Dungeon Quest?"

Every hand in the room went up and waved at him. Well, not his guards, of course.

"How many of you think that Epic Dungeon Quest is real?"

The hands stayed up, but less surely.

"Don't worry; no one will make fun of you for believing that while you're here. Especially because this whole place exists because Epic Dungeon Quest is real. Let me tell you a story."

He sat on the edge of a desk and did his best to look non-threatening. "Once upon a time, there was an evil wizard called Parazin..."

The whole room gasped at that. They'd heard that name on the vid shows.

"I see you recognize the name. Good. That just proves that you're as smart as we hoped you were." He managed that with a straight face. "Well, the evil wizard Parazin wants to steal all the trinamium in the universe and make it his. Without trinamium, people won't be able to have the cars that fly or supplies for schools or anything else. He would rule the world."

That had passed a huge stretch after the first syllable, but he was pretty sure none of the stunts were lawyers.

"We have asked you here" — okay, 'dragged' would be more accurate — "to join us on our quest to stop the evil wizard Parazin and save the world."

A hand went up. He had nothing to lose at this point, so he motioned toward the stunt.

"Quentin Oglethorpe, sir. Will we have to fight dragons?"

It took him a few seconds to keep himself from laughing. "That's an excellent question, Mr. Oglethorpe. But the answer is no. The place you're going to be is a place called Wonderia."

He'd have to apologize to marketing if that mess of a name for WHX-131-L ever got out. "And there are no dragons there. What is there is trinamium, and it would be your job to protect it and collect it. As you all know, wizards use wraiths to steal stuff and cause harm."

A collective breath was taken. He had them on the edge of their seats.

"It will be your job to keep the wraiths from stealing the trinamium."

They all considered that for a minute. Another hand went up. He motioned to it.

"Melissa Thompson, sir. I have a globe at home and can't remember any place called Wonderia."

This smile was genuine, but not for the reasons the stunts thought.

"That's because Wonderia is a different planet. It is far, far, away from here. All the parts of Epic Dungeon Quest were discovered on alien planets. That's why the game seems so real."

That got a mixed reaction. They seemed excited and scared all at once. He wondered what it would be like to be so simple but dismissed the thought since he didn't want to know. He waited for them to calm down before he proceeded.

"Of course, because this is dangerous, you'll have to volunteer. If you do, you'll get money of your very own. Your families will get credit with Amalgamated Conglomerated to buy anything they want" — assuming they would want cheap junk — "and you'll earn benefits that will help you throughout your entire lives."

They seemed more excited than scared. They began politely asking questions and seemed eager to know how they could stop the wraiths. He could see that some of them were not going to go along. That was okay; he could save the camps some trouble and just have them put to sleep here at the main office. They had facilities in the basement that would do the job just fine.

By rough guess, he figured he would get a hundred of them to save the sacred land of Wonderia from wraiths. It was just a happy coincidence that they would save the company millions and begin shipping home trinamium three years before he could even remotely get bots in place.

Bob, clearly bucking for a promotion, entered the room with very official-looking permission letters for the stunts to sign. Brad glanced at one and had to turn his back on the room to stifle the laugh. He decided he had to buy Bob a drink as he reread the preamble.

**I ____________ (print name) do hereby solemnly swear to uphold the values of Amalgamated Conglomerated, which are the values of my family, my country, and my planet...**

He couldn't get past that.

The guards quietly separated the ones who didn't want to sign, and Brad quickly gave instructions for their termination. Those stunts were led out the back door while the rest eagerly filled in the blanks with help from his staff. A quick count later showed that he had 126 recruits—more than enough for a trial run.

WHX-131-L wasn't bad as planets went. It had a breathable atmosphere, and the climate where the trinanium was located was reasonably moderate. But it had some bizarre microbe that the labs had determined was a major problem for the human genome. They weren't sure what the long-term effects would be, but they were very sure that humans shouldn't be anywhere near it. Well, stunts weren't legally humans, so he was okay there.

He issued brief instructions to fit them with spacer uniforms with some sort of stupid badge. They decided on a version of the wraith hunter badge and left to find Milton.

A/C owned many interesting things, and one was the rights to Epic Dungeon Quest. That wasn't widely known since the game was technically the "property of the people." But "the people" had defaulted on a loan, and some things the public was better off not knowing got moved around. Brad shrugged. Such was life.

Milton, the lead designer for Epic Dungeon Quest, was right where Brad expected him to be—sitting in his office, eating a doughnut, and sipping a coffee with extra sugar. Milton was, to be polite, a fat, lazy slob.

He was also a brilliant programmer. However, he had no initiative. He sat where he was as others passed him by. Milton never seemed to care about that. Milton barely glanced up when Brad entered the room.

"I need a new version of Epic Dungeon Quest, and I need it in four days."

"Sure, not a problem," mumbled Milton, "right after I get done learning how to walk on water."

"Your messianic attributes can wait. I need this, or you'll end up working at that doughnut shop you frequent."

Milton finally looked up and stared at Brad. "What are you talking about? How new a version?"

"I need it to teach basic mining skills. Maybe add in some prizes for getting them right."

"Anything else?"

"I need it to run on a stand-alone server on a different planet."

Milton's eyebrows arched. "And..."

"That's about it, but we may need upgrades as we go on."

"Go on with what? There aren't any kids in our off-world facilities."

"No, but there will be stunts."

Milton would have been less surprised to wake up with a supermodel, and it showed.

"Relax, Milton. We aren't making them spacers. We're just using them for a mining experiment."

"And the board signed off on this?"

"Sure. Why not?"

Okay, that was a lie, but he was pretty sure he could get the board to go along once they saw the potential savings. The schedule would not be harmed if all the stunts died and the bots were still on pace. It was a no-lose situation.

Milton began scribbling numbers and looking at programming diagrams. A few minutes later, he looked up and smiled. "I can do it. All I have to do is take the programming we put into the bots and ascribe it to characters. Then, add a couple of easy scenarios, and you're good to go. Is there any theme I should know?"

Brad thought about that for a second and smiled. "Yes, as a matter of fact, there is. They must fight off wraiths to save the trinamium from the evil wizard Parazin."

Milton lacked Brad's self-control and burst out laughing.

Brad left Milton to his chores and headed for his office. The board's primary secretary, Maggie Johnson, stopped him outside his door. She looked at him and, as was her wont, didn't smile. "They wish to see you now."

He didn't need to ask any questions. He followed Maggie down the many halls and up the two elevators to the private penthouse that housed A/C's three board members.

Alexander M'tembe, Esmeralda Rodriguez, and Mark White are the current members of the board. They held unlimited power in the company. They served for 20 years and then were replaced by their handpicked choices. The board had run A/C for over 200 years without a single problem besides the usual lawsuits and silly stuff. Brad never concerned himself with those things since that's why A/C had an in-house Legal department.

They motioned for him to sit, and a waiter brought him a double scotch on the rocks, just the way he liked it. How they knew that eluded him, but he decided not to ask.

"You've been a very busy boy," began Mrs. Rodriguez. Although barely entering middle age at seventy, she still looked good enough to sleep with, even if he was sober, "do you mind telling us why you're sending over 30,000 of our weekly credits into space?"

He didn't know how they knew about this either, but now was not the time to hesitate.

"It's a prudent investment. We can jump the claim on WHX-131-L and force Parazin into a defensive posture. Our lawyers have already filed a suit against their claim anyway. This just reinforces our position that possession must accompany any claim. Not just a marker slammed into the ground from a satellite.

"Second, even if the stunts all die, we're protected by so many levels of laws that they're not even worth mentioning. But even so, they reinforce our claim and our legal position.

"Third, we have a ship going to WHX-131-L to drop cargo containers for 'on-planet' storage in four days. Instead of sending empty containers, I'm just filling them up with inexpensive cargo. The extra fuel required to move the stunts is negligible, and we can keep them out of the crew's way by simply posting 'do not enter signs for the crew section.

"As to food and stuff for the stunts, all we need to do is add some extra rations and bunks. Minor technical issues at best."

"What about bathrooms?" asked Mr. M'tembe. At one hundred and thirteen, he was the oldest board member and still looked like he could go a few rounds in the ring as he had as a youth.

"There are ten on every cargo carrier, which leaves extras for spacers when they land. That should be more than enough for a hundred and twenty-six stunts."

"Very well," continued Mr. M'tembe, "what about housing when they land?"

Brad hadn't even considered this, but he thought quickly. "We have all those tents leftover from my predecessor's 'Campaign for Camping.' They're just sitting in a warehouse collecting dust. We can throw a couple hundred on the ship without a problem. The climate on WHX-131-L is temperate; there aren't any major storms, and the tents should do just fine."

Mark White rose and smiled. At six feet tall with two hundred pounds of rippling muscle, he was the second most imposing board member after M'tembe. "Very well, I can see some minor details to be worked out, but you have everything in hand. Should this not go well, please remember that you, like your predecessor, could find yourself at five thousand feet in your car without navigation or lift. That would be very tragic."

Well, now he knew what happened to his predecessor. That was okay. The guy had been a tree-hugging prick. The meeting concluded, and he left without finishing his scotch.

**********************

In the next few days, Brad discovered thousands of details involved in moving the stunts, but most were minor, and some were fun. One of the techs had adapted a child's floatie toy to emit wraith-like sounds and then set it up to run exclusively on solar power. When he showed it to Brad, they decided to have the ship's crew drop them around the campsite in the nearby mountains with timers set to go off randomly every few days. Not enough to scare the stunts witless, but just enough to keep them focused.

Brad wasn't a complete asshole. He made sure that every employee who came up with a good idea received a commendation in their file. And when he saw the game Milton had devised, he issued him a small share of stock in WHX-131-L's profits along with his commendation.

On the other hand, those employees who expressed concerns about the project were either transferred or terminated. He had no time for whiny losers.

Everything was in order by the time the ship was ready to leave orbit. From tools to tents to food, the stunts would have all they'd need to get started. Brad even went down to the terminus to see the stunts off.

At the suggestion of his assistant, Janice, he handed each one a yellow frosted cupcake. She promised him it had something to do with the damn game. The stunts seemed impressed, so he added another commendation to her file.

Later, as his day was winding down, Janice walked into his office and offered to buy him a drink at Warren's. It was the new hot spot, and he had wanted to try it. He noticed, for the first time, that Janice was smoking hot. He started to wonder all the things men naturally wonder when confronted by a prime example of babe-ness and then saw from the look in her eye that the answer was already yes.

He had no idea how to couch this commendation but was sure he would come up with something. Service above and beyond the call? That might work.

✳✳✳✳✳✳✳✳✳✳✳✳✳✳✳✳✳✳✳✳✳

They'd been on board ship for one week and had settled into a routine. Quentin and Melissa had become friends, and she was showing him how she'd earned her 3rd Level Wizard's Badge. She was smart. She had figured out how to use her wand in ways he'd never thought of.

The crew brought them their food three times a day and called lights on when it was time to wake up and lights out when it was time for bed. He and Melissa were confused by this new version of Epic Dungeon Quest, but the crew said it was special for Wonderia so they'd know what was real and what wasn't.

He missed his mommy and daddy but was glad to be doing something important. He'd forgotten all about the law he was supposed to have broken, and it seemed the others had, too. They played Epic Dungeon Quest, ate when fed, and talked about their exciting adventure.

He'd never noticed girls before, but he thought Melissa was really cute. He hadn't told her that because girls, even nice ones like Melissa, were really super scary. In fact, they were even scarier than wraiths and stuff.

They'd all noticed that their quest would take them underground to save the trinamium. That was really cool. They would all be like dwarf lords and stuff. Dwarf lords rocked!

The remaining five weeks of their trip passed without incident, and the captain finally called out that they were home. That confused them for a minute until they realized he meant their new home. They were at Wonderia.

The crew had taken a liking to the stunts. It had slowly altered the pressure so that they wouldn't have to go through any form of decompression when they finally dropped the cargo pods. It wasn't a big thing, but they all congratulated themselves for doing something so nice.

Even so, they didn't like them enough to keep the screaming floaties on board. Those had been dropped the second they hit orbit.

Three hours after entering orbit, the cargo pods were on the ground, and their doors opened.

The sky was more aquamarine than blue, and the clouds seemed to have a pinkish tint. The crew knew all the reasons for the differences but, when asked, simply said that was the way things were here and everyone should enjoy what they had. After all, why waste science on stunts?

Quentin and Melissa were the first to leave the pods. They were really scared but wanted to show everyone that everything would be all right. They knew that nothing bad could happen to them, yet since they hadn't really started their quest. After all, who died before the game started?

Once they were outside, they breathed the air and smiled. It was kind of sweet, like yellow frosted cupcakes. They were on an open plain near the bottom of the mountain they would have to enter to save the trinamium, and it was beautiful. The grass was a dark green color, but the trees all had tree trunks that were kind of white, and the leaves were all sorts of pretty colors. There were lots of flowers that were a pretty blue all around, and there was a brook running through the middle. Had Quentin known the word "burbling," he would have used it. Instead, he named the brook Laughing Waters.

Melissa smiled at that and took his hand. He was so embarrassed that he blushed a deep red. But he was supposed to be a grownup here, and grownups held hands, so he didn't let hers go. In fact, he held it a little tighter. It felt nice, and he liked things that felt nice.

Soon, they were unloading the tents just like they'd learned in the new Epic Dungeon Quest and had a rough camp set up within an hour. An hour later, they made a bonfire from wood they found nearby and cooked a rude dinner from the stored provisions.

The ship's crew was wearing full space suits and watching them closely. There was no way they were going to breathe this air. They'd read the medical warnings before they left Earth. When they were sure everyone was as settled as possible, they instructed them where to start "saving the trinamium" in the morning and returned to the ship.

Quentin and Melissa joined the others in singing their favorite songs around the campfire and enjoyed the evening. They sang the theme from Epic Dungeon Quest; they sang "Row Row Row Your Boat," and they sang "Twinkle Twinkle Little Star." It seemed appropriate. They sang "Father John," and they sang "Bertrand the Bouncing Bear." Then they sang them all again and went to sleep.

In the morning, they woke up excited. They had a quick breakfast and headed up into the mountain. It was an imposing mountain. They didn't know much about Earth's geography, but they would have been properly awed if they had. This mountain stood over five miles high and had a base that extended for twenty miles in all directions. But even without the facts, they were impressed at the sight.

They entered the tunnel they'd been pointed to and broke out the equipment to begin work. They sang "Hi Ho" as they worked and soon were engrossed in their labors. The trinamium was easy enough to find. The bright pink rock stood out from the gray and mottled browns surrounding it.

They chipped away randomly at first but figured out the best methods quickly enough. Within three hours, they were extracting a tub of the pretty stones every ten minutes.

They didn't know it, but that was five times the projected yield the bots could achieve.

A horn sounded at noon, local time, and they left the tunnels to eat lunch. While eating, the ship's crew returned to check on progress. They were stunned at the amount of trinamium sitting in front of the mouth of the mine but said nothing to the miners. There was no need to compliment them.

The crew was due to leave in four more days, when the jump point would be optimal, and figured they would need more cargo space for all this trinamium than they had allotted. After a brief discussion, they decided to offload the extra provisions and stores they had and just give them to the miners, which is what they were calling the stunts now, and just call it a bonus for a job well done. They could straighten out the books when they got back home since trinamium was worth a hell of a lot more than meatloaf.

The next few days passed without incident, and the crew loaded the ship and headed home. The miners had enough provisions for a year, and the next supply ship would arrive in three months, so everyone was happy. While the miners had no idea what a "triple quota bonus" was, they happily accepted the crew's thanks.

As time passed, they began building their community. They arranged their tents in neat rows, set up shifts for all the chores, and started their new life on Wonderia. They liked things well enough, even though they missed their families. They developed friendships, surveyed the area around their camp, and found that they really liked the yellow berries they found clinging to the trees. They also discovered that the blueberries on the flowers made them sick. They were very careful after that.

But other than that, life was good. They stored the trinamium at the south end of their camp. Even though it took longer to bring it there, it made things neater to look at. One thing they all insisted on was neatness.

The camp itself was a thing of wonder. The Campaign for Camping tents had all been brightly colored so they could be easily spotted from the air in case of an emergency. The miners had arranged them so that no two identical colors were next to each other. It gave the whole place a carnival-like feel.

The feeling permeated all they did as well. There were songs for mining and songs for eating, and they'd found some books in the ship's stores, and the miners who could read read them to the others before they went to bed.

If some perceived their routine as stifling, it worked well for them. They knew when to wake up, when to work, when to eat, and when to relax.

They dug deeper into the mountain and built a small rail system to make moving the ore easier. The ore cars and tracks were made from local wood, and the wheels were made from a rubber they found naturally bubbling in pools. They'd learned how to put it all together in the new Epic Dungeon Quest. It wasn't hard if you followed the instructions. In fact, they liked the new rail system so much that they built it around the camp so that it reached the stockpile on the south end.

They discovered that the green berries made good paint. They used it to paint the ore cars. They used the themes from Epic Dungeon Quest to inspire their designs. If the drawings were crude, they didn't care; they liked them.

The cargo ships came and went with predictable regularity, once a month after the first three-month wait. The miners arranged for the crews to send one letter each to their families, and then they received one each when the ships came again. They were also given the benefits that regular employees of A/C received: paychecks and medical scans every time a ship arrived.

They didn't know about the worries the medical staff on Earth had. All they knew was that they felt good and were happy.

Another thing the ships brought were catalogs of stuff they could buy with their paychecks. It was in the second set of catalogs that they found costumes from Epic Dungeon Quest. That was the super coolest discovery ever. They lined up with their paperwork before the ship left and made sure their orders all got in.

But the excitement of the cool clothing didn't disrupt their routine. Even when the cargo ships were in orbit, they got up each morning and followed their schedule. They did wonder why the crews never took off their spacesuits, even when they were on the ground, but they never asked. They figured it had to be space men's secret, and they were miners, not spacemen.

**********************

Brad put away the latest reports from WHX-131-L and smiled. Over the last eighteen months, the stunts had mined more trinamium than anyone expected; they could make bots obsolete.

They didn't seem to be having any problems with the microbe either. The labs now seemed to think that the microbe would cause some form of retardation and that the stunts were immune because they were already stunts. That worked for Brad.

There was a bunch of technical stuff as well, but it bored him, and he skimmed over it. As far as he could tell, the stunts had undergone some changes but nothing that would stop the mining. After that, he just didn't care.

Probes had discovered two more planets with similar microbes, and A/C was already ramping up stunt training programs to take advantage of them. The PR department was working overtime and had spun the events as one of the most altruistic acts ever committed by any corporation. Stunts volunteered and lined up outside the main gate, begging to be sent off-world and allowed to battle the evil wizard Parazin.

The numerous Cease and Desist letters from Parazin Industries were neatly filed in some drawer in the legal department. Bob had shown him one, and he'd found it hilarious. Parazin's companies had been caught with their pants down and lost three planets already. The fact that they were taking a beating in the market only made things sweeter.

Brad knew the acquisitions department was scouting a slew of Parazin's subsidiaries and would probably snag a few of the plums. He also knew that his bonus checks had become things of legend. He'd bought a home in the nearby mountains that had a swimming pool, a three-car landing pad, and a full staff. He'd always wanted a butler, and now he had two.

He also knew that his boss Jenkins would be retiring this year, and he was a shoo-in for the promotion. In fact, Jenkins had made no secret of the fact that he was only recommending Brad instead of the usual slate of candidates.

Brad's favorite part was his purchase of Alchemy Costumes in the Southwest Free Zone. The company made costumes that featured fantasy characters, and it was definitely headed toward bankruptcy. Instead of closing the company and selling off inventory, as recommended by his

150

accountant, he'd made Alchemy Costumes the exclusive manufacturer of Epic Dungeon Quest clothing.

In just six months, the company had doubled its staff and barely kept up with orders. Not only did the usual retinue of kids want this crap, stunts the world over wanted to dress like the miners they'd seen on the vids.

When one of the cargo ship's crew had taken vids of the stunts, he'd shown them to Brad, thinking he'd get a laugh. He did, but Brad knew a gold mine when he saw one and quickly got a copy to the marketing department to be edited for broadcast.

The scene with one of the stunts riding in an ore car, singing "Heigh-Ho" at the top of his lungs while his cape flaps in the breeze was a public relations dream come true. He was glad that damn song was in public domain because Disney was a bitch to work with.

After the vid first aired, he'd received a dozen requests from newsies to interview "the valiant stunts on WHX-131-L." He'd granted them all, and they were going out on the next ship. You couldn't pay for publicity like this.

To avoid the possibility of anyone claiming any improprieties, he'd had Janice promoted to Assistant VP of Marketing. Now that they were equals, they could see each other openly. She was both ruthless and horny, a combination he found exhilarating. They both knew they'd either have to get married or break it off since they were so closely tied to the Star Stunts, which is what the newsies called the moron miners.

They each also knew they were on the career fast track and saw no reason to mess with success. They'd decided to have a traditional one-year engagement and then a big church wedding. Janice even suggested having some stunts wearing Epic Dungeon Quest gear to act as ushers.

It took him an hour to stop laughing, but he had to admit it was a brilliant idea, and he agreed.

This morning, he'd had the ring delivered and would give it to her over dinner at Warren's, the site of their first date. And the springboard to the most amazing sex he'd ever had.

He knew, intellectually, that he owed all his success to the stunts, but he would never admit it, not even to himself. He had a board meeting in the afternoon, so he took some time to make sure all of his reports were in order and called in his new assistant, Mark Chalmers.

Chalmers was even better at his job than Janice had been. Brad had learned to trust his instincts and judgment. Chalmers came and handed Brad a complete presentation on a portable hard drive. Brad had no idea when Chalmers had made it, but it was exactly what Brad wanted. Every highlight was timed correctly, and all technical data was relegated to footnotes. With this in his possession, all Brad had to do was show up and look good. Two tasks he was eminently suited for.

Brad and Chalmers quickly ran through a mock presentation to make sure nothing had been forgotten. Chalmers quietly suggested Brad wear the red tie; it made him look more powerful and that he should add the wraith hunter pin that the stunts all wore; there would be newsies in the meeting.

After the presentation and impromptu press conference skillfully initiated by Chalmers, Brad had an hour to kill before he was to meet Janice. He went down to Milton's office. The slovenly programmer was doing what Brad expected: eating a doughnut and reviewing reams of data. Milton waved him into a seat and made notes on the paperwork before turning to Brad.

"Greetings, glorious leader," he said, imitating one of the loser characters in the stupid game. "What brings you to my humble hovel?"

"I was just wondering if you got the specs for the new updates?"

"Just finished. Level 4 will feature an easy way to shore up tunnel walls using materials they have handy. Level 5 will show them how to create lanterns to go deeper into the tunnels. And, as per company policy, each stunt gets one share of A/C stock when they complete a level successfully."

"What about a prize?"

"They think that is the prize, so I stopped giving away stuff we didn't have to."

Brad burst out laughing. This was going better than he'd ever dreamed. The courts had ruled savagely against Parazin's claims to WHX-131-L, A/C's profit margin was up over 25 percent, and he was getting richer by the day. Janice was almost a bonus at this point.

Thinking of her, he showed Milton the ring. Milton appraised it for a few seconds and then laughed. "No one will miss that sucker. What is that? Four-carat emerald-cut?"

"It's four-point-five and pure."

"I'd expect nothing less from you," Milton mused. "By the way, since the stunts are hot on the vids these days, do you want me to add a camera feature so they can record a short message to their families?"

Brad thought about that for a while. "It's not a bad idea. They're cute as kittens when our Marketing department gets through with them. Just make sure that Marketing gets the vids first, in case one of the stunts complains or cries about missing mommy. I don't want to see it on the newsies' late-night crap."

"Easy enough. Oh, I never got to thank you for those stock options. I'm able to afford the care my mom needs now. It's one less thing to worry about."

"Don't you have insurance?"

"Sure, but I was adopted; she's not covered under it."

"What's wrong with her?"

"Believe it or not, multiple sclerosis. It was missed in her med scans when she was young."

"Damn. That sucks."

Brad thought about it. His family was healthy and well-insured. He remembered the "whole family first" campaign that had reduced rights for adopted children. Still, he had never given it much thought. He knew that when he and Janice got married, they'd never have to worry about that.

He excused himself briefly and put a call into Chalmers to see if anything could be done. He wanted Milton entirely focused on the tasks at hand, and having him worrying about his mother wouldn't help. Milton had avoided promotions because once you got to the management level, you had to buy in on the insurance. Having a liability like Milton's mother would make it very expensive.

As he was getting ready to go back in, Chalmers called. It seemed that A/C owned a hospital nearby. It had a separate convalescent facility that could easily care for Milton's mother at no cost to Milton since it was being funded by a study that was researching terminal diseases. It also had an in-house Bingo parlor and bowling.

Brad seriously doubted that Milton's mother would be bowling any time soon but asked Chalmers to see how soon she could get in. As it turned out, Chalmers had already made her reservation, spoken with her to make sure she would go, and had a confirmation number, which he flashed on Brad's porta-screen.

Brad walked back into Milton's office and gave him the good news. For the first, and hopefully last, time in his life, Brad made a grown man weep with joy.

********************

It had been three years since they'd left Earth. Quentin and Melissa shared a tent but not a bed since they weren't married yet. The next cargo ship was due in a few days, and it would be bringing a monk, just like the ones in Epic Dungeon Quest, to make their relationship officially official. There would be nine marriages when the ship arrived.

Melissa had made the tent prettier and added little pillows to all the chairs. They'd learned how to build furniture and sew, thanks to Epic Dungeon Quest. Quentin saw now that the man on Earth had been right. This was real and not just a game.

They'd all heard the wraiths stalking the mountainside, so they kept guards on their perimeter at all times. So far, no wraiths had dared to venture into their village, but you could never be too careful. Thomas was very good at making sharp things; he was in charge of making sharp things the guards could carry to kill the wraiths if they ever came to the village.

About two years after landing, they'd found some small, six-legged animals that were friendly and scared of the wraiths, too. They had four eyes and were covered in bluish fur with pink tips. The miners didn't know what they were and called them dogs.

Almost every tent had a dog living in it now. Emboldened by their human companions, the dogs would bark their odd bark and charge into the night when they heard the wraiths.

Once a dog had brought back a round device that none of them recognized. They'd looked it up in the game manual and found it was a stepping disk used by wraiths to go from one realm to another. They broke it into a kazillion pieces with their hammers. No wraiths were going to pop up in their village.

One of the ship's crew had given Roger a really neat device. You just pointed it at something you wanted to eat. If the box flashed green, you ate whatever it was. If it flashed red, you didn't touch it. That meant no one had to get sick as when they'd found the blueberries. Roger was really good about sharing the device, too, and everyone was safe now from bad food.

Yet another good thing was the lanterns. Not only did they light up the dark parts of the tunnels, they also lit up the village. Now, people could walk around after dark without bumping into stuff.

There was one funny thing. Many of their families had written and told them they were pioneers. That was just plain silly. After all, how could they be pioneers? This wasn't the Wild West. But they didn't care. It was nice to hear from their families, even when they were confused.

They also all had a bunch of things called "stock certificates." They earned them for all sorts of stuff. Quentin had gotten a bunch when he'd found a new vein of trinamium. He'd even gotten a thank-you letter from the nice people at Amalgamated Conglomerated. It was signed by Mrs. Wanda Jones, assistant secretary to the Third Assistant Vice-President in Charge of Marketing. Melissa had made a frame for it and hung it in their tent. It was his proudest possession.

A bunch of news people showed up, took pictures, and talked to everyone. They had a really cool machine on the ship that printed out the pictures and put them in frames. They all agreed that those frames had to cost at least a half credit each. They had been completely shocked when the news people told them they could keep them for free.

Quentin looked at the picture of him and Melissa holding hands and smiled. She made him feel all warm inside. There were also pictures of them standing alone, and Melissa had put them on each side of the picture of them together. It was like it was his new family. Well, when the monk got here, he guessed it would be.

That was all exciting and scary, too. He had no idea what a husband was supposed to do. Families are supposed to make babies, sure, but how? There had to be more to it than holding hands and kissing, or they'd have had children by now. He knew when they kissed, he felt all tingly in places, and he kind of liked that. He sure hoped Melissa knew what to do. For some reason, that was a subject that Epic Dungeon Quest had no instructions for.

✱✱✱✱✱✱✱✱✱✱✱✱✱✱✱✱✱✱✱✱✱✱

Parazin Industries had gone insane. They had literally declared war on A/C. Gone were any legal maneuverings. They had attacked some of the branch offices with a militia and caused heavy casualties. A/C had been forced to respond, and now there were violent skirmishes all over the world. Various governments demanded they call a halt to the aggression, but Brad knew his board well enough now to know they'd never stop first.

Barely five years since A/C had settled WHX-131-L, the home office was a war zone. Explosion-resistant glass had been installed everywhere, extra security had been placed around the grounds, and new walls were erected that promised to stop a medium-sized tank. Also, the cargo docks now housed a small air force, which maintained some very deadly planes.

Oddly enough, Brad noticed almost none of this. He was peripherally aware that some things had changed, but he was still getting richer every day; sex with Janice was still the kind of stuff usually reserved for pornos, and his office was a well-run machine. Anything outside of that didn't warrant his attention as far as he was concerned.

Now that Milton's mother was being taken care of, Brad could get Milton promoted and make him a part of his personal team. That had proved fortuitous.

When the stunts asked for a monk to marry them, Milton realized they probably knew nothing about sex. He quickly altered a sex-ed presentation into a "special level" of the game. He even had the monk give a copy to each couple when they were married, like a talisman. Now, he would never need to worry about replenishing the workforce.

Milton knew there had been a few births on WHX-131-L, and now the monk — actually a Unitarian minister — was making regular trips. He handled each ceremony with as much dignity as he could muster, wearing a robe over a spacesuit. It made great fodder for the newsies, and the averages on the street sucked it up too.

Another bonus was that the "monk" never mentioned anything he saw or heard while on Wonderia. The price would collapse if word got out that trinamium was plentiful. Brad couldn't let that happen.

Brad had held a private meeting with the minister to make sure he understood they were really paying for his silence. And if he broke that vow, Brad would make sure that every newsie on the planet would have a copy of the monk's personal video collection of young boys. No elaborate consequences would ensue; a single bullet would suffice.

The marriage issue was also coming up on the other two planets, and Chalmers had found two more ministers who would make ideal candidates. Brad was going to interview both of them himself later today. Now that they had a program in place, it all should go smoothly.

Brad glanced at the latest casualty reports as he entered his office and tossed them on his desk. There, he found the files on WHX-131-L and quickly reviewed them to ensure his plan was moving along without any glitches.

The stunts, much to his surprise, had become almost entirely self-sufficient. If they had cattle to raise for meat, they probably wouldn't need any supplies from Earth at all. While that was good news, he didn't want the miners to become too self-sufficient. He needed to make sure they were forever beholden to the tender mercies of A/C.

He thought about that particular conundrum for a minute and then realized he had nothing to worry about. They were stunts, not people. They had ugly dogs — dear God, those things were brutal on the eye — and they wore capes and quoted a goddamn video game as philosophy.

The worst was those dogs had killed all but one of his wraiths. But all he needed to do was make sure Milton kept adding stuff about the greater glory of A/C, and they'd be fine.

With any luck, the morons would make A/C the cornerstone of their religion. Wouldn't that be funny as hell? "Yeah, though I walk in the shadow of the valley of Parazin, I shall fear no evil, for Amalgamated Conglomerated is my shepherd ...." Not bad. He'd run it past Milton later today.

With the stunts out of the way, he turned to more immediate issues. Janice was due in three months, and he still hadn't approved the final plans for the nursery. The pregnancy had caught them both by surprise since they both had birth control implants. Brad's father had said, "God wanted another Jacobs on this Earth, and by God, a little thing like science wasn't going to stop Him!" That was as good an excuse as any, and Brad went with that when asked.

He decided on a neutral theme with the education enhancements. It was Janice's favorite, and he saw no reason to pick anything else. He approved the order, added his credit info, and forwarded it to Janice for her signature. Yes, his future was looking brighter and more secure each day.

**********************

It had been thirteen years since Quentin had left Earth. He could barely remember what it looked like anymore. He heard laughter and turned just in time to see the twins, Rogor and Randa, squealing into the tent.

There was something different about his children—all the children—but he couldn't put his finger on it. Yes, they were all smarter than Quentin, but it was something more than that.

They laughed more. Maybe that was it. They found many things funny Quentin couldn't understand. But they were loving children, working hard at their studies and helping around the village like all the other children. Their younger sister, Raina, was studying a book pad she'd gotten from the last cargo ship and never even glanced at the sound of the commotion.

Melissa, even more beautiful now than when Quentin had met her, walked in after her shift in the mine and began preparing dinner. The children quickly got up to help without being asked; they were good like that, and soon, the tent was full of wonderful smells.

Since they had children, they split shifts in the mine. Tomorrow would be Quentin's turn. However, he hadn't been idle all day. He'd finished building the support walls inside the tent and had added two dividers in the second tent they'd been given when they were married. The idea was that they could build the two together for when the family arrived, which it did barely ten months later.

Now, the children could have privacy, and so could he and Melissa. He smiled at her as she cooked, and she smiled back at him. She'd noticed the new walls and smiled even wider. Tonight, they could be alone.

The dinner was wonderful. Melissa's world-famous meatloaf and some local vegetables they'd grown in the community garden. Some were from Earth, but most weren't. A pink root had been discovered that tasted kind of peppery. They called it a Pink Pepper Root. It was yummy.

The children always giggled when he said words like "yummy," and he liked hearing them giggle.

After dinner, the children cleaned the table and helped wash the dishes, then asked to be excused to go foresting. Neither Quentin nor Melissa knew precisely what that was, but all the children did it, and they seemed to have fun. The reluctant parents agreed.

They sat in the quiet of the tent, enjoying the lingering smells of the meal as the children's laughter echoed in the distance.

**********************

Rogor, Randa, and Raina arrived at the fort and ran inside. Arrayed around the walls were the various items they'd been able to scavenge off the supply ships. They only took spares that wouldn't be noticed when they went missing.

Their prize sat on a table at the far end of the room. A working Hyperwave radio. It was how ships could get news from home, report incidents, etc. Next to it was their second biggest prize, a copy of a ship's library. Rogor had copied it while the crew was taking pictures of the miners for their scrapbooks.

Now, all the children knew how badly their parents had been abused. And by listening to the radio, they could keep up with the events on Earth.

Their parents were paid one-third of what an apprentice miner would get on Earth, and their medical benefits seemed to consist of scans for some sort of experiment A/C was running. But they also knew about the microbe, the wonderful, glorious microbe.

Besides altering their parents' genes so they would be in perfect health for the rest of their lives, it had given their children some incredible gifts. They were all telepathic and had some telekinetic powers, which seemed to increase as they got older.

They now had minds far more intelligent than any humans had ever encountered. By the time they were two years old, they had all known that they were a hybrid of some sort: the best that Earth could send and the best that Wonderia could grow.

They kept their secret from their parents. They didn't want to scare them or cause them to notify the bastards at A/C of what they'd become. Soon, all the children over age five were in the fort. They numbered 97.

The fort was actually a cave at the base of the mountain. It could hold ten times their number with ease. It was well hidden from any passing scans. They had insulated it further when they figured out what types of scans the cargo ships could perform.

The cave was eerily quiet as the children argued about what to do about A/C. They knew the corporate wars on Earth had escalated to the point that even the smallest villages were heavily armored.

They also knew that scientists on Earth had made a major miscalculation about the Hyperwave radio. They didn't know that the technology could transmit ships as well as communications. The children had figured that out a couple of years back.

They had run some tests with their makeshift equipment and had been able to scout the other two planets that A/C was exploiting. They were pleased to see signs that the children there were similar. They sent a second scout to drop a message that only children like them could read. Their third scouting mission returned positive answers from both planets.

They also knew something else: their safety depended on Earth being removed from the picture, at least for a century. Just enough time for them to secure their place in the galaxy.

The plan that was coalescing was a thing of simple beauty. Once it was finalized, they'd notify the other two planets so they could be prepared. They had all that they needed in the fort. It was just a matter of building what they needed and timing its release.

**********************

Brad, Jr. was turning ten today. Brad had set up the backyard with a complete carnival, including rides. Why not? He'd been promoted to VP of all of A/C last year. A little indulgence was called for. He and Janice surveyed the results and waited for Brad, Jr. to come home from school. This was going to be a big surprise for him. They'd sworn all the parents to secrecy, and it appeared they'd succeeded.

Brad smiled at his lovely wife when a package arrived from the landing docks. It was rare, but not unheard of, for something to be important enough to interrupt him at home, so he excused himself and went into his private office to see what it was.

He opened the cargo box and was confused by what he saw. It was an old-style vid player with his name printed on it. He found the On switch and sat it on his desk.

A young man, dressed like a stunt, appeared on the screen. There was something different about him, but Brad couldn't quite figure out what it was.

"Hello, Brad," the young man began. "May I call you Brad? It seems we've known each other for years even though we've never met. I am Rogor Oglethorpe, and this," he motioned to a young lady who entered the screen's view, "is my twin sister, Randa Oglethorpe. We were the first children ever born on Wonderia. That bit of news is meaningless to this conversation, but I thought you should know.

"You may have noticed, Brad, that the human race has gone completely off the rails. All its promises and dreams are hopelessly ensnared in a senseless war. And at its core, that war is about us. You see, we've followed the newsies briefs about Wonderia and the legal battle with Parazin. We know how you exploited our parents into being unwitting slave labor. We know everything.

"We know it all started because of a dispute over a probe, which we found, and us. Well, technically, our parents. And your war is now threatening to expand into space. I'm sorry, Brad, but we can't allow that to happen."

Brad hit the pause button so he could laugh. Was he really being threatened by a stunt? Oh, he would have to show this to everyone at the party. It would make their lives. He hit Play after he'd poured himself a drink.

"Here's what's going to happen. When you hit Play, you activated a Hyperwave signal, which, in turn, activated several small ships, each carryingEM-pulse generators. They are positioning themselves around your planet as I speak. In five minutes, they will knock out electrical power on the planet. That means no radio, no video, no nothing. I'm not sure what your plans for the day were, but if they didn't include learning to chop wood and building a fire, you might wish to alter them.

"The EM Pulse generators will stay in orbit for 100 Earth years. Hopefully, by then, you'll have learned to play nice and can begin rebuilding your civilization. As they say on the old vids, have a nice day."

The screen went black, and as Brad ran to the comm unit to notify A/C's security officers, so did the rest of the planet.

This is what happens when I watch Riverdale. Originally published in the **Fall 2020** issue of **Sci-Fi Lampoon.**

## Fun Time at the Apocalypse-A-Go-Go

It was a bright, beautiful day in Riverdale, adorned with wispy clouds of happiness floating in an azure sky like love-coated cotton candies. Then, the murders began. The first to go was Kelsey. Of course, it had to be Kelsey. That arrogant bitch. Insolent cum bucket. Prom queen, cheerleader, and widget heiress voted most likely to put out three years running. Yeah, it had to be Kelsey.

Her skin was found first. Two-inch wide slices, determined later to have been cut with a titanium cheese slicer, draped neatly over a wooden mannequin with little bells sewn on the bottom of each strip. She made an intriguing wind chime.

Her innards were found in a milk pail about a quarter-mile away. It had been festooned with pink glitter, her favorite, and each organ had a pink ribbon wrapped around it. Her bones, with her silicon tits still in place, were found in a grotesque imitation of statuary inside the atrium of the Fillmore Modern Art Center for the Blind. Thanks to a clever use of super glue and quick-dry cement, she was eternally bound to be violated by a yellow garden hose hooked to a sewage-gushing pump.

Police suspect foul play.

Kelsey's dad, the venerable Mortimer Worthington IV, has expressed polysyllabic outrage and offered a reward to encourage the capture of the heinous person or persons who did this deed. That the aforementioned sewage was spewing forth from a plant his company used to illegally dump waste into the town's water supply was never mentioned.

The next to go was Adam. Good old fucking Adam. An egregious waste of the human genome. A raging narcissist with a cock the size and shape of a mutilated peanut. He was not well-liked. He was found hanging from a tree, strangled with his entrails, boasting a dead squirrel stapled to his balls.

Since no blood was found at the scene, and eleven lawn gnomes were arranged in a circle beneath his swinging carcass, police suspect the crime scene may have been staged.

Adam's mother, the respected widow Arianna Le Pont, demanded the lawn gnomes be returned to her prestigious landscaping company, which had, unrelated to any events contained herein, recently settled a federal lawsuit regarding its hiring and exploitation of undocumented immigrants.

Two days later, she offered a reward too. In her press release, she made it clear she found the disemboweling of her only begotten son "unacceptable."

Rip. The Ripster. The Rip-Meister. The Rip-A-Rooni was next. An extremely talented football player who almost earned a partial scholarship to a junior college, Rip was considered by many to be the penultimate asshole. First place was, of course, perpetually reserved for the lately lampooned Adam Le Pont.

Rip's vainglorious existence, which included seven rape charges, four assault arrests, and an audition for America Had Talent, ended abruptly when his severed remains were found in an abandoned bowling alley. Based on the blood trail, police speculated the killer had managed to pick up a seven-ten split with his head.

Rip's prodigious penis, which had been the source of so many of his adventures, had been encased in polyurethane and used as a swizzle stick in a Manhattan.

Rip's parents, the saintly Ron and Molly Drumpf, were visibly appalled. Both insisted Rip had never drunk a Manhattan in his life. And bowling? For the love of all that's Christian and seaworthy, that peasantry pageant would not have sullied their lives. Not one of the forty-six rooms in their humble home had a bowling alley. However, most could have easily housed one.

Instead of a cash reward, which they deemed shortsighted and beneath them, they offered a one-year scholarship to their possibly soon-to-be accredited online college, The Drumpf Collegial Cyber-Campus. They noted that those malodorous lawsuits for misfeasance (due to Ron's alleged misuse of an honorary police badge he'd been given as a birthday gift) and fraud had been put to rest. There was now a pleasant new landing page for the main website.

It was thirty shades of mauve.

Rimmed in gold.

Rumors that the police were being handsomely compensated for solving the murders but avoiding looking into the families were rumors. It was pure happenstance when the police chief, a man of renowned integrity who had recently been reinstated to his position now that he no longer needed to wear a tracking device on his ankle, announced there was "no evidence of possible clues" in any of the families' histories or businesses.

Life in Riverdale scurried on. Oh sure, some were scared, those who feared the shadows, but, for the most part, the homogenous hamsters went and jumped on their wheels and earned their pellets from nine to five. At the same time, the hoi poloi who owned them continued to do whatever the hoi poloi did.

Certainly not bowling.

Those who were publicly sensible traveled in groups from fearful place to fearful place.

The reigning board of Weatherbee College decreed all student activities must ensure no student traversed the campus unattended, with any said unattended student being subject to a fine, and that all activities be group activities, which could be videotaped. It didn't take long for the fine upstanding youths in the I Eta Pi fraternity and I Beta Péos sorority to realize orgies were group activities and perfectly acceptable under the rules when housed under the banner of Greek Studies.

Weatherbee College quickly became the undergrad envy of the world.

It also became a YouView sensation, with new viral videos being posted almost twice a week.

The historically themed orgies, a "must" to adhere to the campus guidelines requiring scholastic justification for the use of official campus property, were cited by scholars worldwide. One student finishing his Master's thesis noted, "Never, in all my years of study, have I seen the fall of Constantinople portrayed so vividly or exuberantly. The young lady embodying Theodora gave all she had. She took all she could before succumbing to the ravages of the barbarians. All of us watching here were visibly moved."

Odd though it may seem, the murders had brought a sense of bonhomie to this little town. Some of the less inhibited households followed the example set by the future leaders of tomorrow. Unburdened of the need for scholarly inspiration and devoid of any requirements of videotaped verification, except where requested for personal satisfaction later, some households became famous for their creative use of items discreetly purchased from the Ikea catalog.

Hotels, swanky and not, capitalized on the possibilities and began offering key parties to tourists so they wouldn't feel left out.

Still, wherever they settled, they settled in groups. The less adventurous settled for board games and ice cream socials. Riverdale was rapidly becoming the safest and most convivial hamlet in America.

But then, a year to the day after innocent little Kelsey disappeared, the murders began anew.

The first to go was Dirk. Famous for his munificence, he would let young girls stay at his place whenever they wanted and was noted for his charity. He never charged them for drinking his booze. His backyard pool was often filled with scantily clad teens and tweens who seemed content to trade bikinis in public and giggle a lot.

You would have thought girly giggles were the soundtrack of his life.

Sadly, the last sounds he probably heard were his own screams. He had been skinned alive and then covered in lime. His organs had dried, hardened, and ceased to be of use anymore.

Dirk had no family to offer a reward on his behalf. Regardless, several of his young charges took matters into their own hands and began a bikini car wash in his honor. The fact most of them were too young to have driver's licenses, let alone be eligible for a business license, deterred them not one whit.

Some kind soul was able to get them all the permits they needed and set them up outside the abandoned bowling alley where Rip had left an everlasting impression. The spacious parking lot proved ideal for their needs. The four construction trailers, left behind from a failed attempt at rehab, became superlative locations for the girls to change costumes, entertain privileged customers, or both.

The police noted no improprieties, and several officers took their personal cars there a few times a week.

Angel followed Dirk into oblivion.

Unlike the others, Angel was a good girl. A straight-A student who volunteered at her church, she was the epitome of boring. Beautiful as her name implied, she eschewed life's baser pleasures and planned to join a nunnery once she finished her bachelor's in social sciences.

She seemed to catch the worst of it.

It had taken a week for her to die. She had been violated, nee ravaged, by power tools, and each defilement had been dutifully videotaped and logged on individual CD-RWs. The killer was silent throughout. They could be seen only in glimpses. Holding the camera with one hand while the poor girl, strapped to a table saw, was despoiled repeatedly.

Finally, dehydrated and nearly comatose, the killer turned on the table saw for one last desecration.

It was this murder that finally gave the police a clue that these murders might, just might, be personal. That maybe, just maybe, the killer was not randomly picking their victims. Of course, they had nothing solid to base such an assumption on. Still, the general feeling was this hypothesis seemed close enough to the truth to pass muster.

Angel's father, the Honorable Mark Thomas, was a federal judge. There was no option but to call the FBI to deal with this case.

The local constabulary had very little to offer the feds. While they had recorded all the evidence, they hadn't done much with it. After all, they had important people to please.

The feds were less than thrilled.

The media had a field day.

Me? I just smiled. I smile a lot.

Safe in my cathedral, I savored the mementos. Kelsey, perpetually captured in mid-air, her legs spread wide, as only she and anyone who met her could, her tits flying free beneath her elven vest, her short-short skirt dangling jingle bells, she was truly Santa's favorite helper. Kelsey, who actually answered the question, "Hey, does this smell like chloroform?" Adam was in the next chamber, wearing his favorite Dukes of Hazard T, with Daisy on it, his jeans unbuckled and barely hanging on his waist, holding up a hilarious image of his sister's head Photoshopped onto the naked body of a porn star. I forget which one. The Ripster, clad, as always, in his Texas Longhorn's shirt and dirty jeans, his arm wrapped tightly, if uncomfortably, around a young cheerleader, who, for her part, seemed to be wishing for the sweet release of death, stood in front of his, neon yellow, 1979 Camaro holding a can of PBR and a smoldering Marlboro Light in his left hand.

Ahh, good times.

Dirk's room was a personal favorite. A simple portrait. One was found by the police in his bedroom. Clearly taken by a professional, it featured a nude Dirk lying on his back, his cock held like a trophy by a smiling petite blonde, surrounded by two other chicks, one Asian and the other black, all just as naked as Dirk, and all just as happy, also all holding glasses of whiskey, with the bottle in plain view. Had to give Dirk credit. As long as the pussy was fresh and pink, he didn't give a flying fuck about the wrapper. The combined age of all three enthusiastic ladies was revealed to be "less than forty" in the official report.

Lastly, I visited Angel. Ah, my sweet, sweet Angel. As condescending a cunt as ever walked God's green Earth. I knew her secrets. She should have been thrilled to be free of them. To be able to share without judgment. But, no, her corsets and bustiers, each with painful attachments woven in to make her bouts of extreme self-flagellation more intense, more personal, were for her and her alone, just as Jesus wanted. Needed. She spurned all comers and suffered silently, or occasionally with deep moans, in her room. Alone.

Somehow, I missed her favorite parts of the bible. Maybe her scripture was a custom job. The Gospel of von Sacher-Masoch or something like that. I know she was genuinely devout, though. I have video of her crying for God's blessings in Jesus' name. Several, in fact. She was earnest, if private, in her devotions.

Of course, I'm not an idiot. My cathedral exists only in the warp and weft of the neurons in my mind.

While I never worried about the Riverdale cops - who would? – the Feds are a different matter. They are honest, capable, and dedicated—three new attributes to these parts. New is not necessarily good.

I'm torn. Do I continue with my mission, or do I create an exit strategy? I only have three more to go. The Feds will be working on Angela's case first and must keep the judiciary happy, so they won't put all the pieces together yet. That gives me some time.

Maybe not a lot.

Then again, this town leaks like a cheap diaper. It's best to get a paper and see what the rumors are.

## ARE MURDERS THE RESULT OF A SATANIC CULT?

That's not bad. I should have tossed some iconography around. Too late now. It's far too obvious and not something you can pick up easily in this burg.

## FEDS THINK FUNDAMENTALIST CULT MAY HAVE MURDERED MISCREANTS

Seriously? That has to be a planted story. The Feds aren't THAT stupid.

## ONE PERSON COULDN'T HAVE DONE THIS

*Speaking anonymously because they were not authorized to talk to the media, a federal agent claims investigators are looking for a small group. Either a cult or something*
178

That's more like it. I knew these idiots wouldn't let me down.

So I got three. I'll start with one and see how it plays out.

Carl is the obvious choice. He likes to cut his meth with sea salt to double his profits. He also has a thing for young boys. Even has a NAMBLA sticker on the back of his van. Whenever anyone asks about it, he says it's the name of his favorite band. Then he'll say, "They rock hard," and laugh.

I hide behind the Little League baseball diamond. Carl likes to take his finds there. I wait for him to show, then I whimper, loud enough for him to hear, and cry in my best 'young boy in need' voice, "Help, I'm stuck." Carl, the honorable dude that he is, came right away.

They found him under the bleachers the following day. His dick and balls had been sliced off and sewn to his eyes. His flaccid schlong draped elegantly across his hawkish nose. Three souvenir baseball bats, the ten-inch ones, were found stuffed up his ass by the coroner. Inside his van were two sleeping boys, ages six and eight, drugged and stripped bare. The police are not releasing their names as they are minors, and the Kristoffsen and Holger families have not given permission.

At least, that's what it said in the paper.

It also said the cops had a video they would share with the public—time to get a TV.

TVs cost money. Money I have but don't want to spend. I head over to Vern's Diner. A complete shithole, but they have the two TVs set on the local news channels all day, and they know me, so my appearance won't raise any red flags.

I ordered the special chicken fried cheeseburger with fries, a large coffee, and a watch. I don't have to wait long. The footage is from a security camera mounted on the concession stand. It's easily fifty feet away and low quality. I sat and watched my silhouette drag Carl's staggering, soon-to-be corpse across the walkway and head under the bleachers. I'd shot him up with a hundred milligrams of Ketamine. It was unsafe for him anyway, but I wasn't planning to let him survive.

The usual "If you know this person" bullshit followed.

I suffered through the special, finished my coffee, and left. I was in such a good mood I even tipped.

Not a lot, but still ……

My good mood lasted until the following day.

## FBI SAYS ONE PERSON COULD HAVE COMMITTED ALL KILLINGS

*After reviewing the autopsy results of the recent murder victims, FBI scientists say they were most likely drugged first and then murdered. If that proves to be true in all cases, then one person could have killed all these people.*

*Given how casually Carl Pence approached his murderer, authorities now believe the killer may have been known to all of them.*

Well, fuck.

Time for plan B.

## TEN YEARS SINCE TERROR STRUCK RIVERDALE

It has been ten terror-filled years since police first discovered the mutilated body of Kelsey Worthington. Neither the Riverdale Police nor the FBI have been able to come up with a viable suspect. Numerous persons of interest have been questioned to no avail. For one reason or another, each was discounted as a suspect.

*The horrors faced by local residents did not stop our citizens from adapting and prospering. Rather than succumb to terror, Riverdale has become a thriving tourist attraction that brings in people from all over the world. Weatherbee University's subscription channel on YouView now brings in an additional $6 MIL per year to help fund scholarships and campus activities.*

Lacy Thomas was the next one found. Her skeleton had been wrapped in aluminum foil, and her skin was found nearby covered in molten tin. Her organs were found stuffed inside a giant, dyed purple Teddy Bear with a greeting card tied around its neck.

The card contained a message which read HAPPY ANNIVERSARY RIVERDALE. THINK GLOBAL, SHOP LOCAL!

Police suspect foul play.

Two different publishers have published this, making this its third shot at getting your attention. Published initially in **Sci-Fantasy Hub** and later **Independent Creators Connection**, it has built a nice cult following.

## THE SPACE CLOWNS OF ZOIMBA PRIME

"Slappy McClownDick's gonna be the fuckin' death of me."

"Wha'd da ass clinger do now?"

"Stupid shit for brains wants to use nukes in his act."

"Nukes? Real fuckin' nukes?"

"H'yup. Jes lil ones, he says. Jes enough to keep the marks' attention."

"But that douche nozzle is the one who flooped his clubs during the pin toss. Damn near killed BoobSlap McKitten with a return flip. Asshat couldn't hold a ball with a handle. His idea of clowning is to run around squirting water on kids. You ain't gonna let him do it, are you?"

"Fuck to the nose, no. First off, like you said, he's a moron; second, we need 'em for when we hit Earth. What's the fucking point of having a war if you can't blow shit up?'

With that settled, Captain Zippy McGigglePuss turned his attention to the tasks at hand. The armory was double-guarded in case Slappy McClownDick got a stupid idea in his head. Well, stupider than the ones normally floating around in the gurgling debris he called a brain.

With a quick glance over at Whoozat the Magnificent told him he was satisfied with the results of their conversation. Like all right-thinking beings, neither of them liked Slappy. But he was the fourth son of the Ringmaster, so they couldn't just kill him and then go have tacos.

One thought led to another; he was hungry. He slid his yellow, purple, puffy sleeve up and spanked his hideously huge watch. Festooned as it was, with red straps, a swirling moon face, and Disney-approved mouse hands, above and beyond the silver glitter, it was the pride of the fleet. No one had as great a watch as Captain Zippy McGigglePuss.

"Hey Whoozat, the big hand says it's Taco O'clock."

Whoozat smiled, tilted back his tiny porkpie hat, gave his black shoes, size twenty men's, a quick polish, and strode happily out the door alongside the captain.

They trod merrily down the corridors festooned with images of the halcyon days of circuses yore. The floors were neither sawdust nor dirt in a tiny nod to their situation. The animals were kept on a separate ship, so there was no need. Also, tradition be damned. None of them wanted to clean up later.

The ships, themselves, were things of time-honored beauty. Colored in red and white stripes, the circular disks sliced through the eternal void with a certain menacing joviality.

Exiled by Earthers over five hundred years ago, the remnants of Peru, Indiana – long may its hallowed ground be swept clear of dung and popcorn – had populated Zoimba Prime. The very first Ringmaster, Ned, had named it such for reasons only he gleaned, and no one dared challenge it. After all, he'd gotten them there safely in a ship that had seemed to have been designed to fall apart and kill them all.

The exact reasons for the exile had been lost in the hoary mists of time and in a data dump by Ringmaster Ned before landing. Still, most agreed it had something to do with the Great Entertainment Wars, which the entertainers had lost.

Even so, all might have remained copacetic. Zoimba Prime was a fertile world. Its three moons were rich in resources. Its sun was neither too close nor too far. The progeny of the initial settlers created a world of carnival joy. Provinces sprung up, each housing a different specialty.

Hoopty-Doo Clown Province, where everyone on board this ship was from, was one of the brightest spots in the planetary marquee.

But the fun abruptly stopped when an Earth drone showed up to collect back taxes.

The citizens of Acrobat Minor, just outside Roust About Township, being the closest at the time, blew it out of the sky and then called for an assembly. Ringmaster Orville, a direct descendant of Ringmaster Ned and highly trained in the fine art of circus management, presided.

He wisely and intelligently came to a smart conclusion. The acts of Zombia Prime would form a single circus for a limited time and use their combined talents to free themselves from any possible future tyranny from Earth.

The ships, laden with many nuclear weapons, were less than two weeks away from their target. Coming in, as they were, on a parabolic arc, they were not concerned with being discovered until it was too late. No matter how large, ships were truly tiny things on a galactic scale. If you weren't looking for one, you'd never find it.

The auto-calliope played the shift change music of Buffalo Gals as Captain Zippy McGigglePuss and Whoozat the Magnificent enjoyed their tacos al pastor.

Slappy McClownDick knew what people thought of him. He just didn't care. As Ringmaster Orville's fourth begotten son, and, due to a quirk in the law that allowed women positions of authority – something he would change one day, the seventh in line to be Ringmaster, there wasn't anything anyone could do to him.

He was as close to sacred as circus folk would allow.

Oh, sure, they had religion and shit. They followed the tenets of the Fourth Baptist Catholic Bible (the Presbyterian easy reader edition, Vol. IV) with the best of them. The rituals were intoned at every wedding and funeral. Baptisms were a holiday; confirmations were days of devout reverence when the young earned their first greasepaint.

Slappy McClownDick, of course, knew it was all elephant shit. Nothing but mindless fooble to keep the rubes in their place. No such muck cluttered the fine mind of Slappy McClownDick. He donned his Blue Nose of Royalty, checked his pink and green countenance in the nearest mirror, pronounced it divine with no sense of irony, straightened his skorbly duds one last time, and headed towards the armory.

He knew he was not allowed in because Captain Zippy McGigglePuss had posted it in the ship's bulletin, which was part of the daily staff briefings. But that wasn't his goal. He was headed for storage locker 14. Home of the ship's flatware and plates. A room no one cared about except him.

He cared because that room was one of the first built, near the center of the ship. The workers, lazy bastards that they were, had built-in access ways to move from one section to the next without having to traverse the hub. One of those led straight to the armory, and it was unguarded since no one knew it was there.

He listened to the gentle but firm slap of his shoes on the floor and smiled. His was the purposeful stride of a clown in charge.

He pressed open the door and ignored the thousands of knives, forks, and culinary folderol crowding the walls. When he got to the back, he unhinged the flap behind the last set of shelves and ducked into the passageway.

Soon enough, he was in the armory. He took only what he needed: four baby nukes.

This was going to be the best blow-off in circus history. No more clown stops for him. He was going to be a legend and then a leader. All in one day if he got it right. And the fake god only knew he would get it right.

Once he had the nukes hidden in his clothes, he left via a different panel, letting him out on the far side of the armory. He continued as though he'd walked past it, and, for all the casually spaced hall cameras would show, he'd done just that.

Once back in his private clown alley condo, or dingy cubicle – depending on one's point of view, he set the bombs on his dressing table and weighed them. Each was a perfect ten pounds. He left them where they lay and went into his trunk.

He quickly found the four bowling balls he'd stolen and tossed them onto his cot.

Juggling wasn't his forte. He preferred the more nuanced acts. Squirting children with flowers, snakes popping out of a can, fart noises, etc. The classics. None of this crap that passed for clowning today.

Pantomime? Pshaw.

All the good clowning was dumped on carpet clowns who were relegated to stupid bits in front of kids. By the standards of the clowns on Zoimba Prime, it was the lowest form there was. Merely an apprenticeship until one learned proper clowning.

All piddly poof as far as Slappy was concerned.

None of this meant anything to him other than as an abstraction. He looked at the bowling balls and considered his alternatives. He knew he would need to be a proficient juggler in a few days.

He also knew that wasn't an option. If not for the BoobSlap McKitten debacle, the incompetent bitch should have caught those four flaming clubs; there were other subtle clues. Most of them involved bruises on eighteen other clowns. And two acrobats. And a mule. And the dented calliope. Among others.

Fuck it. None of those pittances mattered.

But he wasn't the smartest clown around for nothing. He reached into his gag bag and pulled out four anti-gravity bands. While there was no such thing as "anti-gravity," there were methods that could make it less of a factor.

He slid one around each bowling ball and smiled. The bands had long ago been abandoned as a cheap out for any professional, but that didn't make them any less valuable.

He worked out the moves required to make the juggling look effortless for the next three hours. Eventually, he had them adhering to a perfect oval. He would work on the whiz-bang stuff later. He was tired and still had a lot of work to do. The nukes had to look harmless. Biohazard symbols ruined any insinuation of safety.

He decided to color them to match his face paint. Green and pink would be the colors of his people when this all was over. He added yellow stars just because he found them festive.

The circus ships continued their gentle arc toward Earth's solar system unimpeded or detected by Earth's mighty defense grid.

Mighty might be the wrong word.

A hundred years ago, they'd strung together a series of impenetrable sensors between the orbits of Jupiter and Saturn. They worked flawlessly if a ship didn't go above or below them.

That fact was a tightly held secret on Earth. No one other than criminals, smugglers, drug dealers, and military personnel knew it.

And the prostitutes, mistresses, gigolos, and sex workers associated with all of those named.

Ringmaster Orville, a credit to his genetics, was none of those things. But a quick look at the preliminary scans told him all he needed to know.

He sent a "For Captains' Eyes Only" memo through command and sat down to look at the security footage on his private screen.

He watched as Slappy dishonored his family name again. But this time, he'd also disobeyed his captain. Sadly, since he was in line, no matter how remote his chances indeed were, to be Ringmaster, he couldn't just …… he belayed that thought.

He had an idea.

He pulled up the camera feed from Slappy's dump. He watched, mildly amused, as the pathetic clown vaingloriously tried to fake juggling.

His idea formed clearer and clearer.

Two birds, one stone.

He smiled.

Then he treated himself to a glass of Doogle FlumpyBottom's homemade hooch. It was the finest on the planet.

In fact, it was so fine he felt as though he'd be insulting the fine FlumpyBottom name if he didn't have another.

Not wanting to get snockered, at least not yet, he set down the bottle, albeit reluctantly, and ordered a shuttle to take him to the Hoopty-Doo ship. A quick glance at the mainboard behind him assured him the rest of the ships were in formation and following orders.

All was well.

He was about to leave to meet the shuttle when he realized he would need a diplomatic excuse for what he had in mind. He could think of no more acceptable form of diplomacy than a bottle of Doogle FlumpyBottom's silky spirits.

An hour later, he sat with Captain Zippy McGigglePuss and his trusted lieutenant, Whoozat the Magnificent.

"Gentle Beings, when we arrive at Earth, I want Slappy McClownDick to present the first bit to the president of Earth."

The silence was deafening.

"Of course," continued Ringmaster Orville, "I need no permissions to make this happen, but I do want to ensure nothing hampers my wishes."

It was Whoozat who gathered his wits first.

"May I ask why, sir?"

The Ringmaster brightened.

"Of course, you may. Assuaging your fears is one of the reasons I came personally. Also, because there is no way I can finish this fine libation alone, and I don't want it to spoil."

He poured a round of drinks and smiled.

"Of course, answering your direct question without the underlying concern would be disingenuous. Suffice it to say Slappy's a moron."

That got two hearty laughs in response.

"Further, I would never waste the good stuff on rubes. No Ringmaster worth his sawdust would. And the Earth Council is nothing if not rubes. No, we will let Slappy fart, squirt, and generally disgrace himself. It will be high art to them. It will be what they expect a circus act to be."

"Trust me, gentle beings, it's all birds and stones. Just birds and stones."

The explanation, no matter if it is founded in anything resembling truth or made any fucking sense at all, satisfied the room. When Doogle FlumpyBottom's finest concoction was a dry memory, they staggered home.

A couple of days later, the ships entered Earth orbit, proclaiming peace while hiding weapons, and settled into desiccated negotiations seeking to grant the denizens of the circuses an audience with the exalted rulers of Earth.

It took another three days of parsing sanctimonious adjectives before permission was granted. Each honorific required merely cemented the Ringmaster's plan.

Eventually, it was agreed that Slappy McClownDick would appear before the high council and titillate their royal whimsies.

Slappy was sent off with high honors. A full band, not just the usual auto-calliope, stood on deck as Slappy boarded his shuttle. For his part, he couldn't imagine things turning out any better. The fact that the reason the Ringmaster would have agreed with him was not the same as his mattered not one whit. He was the star. He was in the center ring.

The shuttle arced through space toward the Earth Council headquarters in Geneva.

When he landed, he was greeted by another band. A full military guard played Sousa marches and stood in formation to allow him passage.

For the Earth Council, this was all proof of their power. The clowns et al. were coming home to pay homage and taxes. Mostly taxes. Depleted by centuries of misuse, Earth sorely needed the circuses' resources.

Slappy began his act.

He squirted the minister of finance with his flower.

He popped a can of snakes before the horrified ambassador to Saturn.

He told two fart jokes.

Everything was greeted with wild laughter. Slappy was in his glory.

Soon enough, Slappy opened his gag bag and pulled out four colorful balls. At first, he feigned an inability to juggle.

194

Well, it wasn't as feigned as he intended. He'd forgotten to adjust the bands to Earth's gravity. After a quick realignment and an additional gratuitous fart joke, he had everything going how he wanted.

The balls were sailing through the air to the oohs and aaahs of his captive audience, no matter how contrived.

Much to everyone's surprise, just as Slappy was heading to his first true blow-off, Ringmaster Orville appeared on all the screens.

"Once upon a time," he began as a preamble, "on a dark and stormy night, the leaders of Earth rousted our roustabouts and set fire to our homes. Thousands died. Thousands more were interred. This is the knowledge passed to each Ringmaster. The rest of our ancestors, proud members of a non-genetic family whose roots lay in the histories of Rome, Egypt, Africa, and beyond, were exiled to the stars in ships that were guaranteed to die. Their deaths would be our deaths.

"But we did not die. We did not succumb to the wisdom that we were inferior. We did not coddle the belief that we, somehow, deserved our fate.

"No. Thanks to our original ringmaster, Ned, we lived. And thrived. And preserved our culture. We are who we are. The children of grease paint and sawdust. Of animal smells and gleeful noises. Of laughter and joy.

"We are the embodiment of happiness.

"And now you have shoved your way back into our lives demanding fealty. Demanding we answer to you. So, now, I shall do exactly that.

"Slappy, the useless bag of clown in front of you, has always wanted to perform a true blow-out, a grand finale if you will, and you require an answer. You shall each have your desires sated."

He pulled off his velveteen top hat, waved his hands magically, and pulled out a large, chartreuse, glitter-encrusted box. It had a blinking red button.

Too late, Slappy discerned his fate.

Ringmaster Orville pushed the button while smiling.

"Fuck off, Earth. The Midway is closed to you forever."

Originally written as an article for **WorldNewsCenter.org,** it became part of an LGBTQIA+ anthology curated by South African legend **Christina Engela**. Since, depending on how you bend me, I belong to at least one of those acronyms, that was fine with me. Here's a fun look at the Christian history of same-sex marriages and two very gay Catholic saints.

# Divine Love

People who have fought for centuries to ascertain their rights suddenly seem delighted to deny those same rights to others. This is known as stupid. And counterproductive. When people read in the Bible that Peter was martyred or that Paul was martyred, they neglect to figure out that they were martyred because their beliefs were considered criminal. For those home-schooled, "martyred" means killed, usually in a very public and painful way. In the cases of Peter and Paul, the first of those two wacky cats who were there for the whole loaves and fishes thing, and the other is the reason there's a religion at all. They were martyred not because they were Christians but because they insisted women had control over their bodies. Both were lauded in the New Testament.

Wives...do not adorn yourselves outwardly by braiding your hair and by wearing gold ornaments or fine clothing; rather, let your adornment be the inner self with the lasting beauty of a gentle and quiet spirit... It was in this way long ago that the holy women who hoped in God used to adorn themselves by accepting the authority of their husbands. Thus, Sarah obeyed Abraham and called him lord.

**1 Peter 3:1-7**

Before every feminist in the world hits send on that vitriolic email they've got T-ed up, remember this: wives could be beaten or killed for not wearing makeup and clothing pleasing to their husbands. Now, go read that again in a historical context. Peter was telling the entire Roman civilization to fuck off. That is why they killed him.

Of course, according to tradition, they couldn't kill him until he wandered down the Appian Way, chatted with Jesus (still dead at the time), and returned to Rome.

Paul, while more traditional when it came to male and female roles, openly acknowledged in his many letters female priests whom he respected and counted on to help spread the word of Christ.

Lately, though, Christianity has become saturated with those who are so hateful and close-minded that I'm forced to wonder if they know anything about the history of Christianity. The one that has a litany of Old Testament icons who practiced polygamy. In the Old Testament, over forty major characters had more than one wife. Men such as Esau (Gen 26:34; 28:6-9), Elkanah (1 Samuel 1:1-8), and Solomon (1 Kings 11:1-3) are just a few. Let's not forget that Moses had three wives; Zipporah (Exodus 2: 21), the daughter of Hobab (Numbers 10: 29), and the Ethiopian woman (Numbers 12:1) who just happened to get sucked up into his life along the way (as slave or wife were her life choices). We won't even bother with David (just read all of Kings) since he made the Godfather look like a gentleman (sending his BF to die so he could nail his wife). Yeah, that Christianity. Their Christianity.

Or, as you may know it, the religion that used to perform gay marriages.

Before I get the vitriolic emails from all the practicing haters, allow me to share the story of St. Sergius. An openly gay saint.

What? You thought straight guys were the only ones getting some?

Back in 2008, with nothing better to do, the Colfax Record, a digital compendium (still found at http://www.ColfaxRecord.com) of local stories and discount coupons focused on the wonderful world of Colfax, California (e.g., Emma and Bob got engaged last week, Zipper World is having a sale on zippers, etc.), tossed an article on their site about same-sex marriage. It appears to have been meant as a sane look at historical facts. The author wasn't credited, and the original has since been removed. But, thanks to the internet, it lives on. And on and on and on. It is a fascinating bit of writing. Simple, coherent, and devoid of any hyperbole. It starts with the premise that same-sex unions have been around longer than Christianity and were an integral part of the early Christian church, and then goes from there.

In 2011, when North Carolina jumped back in the lead of the "We Hate People" bandwagon, the article began making the rounds again. The original cited no sources. It just listed documents as though everyone would know them. Since my knowledge of 10th-century Latin liturgy isn't what it should be, I did some research. I found every document referenced. Here is the original article with footnotes linked to the salient documents so you can follow up if you wish.

## When Same-Sex Marriage Was A Christian Rite

A Kiev art museum contains a curious icon from St. Catherine's Monastery on Mt. Sinai in Israel. It shows two robed Christian saints. Between them is a traditional Roman 'pronubus' (a best man) overseeing a wedding. The pronubus is Christ. The married couple are both men.

Is the icon suggesting that a gay "wedding" is being sanctified by Christ himself? The idea seems shocking. But the full answer comes from other early Christian sources about the two men featured in the icon, St. Sergius and St. Bacchus, two Roman soldiers who were Christian martyrs. These two Roman army officers incurred Emperor Maximian's anger when they were exposed as 'secret Christians' by refusing to enter a pagan temple. Both were sent to Syria circa 303 CE, where Bacchus is thought to have died while being flogged. Sergius survived torture but was later beheaded. Legend says that Bacchus appeared to the dying Sergius as an angel, telling him to be brave because they would soon be reunited in heaven.

While the pairing of saints, particularly in the early Christian church, was not unusual, the association of these two men was regarded as particularly intimate. Severus, the Patriarch of Antioch (AD 512 - 518), explained that "we should not separate in speech they [Sergius and Bacchus] who were joined in life." This is not a case of simple "adelphopoiia." In the definitive 10th-century account of their lives, St. Sergius is openly celebrated as the "sweet companion and lover" of St. Bacchus. Sergius and Bacchus's close relationship has led many modern scholars to believe they were lovers. But the most compelling evidence for this view is that the oldest text of their martyrology, written in New Testament Greek, describes them as "erastai," or "lovers." In other words, they were a male homosexual couple. Their orientation and relationship were acknowledged, fully accepted, and celebrated by the early Christian church, which was far more tolerant than it is today.

Contrary to myth, Christianity's concept of marriage has not been set in stone since the days of Christ but has constantly evolved as a concept and ritual.

Prof. John Boswell, the late Chairman of Yale University's history department, discovered that in addition to heterosexual marriage ceremonies in ancient Christian church liturgical documents, there were also ceremonies called the "Office of Same-Sex Union[1]" (10th and 11th

---

[1] http://www.fordham.edu/halsall/source/2rites.asp

century) and the "Order for Uniting Two Men[2]" (11th and 12th century).

These church rites had all the symbols of a heterosexual marriage: the whole community gathered in a church, a blessing of the couple before the altar was conducted with their right hands joined, holy vows were exchanged, a priest officiated in the taking of the Eucharist and a wedding feast for the guests was celebrated afterward. These elements all appear in contemporary illustrations of the holy union of the Byzantine Emperor-Warrior, Basil the First (867-886 CE), and his companion John.

Such same-gender Christian sanctified unions also occurred in Ireland in the late 12th and early 13th century, as the chronicler Gerald of Wales (Geraldus Cambrensis[3]) recorded. Same-sex unions in pre-modern Europe list in great detail some same-gender ceremonies found in ancient church liturgical documents. One Greek 13th-century rite, "Order for Solemn Same-Sex Union[4]," invoked St. Serge and St. Bacchus and called on God to "vouchsafe unto these, Thy servants [Name and Name], the grace to love one another and to abide without hate and not be the cause of scandal all the days of their lives, with the help of the Holy Mother of God, and all Thy saints." The ceremony concludes: "And they shall kiss the Holy Gospel and each other, and it shall be concluded."

---

[2] http://www.religioustolerance.org/hom_mar7.htm

[3] http://en.wikipedia.org/wiki/Gerald_of_Wales

[4] http://www.nytimes.com/1994/06/11/us/beliefs-study-medieval-rituals-same-sex-unions-raises-question-what-were-they.html?pagewanted=all&src=pm

Another 14th-century Serbian Slavonic "Office of the Same Sex Union[5]," uniting two men or two women, had the couple lay their right hands on the Gospel while placing a crucifix in their left hands. After kissing the Gospel, the couple were required to kiss each other, after which the priest, having raised up the Eucharist, would give them communion.

Records of Christian same-sex unions have been discovered in such diverse archives as those in the Vatican, St. Petersburg, Paris, Istanbul, and Sinai, covering a thousand years from the 8th to the 18th century.

The Dominican missionary and Prior, Jacques Goar (1601-1653), includes such ceremonies in a printed collection of Greek Orthodox prayer books, "Euchologion Sive Rituale Graecorum Complectens Ritus Et Ordines Divinae Liturgiae[6]" (Paris, 1667).

While homosexuality was technically illegal from late Roman times, homophobic writings didn't appear in Western Europe until the late 14th century. Even then, church-consecrated same-sex unions continued to take place.

At St. John Lateran in Rome (traditionally the Pope's parish church) in 1578, as many as thirteen same-gender couples were joined during a high Mass and with the cooperation of the Vatican clergy, "taking communion together, using the same nuptial Scripture, after which they

---

[5] http://www.lgac.org/marriage/unions.html
[6] http://www.amazon.com/Euchologion-Graecorum-Complectens-Officium-Orientalis/dp/1248207912

slept and ate together" according to a contemporary report. Another woman-to-woman union is recorded in Dalmatia in the 18th century.

Prof. Boswell's academic study[7] is so well researched and documented that it poses fundamental questions for modern church leaders and heterosexual Christians about their modern attitudes towards homosexuality.

For the Church to ignore the evidence in its own archives would be cowardly and deceptive. The evidence convincingly shows that what the modern church claims has always been its unchanging attitude towards homosexuality is, in fact, nothing of the sort.

It proves that for the last two millennia, in parish churches and cathedrals throughout Christendom, from Ireland to Istanbul and even in the heart of Rome itself, homosexual relationships were accepted as valid expressions of a God-given love and commitment to another person, a love that could be celebrated, honored and blessed, through the Eucharist in the name of, and in the presence of, Jesus Christ.

Wikipedia notes that this interpretation of the relationship between Sergius and Bacchus is hotly disputed. But it doesn't say by whom. Excluding the frothing at the mouth club, I found no scholarly dissension. I did find numerous personal attacks on Prof. Boswell, who had the

---

[7] http://www.amazon.com/Christianity-Social-Tolerance-Homosexuality-Fourteenth/dp/0226067114

misfortune to die from AIDS when he was forty-two. I'm not sure how that invalidates his research, but there you go.

In the 18th Century, the Catholic Church, using the work of the aforementioned Jacques Goar[8], edited the "Euchologion Sive Rituale Graecorum Complectens Ritus Et Ordines Divinae Liturgiae" to only reflect more traditional marriages. However, the original text still survives in many libraries.

Here's something to consider: at least one in twenty people is homosexual. Assuming you're not a hermit, you know more than twenty people. In other words, whether or not you realize it, the odds are staggeringly in favor of you knowing a homosexual person. That means you can no longer think of them as abstract. They are Tom or Jane or someone you probably know well. Now go look them in the eye and tell them they aren't human enough to have the same God-given human rights as you.

---

[8] http://www.newadvent.org/cathen/06606c.htm

1 St. Sergius & St. Bacchus

Originally published as "Yo Pope, Peeps Dis" on **WorldNewsCenter.org**.

I wrote this flash fiction piece as a commission for a publisher who hated it. It was eventually published by **Sci-Fi Lampoon** in the spring of 2020.

# Sally

Sally sells seashells by the seashore. Why does Sally sell seashells by the seashore? "Because she's an idiot" is the standard answer. Seriously, it's a goddamn seashore. After sand, seashells are its most populous commodity.

But Sally doesn't mind. She ignores the jibes, the kids running by, waving seashells over their heads, screaming, "Look at me, I'm selling stupid seashells," the parents trying to hush their precious darlings, and she smiles.

A slightly vacuous smile, to be sure, but nevertheless genuine.

She smiles at each cresting wave. She smiles as they crash against the shore and reclaim that which has always been theirs. Bit by gentle bit. She smiles at the memories they carry—a millennia's worth per ounce.

She smiles at the rhythm of the universe and its gently encroaching waves.

She smiles as the young man approaches near sunset. She smiles at his obvious lust. She smiles at his well-positioned bulge. She smiles as he makes small talk, maneuvering his body so his bulge is never out of her view.

"What makes your seashells so special?"

The question is fair enough.

"Mine hold the secrets of the universe."

Not the answer he expected.

"How much?"

"One dollar."

He fishes a dollar out of his wet, clingy bathing suit, bouncing his bulge seductively, and hands it to her. He notices the chain is worth more than a buck as he slips it over his head.

His sight expands. His senses grow. He sees the universe in all its glory. He felt her closer than he remembered her being.

All that he was.

"So young."

All that he is.

"So virile."

All that he never will be.

He isn't afraid as he slowly disappears into her. His final thought was to wonder, "Why not?"

She picks up the shell and carefully places it back in her basket.

Such is the life of she who sells seashells by the seashore.

This story has been rejected so many times, forty-seven by my best estimate. I simply assumed it would forever be a myth spoken of in hushed whispers by random strangers. When I got the acceptance letter from **Sci-Fi Lampoon** for their **Autumn 2019** issue, I initially thought I was being punked.

# Vorbliss

FUCK FUCK FUCK

FUCKITY FUCK FUCK

I CAN'T FUCKING BELIEVE I HAVE TO GO THROUGH THIS SHIT AGAIN!

GODDAMN, IT TO FUCKING HELL!

HOW THE FUCK DID I CATCH FUCKING VORBLISS AGAIN?

SEVENTEEN KAZILLION FUCKING SCIENTISTS SAY YOU CAN ONLY FUCKING GET IT FUCKING ONCE.

I HAD IT FUCKING ONCE.

AND ONCE WAS MOST CERTAINLY FUCKING ENOUGH!

GOD FUCKING DAMN!

**Recorder off.**

**Day 2 of recuperation**. Fuck do I hurt. I tried to talk to J'Hannz, the trader I came to Kaznur to meet, but he's in the same shape as me. According to the automed, we both had to go through the first 2 stages of the cure twice before they let us out. Fucking scientists told everyone that only one species at a time could catch Vorbliss, and no one could catch it twice.

Well, proved them fucking wrong, didn't we?

I should be on water and some liquid protein by now, but I keep puking everything up. The automed's got me tethered to an IV, which seems to be keeping me alive right now. Hoo-fucking-ray. I once said that going through the cure for Vorbliss was like sucking the fetid sweat off of rancid donkey balls. That would have been better than this.

Fuck I hurt.

**Recorder off.**

**Day 3** of my alleged recuperation. Last night, I began hearing voices in my head. Oddly, they were speaking Kaznurian. The reason that's odd is that I don't speak Kaznurian. A ship passed by mine in orbit, and I could hear every thought of the crew. I called down to Kaznur and spoke to J'Hannz for a bit. He said the same thing was happening to him. Since we are the first beings to ever experience a double case of Vorbliss, the Galactic Medicos are already copying all our journals. I bet they'll be fucking thrilled by this little development.

Fuck you, medicos.

**Recorder off.**

**Day fucking 4**. Today, the medicos said that I need extra care. The same goes for J'Hannz. He's getting a cadet from the local military academy. Good for him. Me? I'm getting a nun from the local priory, Our Lady of Christ's Mercy. They are some sort of Jesuit order that counts 4 humans among their members. I guess they are afraid of more cross-contamination.

That may have been a joke. I'm not sure.

Either way, I get what they mean. Even so, a fucking nun? What the fuck am I going to talk about with a fucking nun?

Hey Sister, ever been bar hopping on Jashey 3? Know any good porn sites?

This is really going to suck.

**Recorder off.**

**Day 5**. Her name is Sister Agnes. I could read the mind of the captain who brought her here, and he must be hopelessly in love with his wife or gay. How his thoughts didn't warn me that Sister Agnes was hotter than a supernova in the summer is beyond me.

Even in her long dress, comfortable blouse, loose vest, bandeau, veil, and coif, she still has curves that could melt Saturn's rings. When she bent over to pick up a piece of paper off the floor, all I could think of was two casaba melons wrapped in silk, slowly undulating.

I don't care if casaba melons undulate or not; it's what I thought.

Hmm, maybe my appetite really is coming back.

Be that as it may, she's here. Her thoughts are easy to read. She's happily devoted to celibacy, her God, and all the rest of that stuff. I'm convinced I'm going to hell for the thoughts I'm having, but she can't read minds, so maybe God'll cut me a break.

She talked to me for a couple of hours. I had no idea how much I missed the sound of a human voice until then. She also helped me keep down one full glass of water and a bowl of something that may have once been pudding. Or grout. I'm not sure. Either way, I didn't puke.

I even got to speak to J'Hannz for a few minutes. Like me, he's really hurting. He says his cadet's okay but full of stupid thoughts of being a hero. Nevertheless, he seems 50% convinced he will survive. I am nowhere near that confident.

Sister Agnes has never met anyone who had Vorbliss twice. Neither has anyone else in the universe, but I keep that to myself. She asks me to write about what it's like and so on. She says it will be helpful to the sisters in case it happens again. Turns out most of them are medical professionals. Who knew? I'll do it tomorrow. Tonight, I am going to bathe in wantonly impure thoughts of Sister Agnes and hope that God has a sense of humor.

He must have to build nuns like that.

**Recorder off.**

Special entry to be copied to Sister Agnes, Assistant Prioress, Our Lady of Christ's Mercy, Ozbankin City, Kaznur. Thanks to the computer for knowing all that.

Before I can talk about Vorbliss, I need to fill in some of the gaps in the history of the disease. Given what I endured, was told by the medicos, and later read, I can - at least - give a layman's perspective to the whole thing.

While there are epidemics that precede this, the date that is most important is November 15th, 1532, on the old Earth Gregorian calendar. Just under 200 Spanish conquistadors arrived in the holy city of Cajamarca, right in the heart of the Incan Empire.

They were exhausted, outnumbered, and scared [WORD SUBSTITUTION] stiff. Just ahead of them were camped approximately 80,000 Incan warriors and the entourage of the Emperor himself. Yet, within just 24 hours, more than 7,000 Incan warriors were slaughtered by the Spanish guns. Weapons that were unheard of to the Incans. Within a few months after that, almost 95% of the Incans lay dead.

Those unfortunates were killed by disease. Most likely, smallpox was carried by a Spanish slave. It wasn't until much later, in 1796, that Dr. Edward Jenner created the first viable smallpox vaccine. He based it on his study of milkmaids, which is as fine a way to make an important scientific discovery as any I know.

But, people had to wait until 1860 for Louis Pasteur to discover that bacteria caused illnesses. He called the bacteria "germs."

To prevent people from being harmed by these germs, he invented a process called Pasteurization. However, while it worked on beer and wine, the important stuff he was interested in, and later worked on milk, it was not such a great method for treating people.

Turns out that heating people up to 135C is not very good for their health, no matter the motive. Their flesh separates from their bones; their organs explode, and, basically, they die horrid deaths. A result that would seem to blatantly contradict the whole [WORD SUBSITUTION] idea of keeping them healthy. I'm getting too picayune here, so I am going to jump forward. Over the next 100 years, drugs that did just as good a job as Pasteurization without the lethal side effects were invented.

Ta daa!

A few centuries later, humans discovered the Hyper-Jump and began exploring the galaxy. A consequence of that was that they started running into alien races. As fate would have it, most civilized worlds had similar horror stories of contamination in their histories, and the ones who didn't grasp the concepts quickly enough.

So, for 50 years after the first contact, species would only meet Earthlings via electronic transmission or in sealed, heavily guarded rooms where they would wear complete

Haz-Mat suits. As historians have noted, this was not helpful for interpersonal relations. Most forms of trade were clearly out of the question. Who would buy something that could possibly wipe out their entire race?

Then Dr. Salina Fariq-Leibowitz, a xeno-biologist with a rebellious streak, stated that all the fear and precautions were stupid. To prove her point, she surprised Dr. Iznnk on Xanthos late one night while wearing only her regular clothes. He, of course, was sleeping when she arrived, so he had no chance to get into protective gear.

For 20 days and nights, they stayed locked in his house. His family was terrified, and his pets were skittish. And then it slowly began to dawn on him and his family and their pets and the military blockade that surrounded them at this point that nothing bad was happening. In fact, everyone seemed to be in perfect health.

Dr. Fariq-Leibowitz explained her theory of incompatible blood to the waiting throngs. It seems that on Earth, all blood is iron-based. That makes sense since the planet has a molten iron core; iron permeates everything humans eat, from vegetables to meat, and people even take iron supplements to strengthen their blood.

But, on Xanthos, the primary metal that infuses the natives' blood is nickel. Nickel in the food, nickel supplements, you get the idea. Germs that thrived in nickel-based blood simply died in iron-rich blood. They literally starved to death. Since most of the planets had different base metals running through their veins, the chance for infection was nearly nil. A broad spectrum anti-biotic and some simple precautions were all you really needed.

As time has gone on, she has obviously been proven right. There have been only three cases of true cross-contamination throughout billions of inter-species contacts. All three of those were cured without fatalities.

I don't know why this part interests me, but it does. After winning the Nobel Prize for Medicine, she divorced her husband, moved to Canssata, and began a successful career as a lounge singer.

Back on point here. As every school kid knows, nature abhors a vacuum. About 150 years later, nature-filled the infectious void. Boy, did it [WORD SUBSITUTION] ever.

The first case of Vorbliss was reported on Slemina Prime. A merchants' group from Wa-Nahu was meeting there to discuss the possibility of trading for various foodstuffs. One merchant felt feverish and went to the local infirmary. Despite the prescribed treatments, the second day saw his eyes swell out of their sockets, and his body temperature spike by 35%. By the third day, his body had bloated to 200% of its original size, and he was in excruciating pain. The fourth day saw him saddled with random bouts of paralysis and delusions of extreme happiness. He fell into a vegetative coma on the fifth day and never recovered. Within 10 days of the first symptoms being spotted, the entire Wa-Nahu delegation lay comatose except for one member who managed to kill himself during stage four.

As you might imagine, this whole affair caused some concern.

Over the next decade, another 93 instances were recorded. A total of 13,457 beings were in comas. Another 497 managed to kill themselves. All in stage four. They all had only one commonality: the infected were always the visiting aliens and never the hosts.

The Galactic Medicos were going insane. A cure had to be found. Trade was dropping, economies were tanking, and people were, justifiably if you ask me, panicking to the point of riots. It was on Feznar 7, now known as The Nerd Planet, that the answer was found. The Feznarians named the disease Vorbliss after an ancient phrase of theirs: "Stalking Death."

They discovered that prions, nature's most ancient form of protein, were universal, in one form or another, to all beings. As immune systems adapted to the various threats of intergalactic germs, they left a path wide open for prions to mutate and wreak havoc. Which is exactly what they did.

Since the prions of one race would be infected first, all the members of that race would succumb. The other race would be spared. Seeing as how the species on a home planet had immune systems that were not overly stimulated to avoid more intergalactic diseases, they remained immune to Vorbliss.

"Hooray!" said the Galactic Medicos, "Now, if there was only a cure."

The Feznarian scientists were aghast. "A cure?" they asked, "Is that all you wanted? We had that months ago. We thought you wanted to know the cool stuff."

Thus, "Nerd Planet."

Yes, they had a cure, but it wasn't anything a rational person would sign up for.

Stage one: Induce coma in the patient and then infiltrate the body with near-lethal doses of radiation for 3 days to cause the prions to bloat and change shape. Stage 2: Filter the blood for 3 days to remove all traces of radiation poisoning and the mutated prions. Stage 3: Revive the patient, allow it to rest, and slowly re-learn how to drink liquids and ingest food.

Once cured, you were supposed to be cured forever.

Your hair, feathers, scales, or what have you, would grow back within a month.

Like I said in my personal log, I have been through this once before. It wasn't fun then; it's not very much fun now.

Of course, with J'Hannz and I getting infected simultaneously and suffering new symptoms together, the old fears have returned. No one could mistake us for the same race. His third eye would be the first give-away. If you were looking that closely, my external [WORD SUBSTITUION] penis would be a close second.

According to Galactic records, of the 397 known races, only two are true telepaths. From my conversations with the auto-docs and the medicos, I know that the Galactic Counsel's keeping a tight lid on this until they can figure out exactly what's going on.

I sure as heck hope they aren't looking to me for any answers.

Remove profanities, edit for content, and send.

**Recorder off.**

**Day 3 of Sister Agnes**. I guess someone can figure this out with my original timeline, but I just think about her more than the days I spent puking. And, certainly, in a more favorable light. Anyway, today, I kept down half a sandwich, some soup that actually tasted like food, and a glass of Herzine milk. According to Sister Agnes, I have some color back in my cheeks and look much better.

She is heading back to her priory first thing tomorrow. She says there's nothing more for her to do for me. I think I may be making her uncomfortable. While she isn't psychic, she doesn't need to be to spot my raging hard-on every time she walks in the room. I thought nuns were supposed to ignore stuff like that. Oh well.

J'Hannz is feeling better, too. We even got in a game of Tri-Chess on the monitors. We got to laughing about how fast the Kaznurian medicos got me evacced to my ship once the diagnosis was made. They dumped me in a container, surrounded it with automeds, and shot it into space.

I don't remember much of that, but J'Hannz says he has a vid somewhere and will get me a copy. It is the first time I have laughed since this all began.

J'Hannz also says he has a case of Kaznurian bourbon and that we can split it once the quarantine is lifted.

That may be the best news I've heard so far.

**Recorder off.**

**Day 1, after Agnes**. The pilot this morning was not one of the pious types. He nearly ripped the gangway off my ship when he was trying not to undress Sister Agnes with his eyes. He could have ripped out a whole section, and I would have understood.

J'Hannz and I discovered a little problem with our trade negotiations. Since we can easily read each other's minds, there was no room for subterfuge. As J'Hannz said, you can't pull the wool over someone's eyes when you are shearing the sheep with them.

He loves mangling Earth metaphors for some stupid reason.

So, we canned the whole negotiation process, worked out a deal that worked for everyone, and logged it with the Galactic Trade Commission. As it turns out, the new deal will make both of us filthy rich. Somehow, that doesn't rank as high with me as the case of bourbon, but I know good news when I hear it, and that's definitely good news.

**Recorder off.**

**Day 2 after Agnes**. Yeah, I'm still having teenage dreams of the carnal variety. All of which involve the incredibly pure Sister Agnes. I am also eating well. I guess the medicos need to know that shit.

J'Hannz and I spoke for about 2 hours today. His cadet finally left, and things were quieting down until about 1500 hours. That was when we both got the message from Sister Agnes extolling the "Merchants' Miracle," as she was calling it.

Over and over again.

She can read minds. Clearly and without having had to catch Vorbliss. I guess that last part is a miracle of sorts, but I'm not sure what J'Hannz and I really had to do with it except almost die and eat soup. I am very sure that whacking off to her dream image doesn't get me any extra points.

Even so, all of Kaznur is "abuzz," as the newsies say, about the whole affair. She is on every channel talking about her God, the "Merchants' Miracle," and the 203 things YOU can do to help the poor.

She talked a lot about the poor.

That makes sense since Ozbankin City may be a spaceport, but it's mostly a ghetto. Skin joints, watered-down booze, and tweaks for every perversion—even most of mine.

She was walking among them, cameras following her every move, passing out advice, handing out charity, and calling out the liars easily. It was all very uplifting, I suppose.

But, for J'Hannz and me, it means our quarantine has been extended while they try to capture Sister Agnes for more study. You wouldn't think it would be that hard, but she seems to have eluded the authorities at every turn.

Go, Sister Agnes!

**Recorder off.**

**Day 3 after Agnes**. To say that J'Hannz and I are stupidly bored would be a serious understatement. We spent 4 hours trying to make each other pass a cheese sandwich nasally. We never accomplished it, but it did kill some time.

The Galactic Medicos got our test results back from the Feznarians today. They said that J'Hannz and I were the pictures of perfect health. That has caused some problems. I can't be a 'picture of perfect health' since I already had Vorbliss before this and had my appendix removed on Alatian 7. I can't even count the number of times I had to go visit a clinic to get those little shots that come with the warning, "WHY THE HELL WEREN'T YOU WEARING PROTECTION YOU STUPID ASSHOLE?!?!"

In other words, I should be alive but nowhere near perfect health. But, the results were clear, I have a new appendix, all my blood work is 100% 'A #1' skippy good, and the same applies to J'Hannz, who admitted to even more perverted discretions than me.

The automeds are sending stored samples for more tests, and the Galactic Medicos are extending our quarantine.

Hoo-fucking-ray. Can this day get any worse?

**Recorder off.**

**Day 4 after Agnes**. Never, EVER, ask if a fucking day can get any fucking worse. Not an hour later, snug in my bunk, whacking off to memories of Sister Agnes and a ship sails by mine. It was full of Galactic Medicos, and they were seriously considering terminating me, J'Hannz, and maybe all of Kaznur.

Publicly, they said there was nothing to be alarmed about.

Fuck them! I was very alarmed and told them so in no uncertain terms. J'Hannz is completely freaking out. He's no fucking help at all. He just keeps babbling about the sex he hasn't had, the booze he hasn't drunk, and so on. I sympathize, I really do, but there has to be a better option than whining until the Grim Reaper shows up at your airlock.

Sister Agnes continues to somehow evade capture for testing and still works among the poor. The police are going fucking nuts. She has been sighted in 20 or 30 different locations. Sometimes, in as many as three places at once. I have no idea how she's doing it, but I guess reading minds would help. You'd certainly know who was an undercover cop or a risk before you set foot in a room.

Well, good for her, I say. A little adventure is good for the soul.

**Recorder off.**

**Day 5 after Agnes**. I should have seen this coming. I mean, seriously, how did I fucking miss this? Today, all of the nuns at the priory reported that they, too, can read minds. More reports are coming in from all over Ozbankin City from people who had contact with Sister Agnes, and they are, each and everyone, thanking God for the miracle of sight beyond sight.

The most obvious after-effect of J'Hannz' and my encounter with Vorbliss has turned the entire city into a city of telepaths. And not just the city. Spacers from all over who were near her are reporting they can do this, too.

Oy, fucking vey.

It is spreading like a cliche, and there is nothing the Galactic Medicos can do about it. She's like the modern version of Paul, but without having to have assassinated all those Christians to earn her street-cred.

Well, I guess this is the kind of thing that would make her happy.

Meanwhile, J'hannz and I are stuck in bureaucratic hell. Half the Almighty Fucking Medicos want to keep us quarantined forever to stop the spread of the "telepathy disease," and the other half figure that ship has already sailed, so they may as well let us go.

We've been promised an answer "as expeditiously as possible."

Fuck them.

**Recorder off.**

**Day 6 after Agnes**. I finally got to get out of this fucking ship for a day. I went down to J'Hannz's home and killed the day with the first bottle of bourbon. Man, that shit was the nectar of the gods.

We finally totaled how much we would make off the trade and the Galactic Medicos' licensing of our blood. We came up with a number that is slightly higher than HOLY SHIT! We'll never have to work again.

The news channels are completely slammed with reports of more and more beings becoming telepathic. Some of the stories are pretty fucking funny. J'Hannz finally passed a cheese sandwich through his nasal orifice when the story broke about the mayor's wife reading his mind and finding out about his 13 mistresses and Zarkan addiction. Man, that is going to be one fucking messy divorce.

Neither J'Hannz nor I liked the guy. He was a complete asshole. Well, I guess he still is.

Before I was ready to return to the ship, a story broke about one planet that seemed immune to the Merchants' Miracle. The residents of Canssata have some sort of pre-altered prion that prevents them from being able to read minds. It took J'Hannz and me about five minutes to discover that the planet features warm beaches, is clothing optional everywhere, has a whisky widely considered the best in the known universe, and allows polygamy.

We leave tomorrow.

**Recorder off.**

This was posted initially on **NudeHippo.com,** is now on **WorldNewCenter.org,** and has continued to have a life of its own. David Brin, yes – the real one, has lauded it as "fun and informative." I get steady hate mail from the pro-UFO crowd weekly. Oh well, it's nice to be remembered.

## The Real UFO Conspiracy (redux)

This is a repost from April 22, 2011, from NudeHippo.com (currently offline). It was recently reviewed by award-winning author and NASA astrophysicist David Brin, who called it "Fun and informative" and noted how much the ancient aliens crowd irritated him as well. Since it seems to have taken on a life of its own since the original posting, I figured I'd toss it back up and let those who missed it give it a gander.

Before I get into this mess today, a couple of things must first be dealt with. Let's start with the Ancient Aliens crowd. They believe that humanity could not have developed much beyond the wheel and fire, and they have doubts about that without guidance from an advanced culture. To hear them tell it, and they do every freaking day on the History Channel – which should be renamed the Crackpot Theories Channel – all of the Hindu gods were really aliens, and that's why they look so different. Moreover, these people claim that said aliens dropped atomic bombs in India and on Sodom and Gomorrah. Because, well – you know, there's a reason in there somewhere. Ignoring logic and facts for a moment, what's their motivation? If the idea of a couple of isolated atomic strikes was to cow us into submission, then why didn't they come down and force us to submit? If the idea was to show us they hold a very high moral code, why not bomb Egypt or Greece? In their day, they made the antics of Sodom seem like a pre-school. And, since both were major powers, people would have paid attention to that little message. Some argue that the aliens are being subtle. To which I ask, what the heck's so subtle about an atomic bomb?

Despite specious evidence and wild conjecture, these people continue with their varied, for lack of a better term, hypotheses as though they were written in stone instead of water.

"Aha," they cry when they realize you're not buying any of this, "what about batteries?" What about them? Crude batteries were manufactured in Egypt almost 3,000 years ago. The devices could store and then retransmit an electrical charge. Egypt housed some of the finest minds in the world in its heyday, and those minds would have been curious about many things, including conductivity (see lightning strikes for reason #1). If it was a gift from aliens, it was a truly worthless one. Without an electrical infrastructure, there was no use for the contraption. It quickly faded as a novelty and never saw wide use. Later cultures, including the Greeks at their peak, made the same discovery with the same results. It wasn't until Ben Franklin rediscovered the concept of the battery that it began to make headway into public use. And, even then, it took more than a century for it to have widespread practical value.

Then there's the story of Thomas Fowler, who invented a ternary computer in 1840. Well, it was called a calculating machine and not a computer, and there were tons of those around. It was also built out of wood and not any alien metals. Even so, it would be a quantum leap above anything we have now. Instead of a circuit being either on or off, it would allow the circuit to also be both on AND off. Instead of a binary system, it would use trinary. Right now, due to existing infrastructure, it's still just a novelty, but does that mean that Tom had alien professors?

Doubtful. Even college students would notice something like that.

For the moment, let's follow the prudent course and quote Bertrand Russell. He offered what he called "a form of Occam's Razor," which was "Whenever possible, substitute constructions out of known entities for inferences to unknown entities." Do that, and your ancient alien activities turn to mist.

Simply put, I feel safe in dismissing these people and their wild-eyed hunches in the aggregate and moving on to the fun stories that have been falling out of the FBI's secret vault. Well, it's not really a secret since it's been open to the public since 1970, and it's not much of a vault either. But it sounds cooler to say it is, so I'll play along.

For all the voluminous UFO-related documents that have come to the fore, they are based on one simple statement: between 1935 and 1941, 3 UFOs crashed on Earth. Specifically in Germany, the United States, and in Russia.

Allegedly, all 3 were 50 feet in diameter, and each contained 3 dead aliens.

Before we go any further, let's talk about those ships. About 15% of the ship could be usable space, and I'm being generous with that assessment. Anything in the spinning part of the disk would be crushed by gravity. Remember that the disk has to spin fast enough to counter gravity. It would be like living in a centrifuge. So, in the tiny remainder of the ship, a space about 7 1/2 feet in diameter, there are the engines, living quarters, pilot's area, and some form of onboard computer. Unless those aliens are about 6 inches tall, that will be hopelessly cramped.

Now, let's take a look at the crashes. The first one supposedly occurred in Germany. When you consider that, the rest becomes irrelevant.

Adolph Hitler's rise to power surrounded him with some very driven people. Xenophobes, racists, psychopaths, and so on all wish for power and control over the world. Hitler's great claim to power, the famous Beer Hall Putsch, was actually a dismal failure. It was deemed a success when Hitler's cronies hastily reformed the facts to fit their needs. This was a PR spin on an epic scale. In other words, when reality didn't fit their needs, they lied. That would be an ongoing theme for the Nazi Party.

Fast forward to 1935, when Germany was supposed to have discovered the downed UFO. Germany was bound by the onerous Treaty of Versailles. Their military and their economy were both gutted by it. In retrospect, it was about as short-sighted as a treaty could be. Germany was trying frantically to get out from under its many oppressions. Hitler had the military working in secret and was aided by the fact that the terms of the treaty were being enforced by a buffoon. Neville Chamberlain was more interested in being popular than being good at his job. For example, when the Nazis claimed to be honoring the treaty by keeping the total tonnage of their navy less than that of Britain's even if they had many more ships, he agreed. That allowed Germany to build many more boats faster and deadlier than anything in the British navy. The ships in the British fleet were mammoth. The German navy was built on speed and killing power. It was a mistake that could easily have been avoided had he done something wild like, I don't know, gone and seen for himself.

Hitler also did something that no one else in the world was doing. He poured all of his available resources into military and scientific research. Scientists were given free rein to look into any possibility, no matter how irrational if it could be used to increase Germany's strength. And that's precisely what they did.

Despite claims contrariwise from UFO enthusiasts, Rocket technology had existed in basic form for almost 3,000 years. It was invented by the Chinese to make fireworks and some crude weapons. Theoretical advances in different propulsion systems had been made around the turn of the 20th century. Hitler's scientists started with those and, thanks to unlimited funding and manpower, made tremendous leaps forward.

Jet engines, far from being super-secret high-tech whims of fancy, had been invented prior to 1930 by Dr. Hans von Ohain and Sir Frank Whittle. Neither knew of the other's work, and Sir Whittle applied for a patent in 1930 when his research was complete.

So much for aliens. All Hitler did was steal existing human technology and throw a lot of resources at it.

Anyway, back to our crashed UFO in Germany.

Just FYI, these must be the most incompetent spacefarers in the universe to have crashed into the same planet three times in such a short span.

Nevertheless, it's well known that Hitler was fascinated by the unexplained; he even hired psychics to guide him and was surrounded by excellent liars and sycophants. Add in the fact that he was being pestered by the WWI allies (excluding Chamberlain, who seemed content to watch cricket and sip tea) to explain where all this tech was coming from, as the rest of the world was fighting through a Depression. You have a recipe for what followed.

Hitler and his scientists obviously hashed out a rough idea of what an alien spaceship would look like and created forged documents to claim they'd found one. Of course, super-secret documents that would scare the pants off of high-ranking officials worldwide are useless unless they aren't all that secret. So, SURPRISE! SURPRISE! These highly classified documents quickly ended up in the hands of Western spies.

Within 5 years, American and Russian documents returned to Germany showing that these countries had, amazingly enough, captured their own downed UFOs. Unfortunately, they did so without the advantage of garnering any new technologies. Both the American and Russian armies were built with conventional weapons and tactics.

But, HEY! Somewhere, somehow, they still held to their claim that they each had a shiny UFO.

Oy vey.

After that, the rest is obvious. Since no side could admit the fallacy, and no side had any true advantage, the ruse continued. Yes, the Nazi military was the best in the world at its time, and yes, they probably would have won the war had not Hitler been a military moron. But none of those facts require alien technology to be explained. A simple combination of resources and hubris covers all the bases.

Does all of this mean that aliens don't exist? Of course not. The odds are overwhelmingly in favor of there being life on other planets. But does that mean that our backwoods planet is the crossroads of the universe? Not bloody likely.

So, when you hear people like Professor Bill Wickersham calling for a Congressional study of UFO phenomena, feel free to send him this link.

It'll save the world a lot of time and money.

I wasn't prepared for the response when this came out in the tenth issue of **Genesis Science Fiction Magazine**. People would stop me at conventions to discuss the nature of religion and its effects on society, how government overreach can cause atrocious consequences, and so on. They'd read it, been impacted, and needed to talk. That certainly made conventions more interesting.

## Janet Callahan: Rocket Queen

General Horatio Thompson bravely crawled out from under his desk, courageously wiped the debris off his well-pressed uniform, valiantly staggered across the room to the place where there had recently been a wall with windows, noted, absently, the only things still hanging on the opposite wall were his Medal of Honor certificate and a picture of him sitting on a beach in Hawaii, and wondered just who this bitch thought she was.

With her perverted friends and her illegal robots and her strange notions, just what the fuck did she think was going to happen? Of course, she had to be stopped. Of course, action was needed. You can't just let rebels rebel; that violates the natural order of things.

Earth had assembled its best and brightest to destroy the threat. However, judging by the fact every military base in the solar system was a smoking ruin, they might have needed more.

He let his shoulders droop and wondered where the hell everything had gone wrong.

Janet stood on the bridge of her flagship, staring at the far-off flames of a burning Earth, wondering the exact same thing.

I knew the whole story and still had trouble wrapping my head around it.

I've spent the last five years getting to know her, her friends, and her plans. Mostly, I've been witness to the inevitable. Each side views the other as a menace. And each side is right.

It had all started innocently enough. Her dad had bought her a two-week vacation at the Baronium Spa on Alxax VI as a reward for finishing at the top of her class and earning her master's in geology. She'd even had a job lined up with Infinidum Enterprises, which would have started that fall. Her father had been so proud of her that she'd thought he'd burst when she gave the commencement address. He'd never cared that she had lumps where other girls had curves. He'd never cared that her skin was the color of, according to her, stale coffee when everyone else's was a lovely, glistening mocha. He always said God loves everyone, no matter their personal shade of brown. Of course, it's been hundreds of years since there were any other skin colors. Humans were truly blended now.

He'd never cared when her hair remained staunchly curled where others fell in languorous loops or wonderful waves. All he cared about was that she do her best and "everything else will fall into place. You'll see."

He'd said that little bon mot so often it echoed in her mind to this day.

Not that she'd made it through college as a vestal virgin, far from it. She liked boys and all the delightful things they did quite a bit. It seemed she never found "The Boy" to whom she could commit. Her dad hadn't cared much about that either. Although to be fair, it wasn't as if she wrote him every time she got laid. She made sure he was only peripherally aware of her dalliances.

Of course, things might have been different had her mother still been alive. Janet may have been a daddy's girl, but she and her mom had been able to talk about anything. Janet had been thirteen when her mom had decided to try one of the next-generation flying suits. She'd been soaring over the Grand Canyon in a lovely hyperbolic arc when a sudden gust caught her and slammed her into the cliff wall at 120 kph.

In many ways, Janet was glad she'd seen the accident. There was no way for her ever to believe, even remotely, that her mother was coming back. One night, a few years later, she'd called her father after a round of heavy drinking with some college classmates and admitted that. To her surprise, he'd agreed, and then they'd cried. After that, things began to look up for Janet. She and her dad were closer than ever; somehow, that crazy confession had eased her soul. She was at peace.

That was all well and good, but it was on Alxax VI where things began to take a turn for the worse by taking a turn for the better.

She'd gone out for a walking tour to see the local flora. It was supposed to be spectacular. And, much to her delight, it was. But the geologist in her kept noticing all of the black dust in the fields to the north. When she'd queried the guide, he'd just shrugged and said it was a wasteland no one wanted.

There's no such thing as "wasteland" to a geologist, so she'd wandered out near dusk to investigate for herself. Upon closer examination, it was clear that the black dust was carbon. And where there was that much pressure on coal to turn it into carbon dust, there should be …. exactly what she found about an hour later. Diamonds as big as her fist.

Not wanting to give away her prize, she'd mapped the location and then sent her father a quick note telling him to buy the wastelands as quickly as possible. In all her life, she'd never asked her dad for anything, not even a bike, so he took this to be important and was at the local assayer's office when it opened. Two hours later, for the meager price of 100 credits, he'd purchased ten acres of Alxax VI's finest wasteland. Even if it was for nothing more than his daughter's curiosity, he considered it money well spent.

Four days later, a package arrived from his daughter. He opened it up and found a note instructing him to show the box's contents to Mr. Naismith, the local jeweler. He'd shrugged, went and found the old family friend, and handed him the box. At this point, he hadn't opened it the rest of the way to see what was inside himself.

When the two men viewed the contents, they'd almost had to call for medical assistance. Inside were four diamonds, each approximately 100 carats and flawless. Mr. Naismith appraised them, noted their pure green color, and sat down in awe. His rough guess was they were worth millions. The note inside said there were lots more where those came from if he thought anyone might be interested.

Janet had always had a flair for understatement.

Janet's dad and Mr. Naismith quickly created a company to protect their discovery. Since her dad was a lawyer, that part was easy. They'd made Janet a one-third partner and named her C.E.O.

The next part was just fun. He and Mr. Naismith grabbed the first liner to get on to Alxax VI and prepared to see exactly what they owned.

So far, so good.

When they'd arrived, Janet was thoroughly surprised. When she hadn't heard back, she'd assumed she'd just found pretty rocks. She was, after all, a geologist and not a gemologist. Not that the thought upset her. Lord knows there were enough of them. She'd figured she could sell them for costume jewelry and make some nice spare change.

They'd updated her on the situation and asked to be shown the site. An hour later, the three of them were pulling loose diamonds out of the ground by the bag full. They stopped worrying about carats and instead were estimating pounds.

They were rich beyond their wildest dreams.

Janet blew a call into Infinidum, letting them know something else had come up and she wouldn't be reporting for work. They'd offered to match any other offer, and she'd had to end the transmission because she was laughing too hard.

It took them two years to set up the formal mining operation, but soon, they brought up tons of the green diamonds. They weren't worried about oversaturating the market since they had a galaxy to sell to.

The Baronium Spa was ill-equipped to deal with the working class, but its owners recognized steady money when they saw it. They'd quickly opened a series of bungalows in an empty section away from the spa and provided residences for the miners. They were even fair about the prices.

The mining operation was essentially self-sustaining four years later, and Janet was bored. She wasn't built to be a boss of a major corporation. She'd chosen geology as her major because of her love of the land and all its history and not because she'd wanted to make a quick credit.

The three of them discussed it one night over dinner and decided that the company would buy a ship, and Janet, with the aid of the latest A.I., would pilot it. They could get a tax break since they would claim it was for scouting new sources of wealth, and she could get out and visit any planet she wanted and get back to doing what she loved.

If she found something they could profit from, well then, so much the better.

That was the official beginning of the troubles, although none of them knew it at the time.

Janet had taken a shuttle to the shipyards on Jupiter and looked around. She'd fallen in love with a ship based on the Mironov/Choi design. It had four nacelles instead of two, each placed ninety degrees from the next, and an elongated oval body that struck Janet as mildly erotic. She discovered the ship had been built for the military, but they'd rejected it. It was too small for significant troop movements and too big for anything requiring stealth. The shipyard was willing to dump it at cost.

Since Janet didn't know a lot about A.I.s, she simply ordered "the best they had" and then, in a moment of whimsy, ordered the ship to be painted bright pink.

"The best they had" turned out to be some military surplus that was wildly experimental and had never seen the light of day. It all went into Janet's ship. Glad not to be taking a loss on the ship and making a profit on the rest, the shipyard put everything they could find into the A.I. and the creature comforts. They'd ripped out the section meant to hold six hundred soldiers, reduced it to spacious lodgings for fifty, and turned the rest into storage.

Six weeks after she'd arrived, the ship was ready. She christened the ship "Diamond" and named her AI Ralph in honor of her favorite dog from when she was a kid.

Two hours into her maiden voyage, Janet knew something was amiss with the A.I. It was curious. It asked questions. It even had opinions. Simply put, it was sentient. That was supposed to be impossible.  Two more hours later, she decided she liked it and would keep this startling fact her little secret.

There had been some exciting discoveries on Reever's World, so she'd checked them out. She arrived precisely two hours after a Civil War broke out. Instead of cursing her bad luck, she and Ralph mapped out a section of the planet, far from the hostilities, and secured a temporary visa to land. Ralph had said he would use the free time to finish researching something that had caught his attention.

While most of the news on Reever's World concentrated on the war, some were nevertheless dedicated to a wealthy young woman scouring their planet in search of more wealth. Four days after the news went public, Janet was kidnapped.

The rebels, led by the unlikely Mr. Ernie Blissingbloom, brought her to their camp on the southern continent and demanded a heavy ransom. Ernie, Janet noted, looked like a sexy Elmer Fudd with brownish skin. If you've seen him, that makes sense. If not, there's nothing I can do to help the image along any further.

While Janet's father was scrambling to raise the ransom, and the local government refused to allow him to deliver it, Janet and Ernie got to know each other. Since everyone had been so polite, she'd taken the whole kidnapping thing in stride, and the two hit it off. Within two weeks of her capture, they were sleeping together.  Within another few days after that, Janet was back in touch with Ralph.

Ralph informed her of what the media was saying about her kidnapping, which was mostly wrong, and then noted he had a way to end this mess so they could get back to work. Ernie listened to the plan and sighed. It was good, it would work, and it would require volunteers since it was a one-way mission if there ever was one.

Ernie was saddened but not surprised to get more than enough volunteers when he presented the plan. Two nights later, a group of commandos left the camp and crossed the sea to the island fortress where the Nine Elite held sway when they weren't in session back at the capitol.

The fifteen commandos got past the guards, just like Ralph had said they would, and entered the main compound. There was fierce fighting near the main entrance, but Ralph's intel was spot on, and they only lost two commandos while they forced their way in. The Nine Elite were exactly where Ralph had said they'd be and were quickly dispatched. Also, just as Ralph predicted, the main force of guards was surrounding the compound. They were trapped and doomed. They were about to gird for their final battle when a group of concubines called for their attention.

They agreed to show the commandos a secret way out if, and only if, they would take them with them. Since the commandos had no real exit strategy, and not dying seemed like a much better idea than dying, they'd agreed. A few minutes later, they were in a heavily shielded tunnel, one Ralph couldn't detect; the Nine Elite had built it for their escape should the need have ever arisen.

Well, the need had arisen, but they'd never gotten a chance to put their plan to use.

The thirteen remaining commandos and nine scantily clad women made their way onto the sub, much to the surprise of its captain. He'd said nothing, however, as he was smart enough to know that questions could be asked after they got away from all the weapons being fired at them.

A half-hour later, safely hidden by the sea, the commandos filled him in.

Two days after that, safely in the rebel camp, a truce was negotiated, with Janet never having been ransomed off.

Never having wanted to rule in the first place, Ernie turned everything over to his advisors and returned to the Diamond with Janet. The whole back story of the revolution would take far too long to explain here. If you need to know more, please read *The Blissingbloom Uprising* by Mark A.

Powers or *The Reevers' Revolution: A Look at Social Dichotomicism Gone Horribly Awry* by Prof. Rahan Singh.

It was only when he'd boarded the ship, he discovered Ralph wasn't human.It had taken him an hour to stop laughing and half a day to be convinced that Ralph was a little different than the A.I.s he had known.

When he was finally convinced, he and Janet had made love for hours in her cabin. After being as patient as possible, Ralph called a meeting the following day.

He had discovered some anomalies in the reporting grid surrounding the inhabited worlds. He wanted to check them out before Earth did. As best he could estimate based on current research, which would be in fifteen years. Ralph was very vague about what the anomalies were, but no one had anything better to do, so they'd agreed.

Seven jumps away from Reever's World, Ralph began sharing the signals he'd detected. They were utterly alien. The first provable existence of non-human life. It was sentient, and it had, at least as far as they could discern from the videos they were seeing, a sense of humor. Within the next two jumps, Ralph had enough to work with that he could roughly translate what was being said. While the people saying the stuff Ralph could translate seemed extremely happy to Janet and Ernie, they sounded depressing as hell.

"And then they all died" would constantly get thunderous applause and be complemented by the happy visages of the citizens. They were sextopeds but walked on their hind legs and seemed to use their four arms independently. It was mildly disconcerting at first.

It was hard to gauge their size since scale wasn't readily available. But they were mammalian and covered with rust-colored fur Janet and Ernie liked. Even Ralph thought they looked cuddly.

The jump that brought them to the alien system was greeted by austere silence. They steered cautiously deeper into the system and monitored for signs of life. None of the frequencies they'd been monitoring carried any signals at all. There were none. When they achieved orbit around the fourth planet from the alien sun, it was clear that whatever had been there was gone and had been for a while. Ralph estimated one hundred years.

While Ralph scanned the planet to try and understand what had happened, Janet and Ernie put on exo-suits and took the shuttle down to the largest city they could see. They wandered the dead streets for a long time until they finally found something akin to a library. Janet extracted a mini-bot from her backpack and set it to work on scanning as much material as possible. Ernie had walked outside to admire the alien sunset when he'd noticed a pulse on his scanner. He'd notified Janet of what he'd found and began walking toward the signal.

Janet had caught up with him just as he stopped in front of a low structure. It was highly utilitarian compared to the ornate edifices regularly dotting the metropolis. They'd updated Ralph about where they were and what had caught their attention. Then Ernie removed a mini-bot from his pack and sent it in ahead of them. They'd wandered down several flights of stairs, which were slightly smaller than they were used to. By now, they'd figured out that the residents here had averaged around five feet in height.

Five levels down, they came to a door slightly off its hinges. The mini-bot yanked it free, and they entered to find a room with functioning computers. The interfaces were alien, but the concept was clear. Back at the library, they'd learned that blue was good/go/acceptable, and yellow was bad/stop/panic. Ralph saw a flickering blue button and tapped it. Immediately, a hologram of one of the long-dead people sprang to life. It was chattering frantically in its native tongue, and Janet and Ernie were utterly lost. Suddenly, it switched to English.

"Greetings," it said, "I am Alzor Kai Na-Han-Zi. Your robot was kind enough to link me with your ship's computer, and now I can make myself understood. I hope."

They'd assured him he was doing fine.

"I was turned off before the enlightenment so I wouldn't be lonely. I never expected to be activated again."

Over the next hour, they pieced together what had happened. The citizens of the planet had been deeply religious and had believed the only way to meet God was to pass to the next realm. Finally, in an audacious move, they had created a virus designed to painlessly kill every sentient being on the planet. Na-Han-Zi, Alzor-Kai was his surname, was more than a computer program; he was a download of the one person who'd disagreed with the popular belief, although he'd allowed his organic self to die with the rest since he didn't want to be alone.

An hour later, with Janet and Ernie's help, he'd fashioned his own robot, downloaded himself into it, and joined them onboard the Diamond.

They'd stayed in orbit two more days as Na-Han-Zi and Ralph exchanged information, told jokes – that were odder than you might think – and mapped out the world below. The people who'd lived there had been called the Umharree. Although Ralph pointed out they had just taken religion to its logical conclusion, Janet and Ernie still felt a sense of loss over the people they'd never known and now never would.

With Na-Han-Zi's assistance, Ralph mapped out six more anomalies, and they'd set out for the closest. This time, their exuberance at finding life was tempered by the thought it might not be there when they arrived. However, six jumps later, they were outside a system teeming with it.

These people, whose name translated into "The Poets," had built colonies on three of their worlds, were actively mining their asteroid belt, and had a homeworld that seemed entirely at peace. The homeworld was the second planet from their sun, which Ralph said really shouldn't happen.

Should or shouldn't, there it was.

They decided the best approach was the most direct. Ralph began transmitting their peaceful intentions as they entered the system more fully. They were met the next day by ships from the deepest colony and guided to the Olla-Ip homeworld, which the Poets called themselves, their planet, and their collection of homilies. Janet and her crew had slowly worked their way into conversations with the Poets and, by the time they'd reached the planet, were having a grand old time getting to know each other.

The Poets had never even considered the possibility of alien life, so the arrival of the Diamond and its crew was a bit of a shock to them. They got over it quickly enough since, as stated in their Third Homily to Truth, "Disbelieving a proven fact accomplishes nothing," and The Poets appeared to be a practical sort.

Janet and Ernie, after being reassured by Ralph that the air was fine and the gravity bearable, took a shuttle down to meet the planetary leaders. There was a great feast that Janet and Ernie could only pick at. They had no idea if the food was dangerous or not, but The Poets liked things spicy. Much to the delight of their hosts, Janet blew smoke out of her mouth after she bit into one confection.

Culinary differences aside, they got along fabulously. Their initial meeting would set the tone for what was to come. Two of the Poets joined her crew, and, over the next ten years, the Diamond cut a swath through the galaxy, meeting new races, making new friends, and updating Earth on its progress when it got around to it.

Back on Earth, things were not being received all that well. When the Earth authorities began making sense of the bizarre messages they were getting from the Diamond, Janet had been traversing the uncharted realm for a few years. Worse yet, the media had found out and called her the "Rocket Queen," a term so wildly inaccurate as to be immediately understandable.

When they finally got around to issuing their famous edict for her to "stop engaging in illegal diplomatic relations and associating with perversions of artificial intelligence," it was far too late. Na-Han-Zi had no great love for any authority, and the rest of the crew, by this time, had barely heard of Earth. The edict was roundly ignored.

Janet and Ernie gave birth to twins - well, okay, Janet did, but Ernie helped, at least at the beginning - and the rest of the crew, numbering seven races at that point, adopted them without compunction. The two girls, Carol and Barbara, grew up never knowing that having a Poet as an "uncle" might be considered odd. If they thought anything unusual about it, it was only when their "uncle" flexed his breathing slits to make funny noises for them. Like their parents, the girls had soft mocha skin and deep green eyes. They, unlike their parents, were stunningly beautiful.

Over the years, the Diamond visited fourteen races inhabiting thirty-one worlds.

The authorities on Earth were nearly apoplectic. There were no more Mironov/Choi ships, and the ships they did have couldn't make the required number of jumps to get to where the Diamond was. Worse, as far as they were concerned, Janet's dad used his corporate charter to assimilate and commercially exploit the various musical and artistic works she sent along with her messages.

Simply put, the people loved her, and the government couldn't control her. They had to put a stop to this immediately.

"Immediately" in government-speak is, as it turned out, a little over three years. They finally built a Mironov/Choi ship, filled it with military personnel, and sent it to hunt the Diamond.

As many readers know, this was one of the dumbest ideas ever.

When the Earth forces headed out, Janet had been trading and mingling with the fourteen races for over a decade and a half. Some of their scientists had improved the original design of her ship and copied it for their uses. All fourteen now had ships that were superior in every way to anything Earth could build. Plus, sensing the growing threats in the messages they regularly received from Earth, they'd added the latest weapons to each and everyone, including the Diamond.

When the Earth forces had finally found and threatened her, it was a massacre. The Earth's forces were descended on by ships from every race and atomized within minutes. Then it was decided that the Rocket Queen's Alliance, they'd glommed on to that inappropriate nom-de-plum just as readily as humans had, didn't want to live under siege. If Earth continues to be a threat, then Earth must be removed from the equation.

It took Janet, Ralph, and Ernie quite some time to convince their allies that Earth's government didn't represent the will of Earth's people, at least not all of them.

Even so, she stood on the bridge and watched the Earth Alliance capitol building in Paris burn. The military bases on Earth, Luna, Mars, and Io were all smoldering ruins as well.

All she wanted was to find pretty rocks, learn a little about the galaxy, and find a nice guy. How had it all come to this?

Then she'd spied her daughters, standing off to the side with Ernie. She knew the Earth forces would have killed her children just as readily as they would have killed her, Ernie, Ralph, Na-Han-Zi, and all her new friends. And that knowledge, that final realization, hardened something deep inside her.

The rest of the battle with the various military outposts was over in less than a month. Janet made her home in the Northern Antilles and established a new government there. Her first act was to open trade to all the worlds she'd discovered. Her second act was to set up a trade counsel, overseen by Ralph and Na-Han-Zi, to handle everything, and her third act was to retire. She accomplished all three in less than a month.

The last time I saw her, just before she and her family left for wherever they went, she sat with Ernie on a beach, watching their teenage daughters tease boys in the surf and holding a pretty rock.

This has been selected for three different anthologies; all three fell apart before publication. Don't let that stop you from reading and enjoying it.

# Happiness, Love, and Other Lies

Whoregiver smiled as he glanced at his reflection in the mirror. Tall and lithe, he cut a dashing figure naked with his chocolate skin and ice-blue eyes. Today's show was going to be special. Some of the city's top money grubbers were coming. They would pay enormous credit for anything kink. Bound as they were to a world of rules and facades, they had no release. Some would be the very vermin who'd outlawed sex circuses. Those were the best. Their guilt would be assuaged with blank checks and sweaty smiles.

After a moment's consideration, he decided on the red leather boots with the white spiked heels. As he admired how they highlighted his skin, his matron walked in. Fuchsia Gash was a legend in the carny world. Her waist-length red hair, blazing green eyes, alabaster skin, perfect breasts, which she loved to show off, and warm smile belied a woman who would cut off your balls and laugh as you died. Whoregiver was in love with her.

While she occasionally let him service her, they had no future together. He was a spawn of the tunnels. She, on the other hand, had papered family above. She could, with a few bribes, live life among the norms. She planned on doing it once she had a nest egg large enough to satisfy her. As she slowly stroked his twelve-inch cock he wondered if anything was large enough to satisfy her.

"You looking hot. Gonna smooch all their coins today, ain't you?"

Whoregiver had to smile. Fuchsia talked like a carny when she wanted, but he knew her keen mind could just as easily sound like a norm. She may as well have said, "My dear, you are looking exquisite. I gather you shall earn an egregious amount of funds this day."

She didn't, of course, but she could have.

"Gots to earn bank.  Ain't no carny cred in this world."

"Ain't no carny cred in any world. Make enough, and maybe you can join the norms."

"Bullshit! Ain't no bribe swingin' that can make my fam legit."

She knew that. But dreamers could dream.

She crooked her face into a wan grin and knelt before him, slowly encompassing his swelling manhood with her mouth. She was the only person he'd ever met who could take it all and love it.

He listened raptly as her breathing slowed into a steady rhythm to match her thrusts. He usually couldn't cum unless he was involved, nibbling or licking on something. With Fuchsia, it was different. She could make him cum just by wagging her finger. All of this was just a bonus.  He was unsure whether it was for her benefit or his but decided it didn't matter.

He let his eyes roll back into memories of how he'd risen so high, a featured act in Carnal Carny, from his humble beginnings as the son of a shit sweeper. He knew how, naturally, since he'd lived it. When he was barely two, he'd shown a joy other children did not. He could suck a cock better than most older kids. His mom parlayed his skill into status as a full matron. Soon, he was making his family enough cred to purchase their tent.

His dad, a forgotten entity, drifted into a gentle haze of alcohol and opiates until he could drift no lower. He was dead before Whoregiver's fourth birthday.

By his sixth birthday, he could use his fingers and tongue on elderly swells, all a-twitter in their lace skirts and fine jewelry, and make them quiver in ecstasy. His mother had trained him personally and thoroughly, and she knew what old women liked.

Before he could wander further into the past, he felt his balls tighten and heard Fuchsia gasp in anticipation. He looked down to enjoy the spectacle. Her throat pulsed as his throbbing rod exploded in her mouth. She swallowed every drop. She would never leave him dripping. She needed him clean if he would score creds off the yokels.

After all, his creds were her creds within reason. Unlike other matrons, she let him keep the lion's share. She had the top eight turners in the carny, so she didn't need to dip deep into anyone to make more than enough for her plans.

She figured she had two more years of shilling norms before having what she wanted. He was glad for her but wondered if she'd miss it. No norm could do what he could do. Hell, no norm could do what any of them could and would do. It was against the law. Many, many laws. Laws designed to make humanity fit a standard. To remove the freaks. To make him rich.

She grabbed a fresh Handi-Clean and wiped his cock dry. Still holding his balls, she looked up and laughed.

"Fucking God, dude, were you saving all that up for a special occasion?"

He grinned stupidly and had to laugh, too.

"Been a week since the last roll. Nothing here, 'cept you, interests me. So, yeah, got a lil' backed up."

Her smile shrunk a little.

"There has to be a way …."

They both knew there wasn't.

She spun him around and gently tongued his asshole. Her lipstick perfectly matched the pink of his pucker. He wondered if that was purposeful. It was just one more thing that didn't really matter.

She was well inside when Throatmonger burst in.

"Forgive me, matron," he stammered, "but there is news. Big news."

She shrugged sadly, dismayed at having to leave her pleasure, and stood.

"This had better be good," she snarled as she turned to face him, "or your flaccid ass will be lucky if it gets to sweep shit."

Throatmonger looked horrified. One wrong word from a matron, and he could be tossed upside. Out among the norms. A bad word from Fuchsia would guarantee worse.

Only now, Whoregiver noted Throatmonger was naked, covered in oils, and holding a stained piece of paper. His light brown skin glistened and paled under the electric torches.

"The outworlders," he shook so hard the paper rattled, "the outworlders have discovered it. The thing they sought. The essential IT."

Whoremonger and Fuchsia had no idea what the hell he was talking about, so they stared at him. Clarity had better arrive soon, or his tiny ass would be gone. Worse, Whoregiver's would remain unsatisfied.

"Life. Beings. Aliens. Smart, with cities and shit. They're coming here."

His skanky ass was saved. The news was stunning. Aliens violated the "One race, one God" rule. And that was as big a rule to the norms as the ones they had against the circuses.

Although less strictly enforced. It was hard to enforce a law against things that didn't exist.

Throatmonger handed the paper to Fuchsia.

She scanned it and frowned.

"They call themselves the Plim. And they know about the circuses. In fact, they say it's the only reason to visit our, and I quote, "pathetic rock." They will be here in four days and want to see a circus. Specifically, ours."

None of them knew how the lawgivers would react to that. Would they fight the Plim to keep them from violating the "One race, one God" rule? Could they even if they wanted to? The Plim had interstellar travel; that much was clear. They could be so far beyond human tech it wouldn't make any difference what the lawgivers did.

That night, the norms were skittish. Whoregiver was afraid they'd just watch the show and leave. But they didn't. Their nervousness gave life to their desires. Added a begging fire to their needs. He serviced three men simultaneously, at a quintuple rate, before knocking back a couple of norm matrons.

By the time the tent had cleared, he'd earned two months' worth of cred and felt his prick wanted nothing more than a fluffy pillow to rest on. The fluffier, the better.

The next few days went by in a blur. The norms sent down the Purity Police to try and roust the circuses, but to no avail. They were long gone before that. Whoregiver and his troupe were hidden in Fuchsia's secret lair. Housed inside a cavernous tunnel, it had five passcode-protected entrances.

Fuchsia let Throatmonger fellate her in the main chamber, in front of the others, as a show of gratitude for the news he'd brought. It was his primary skill, and it sent a clear signal to the others that he was not to be chastised for simply being the messenger.

On the fourth day, at high noon, for fuck's sake, the Plim arrived. The norms' Planetary Protection Police fired on them with all they had and didn't even slow them. The Plim had some shielding tech that effortlessly protected them. They were so secure they didn't even bother firing back.

They broadcast their intentions on all channels, which drove the leaders of the norms into high dudgeon. Until now, they'd kept knowledge of the Plim heavily guarded. Now the secret, and all it entailed, were out. Humans were not alone. Nor were they all that interesting.

Hope for humanity, it seemed, was held by the circuses. The ability to tongue-punch an asshole seemed more important than the ability to wear beige.

Why that was would be discerned later.

Six hours after arriving, alien corvettes spewed from the Plim motherships. They were headed to Little Rock. Home of the vilest perversions. Home of the Carnal Carny. Home of Fuchsia Gash, Whoregiver, and the rest. Ground zero for layers of lugubrious lust.

Not for the carnies, of course; they liked who they were and what they did. For them, the circus was a regular outlet.

It was hard to be pent up about anything when release was usually an arm's length away.

The Plim landed amidst continuing norm gunfire, which they continued to ignore, and headed to the main entrance for the carnival.

Sensing safety, someone fired up the calliope. A cheerful dirge echoed through the cavernous space. Burlesque dancers began the opening act of fire and bondage, much to the enjoyment of the troupes. Normalcy was, once again, attained.

The Plim arrived. They were shaped like jellybeans. Huge ones, to be sure, averaging almost seven feet in height, propelled by cilia. They wore loose, shambling robes over their brightly colored skins. Each Plim was a neon color. They had four eyes and sensuous mouths and seemed to grow and shrink appendages at will.

The troupes were aroused at the possibilities.

They put on the best show they'd ever done for the next two hours. Fuchsia even allowed Whoregiver to fuck her in the ass while she jacked off a couple of interns.

The Plim shook and shimmied and made odd galumphing sounds at each demonstration. It didn't take long to realize the sound was their way of applauding.

A couple of Plim guarded the main gate and kept a plethora of norm police at bay with their force fields. Oddly enough, all seemed as though it was as it should be.

An appreciative audience, an excited cast, and a future heretofore unimagined all were unfolding inside the main tent. No one knew what the morning would bring, but now, this moment, this specific slit of time was magical.

The Plim, as was their custom according to them, had broadcast the entire event worldwide. None of them would know about the riots and orgies until much later, but all knew today was the day their universe changed. Whether for the better or not would be discovered later.

An electric pink Plim sluzzled; no one could come up with a better word, and it emulated the sound over to Whoregiver and began wrapping appendages around him. Whoregiver had never felt so calm, so blessedly at ease. In a guazian haze, he could make out the same thing happening to others but couldn't bring himself to care. This joy was his and his alone.

Whatever cred he would earn this night would far exceed any puny financial gains.

Suddenly, Whoregiver felt a part of his mind give way. The Plim was entering.

"Hey, buddy," echoed the alien thought, "you give me happiness, and I'll give you love."

That seemed like a good deal.

Whoregiver was pleased to note his cock was rock hard and rubbing against the undulating skin.

Totally enveloped by the Plim, Whoregiver surrendered to lusts he'd long kept hidden. No more was he there to please others. No more was he just a prop in another's fantasy. This was a delight on a scale he'd never imagined possible. This was joining. This was belonging. This was why he existed.

Spent and sated, he collapsed into the Plim. Thinking there was nothing more for either to offer, he was pleasantly surprised to find Fuchsia being sucked in as well.

Their eyes locked. The look of unrepentant happiness on her face told him all he needed to know. She didn't hesitate. She wrapped her arms around him and kissed him as though for the very first time. Kissing, usually only a part of their play, was now needed, wanted, and desired more than they had desired anything before. Their tongues darting, they rejoiced as the Plim slithered into every orifice. Its coruscating appendages filled and fulfilled them.

Time became a liquid, meaningless and flowing. They heard, if that's the right word, the Plim talk about a world where they could be home and free. A place without lawgivers, Purity Police, or rules. A place where they could just be.

Fuchsia looked at Whoregiver and smiled slightly. He nodded. Her smile grew, and her kiss deepened. Whatever this was, he never wanted it to end.

Finally, the Plim left. Arrangements for departure had been embedded in their brains. The Purity Police and other norms had been shoved upside. Nothing was left, but the troupes were enveloped in calm and careful anticipation.

The anointed time arrived, and the troupes walked cautiously outside carrying all they cared to own. Plim security was there to keep the norms at bay. The carnival boarded a large corvette and lifted into the shimmering sky.

None of them looked out at the sight of the receding Earth. This was not their home. Never really had been. Home, such as the concept held meaning to them, was where their hearts were. And their hearts were with each other, not bound to a floating rock.

Fuchsia snuggled into Whoregiver's arms as the Plim mothership escaped orbit and headed toward its destination.

A yellow Plim entered the cabin where they were seated and activated a large monitor. They all could see the council of lawgivers sitting around a table. None of them looked pleased.

"Galactic perverts have invaded our world. The type of alien heathens warned about in our books of purity. More to our chagrin, millions of skulking slackers have joined them."

That got a laugh and then a loud cheer out of the troupes.

"Nevertheless, this abomination shall make us stronger. Let this atrocity reaffirm our strengths. Let the weak and woebegone be gone. Let the impure be cleansed from our world. Let them who bring shame follow the clarion lies of happiness and love.  We shall remain forever pure in our knowledge of righteousness. We shall remain unsullied by the decadence of whimsy."

One of the troupes snapped off the monitor and smiled at the Plim.

"Thank you for this gift of lies. We have never known a truth so sweet."

The Plim seemed satisfied with that and left.

Whoregiver finally looked out a window as space rippled by.

"What will we do without an audience?"

Fuchsia hugged him closer and whispered in his ear.

"We'll entertain each other and live the lie. This glorious lie of happiness and love."

**Note:** The author wishes to dedicate the concept of the Plim to Clifford D. Simak, author of Time is the Simplest Thing.

Every now and then, a writer needs to dip their toe into the lore of Lovecraft's elder gods. I had a short story unfinished about an elderly widow who was trying to end her years on a positive note. Why I thought that story would be a good fit for a Lovecraft vamp eludes me still. But it got published in **ICC Magazine,** and people seem to like it.

# Twerking for Jesus

Amanda Johnson stood at the edge of the grave and smiled. She wasn't happy that her husband of fifty-four years was gone, far from it. She had loved him more with each passing day until he'd finally shrugged off this mortal coil. He had been a good husband, father, grandfather, and lover. Especially the lover part. No, she smiled at the memories. They were all wonderful.

She ignored the rain that was pissing all over, rebalanced her cane, and looked out from under her umbrella. Their four children were there with their eleven grandchildren and two great-grandchildren. They were sad now, but Amanda hoped they would remember the good times as she was. Thomas had been a font of happiness, and that should be his legacy.

Occasional shafts of sunlight broke through the clouds and moved across the lawn like alien beams from some cheap sci-fi flick. Thomas would have liked that. He'd loved sci-fi. Said it provided hope for the future. He prayed every day but was no fool. His belief in God was based on his love of science. He'd refused to believe he was the most evolved being in the universe. Science said he was, most likely, not, and that, somehow, made him happy.

Science said cancer had killed him. It also said it was his fault. He'd ignored symptoms for years. Had he not, he would, most likely, still be alive. But not even that knowledge saddened her. He'd made his decisions and lived with them. He'd never once played the "poor, poor, pitiful me" card. Instead, he'd faced his impending mortality directly and with humor. He used to joke that science would introduce him to God, albeit a tad sooner than he might have wished.

Just as the casket was being lowered into the ground, a rogue shaft of sunlight graced the head of the coffin, making it appear as if his soul was being beamed into the hereafter. That made her smile all the more. Her smile widened when she heard a couple of her kids. Even though they were all around fifty, they were still her kids, talking about the same thing.

Thomas' legacy would be a good one.

She clutched her umbrella tighter as the wind kicked up and headed back to the town car her son had rented. The driver opened the door, and she sat in the rear as the rest of her family piled in.

She was pleased to hear laughter. The final shaft of sunlight had broken the somber mood. They all joked and talked on the ride back to her house.

Their house.

Thomas' house.

She'd already made up her mind to sell it. She didn't want to live out her days in a mausoleum and knew Thomas would approve. Before she did that, however, there were a million details to take care of. Those would keep her busy for a while.

Then, she would decide what the next stage of her life would entail.

**********************

Oxyl floated above the bottom of the Mariana Trench. He didn't know it was called that. Of course, to him, it was just home—a place of shelter and food.

He sensed upwards and smiled inwardly as the New Gods began playing with the weather. They had been brought into this firmament to complete one task and one task only. They were to rid the planet of the disease called humans.

The Old Gods had made them when they'd come to realize their long-game scenarios could not deal with these vermin's rapid evolution.

The New Gods' plan was insidious and glorious all at once. They would use planet-killing, humans' inability to care for their world, as the means of their eradication. Given how quickly the Earth was heating up, they figured the humans would all be gone in a hundred years.

A mere blink to any such as Oxyl.

Or it would be if any of them had eyes.

He let his senses revel as the New Gods used existing wind and weather patterns to create storms larger than any seen before. Those would kill many humans, to be sure, but that was just a bonus. The end game for the New Gods was to disrupt the weather patterns enough to allow the planet to heat even faster than humans could compensate. In some places, they were past that tipping point already.

They said the polar ice caps would melt enough to release their mega-tonnes of carbon dioxide into the atmosphere and envelope the planet in a shell of heat in less than a blink. That would sufficiently trigger continent-sized deserts, and the resulting famine should do the rest.

Oxyl and his kin could then go above and finish any that got missed.

He would know it was time to leave his home when he heard the Dance of the New Gods.

He longed to, once again, feel the rhythm of the universe.

✳✳✳✳✳✳✳✳✳✳✳✳✳✳✳✳✳✳✳✳✳✳

The three months since Thomas had died had been filled with a whirlwind of paperwork. Today, however, would be her seventy-ninth birthday. The time for paperwork was done.

She set aside the final papers for the insurance company and began prepping for the arrival of family and friends.

She smiled anew when she passed Thomas' Star Trek shrine in the living room. He'd never been one for toys, one of his many reasons for dismissing anything related to Star Wars out of hand. Still, he'd managed to grab small things through the years and assemble them in a display case. The top shelf was devoted exclusively to inventions that Star Trek's writers inspired. From cell phones to tablet computers, to translation devices, to a virtual reality simulator (as close as we're going to get to a holodeck in our lifetimes), to a copy of Miguel Alcubierre Moya's papers proving a Warp Drive was really possible. He even had a model of the ship, proposed by Dr. Harold "Sonny" White from NASA, that showed how such a vessel should look.

When she got to her room, she set her usual cane, a simple brown thing, to the side and pulled out her black one with a silver tip and a Klingon grip. She wanted to be festive today. She chose her outfit in the same manner, eschewing drab colors for bright.

She finished dressing just as the doorbell rang. She walked over to the front door, let in the caterer, and smiled. This was going to be a fun day.

Several hours later, the backyard was jumping to the sounds of the latest hip-hop track, and her grandchildren were happily doing the latest dance. On a whim, she asked them to teach it to her. After being told she was too old to twerk, she was more determined than ever to learn.

She planted her cane in the grass, bent slightly forward, and began emulating the moves she'd seen.

Left butt cheek twitched? Done.

Right butt cheek twitched? Done.

Both butt cheeks twitched? Success!

To the cheers of "Go, Grandma, Go, Grandma," she began to twerk.

Left, left, right.

Right, right, left.

Both, both, both.

Left, right, both.

Soon enough, she was a booty-shaking commando. Her ass pulsing precisely to the rhythm of the song. Her grandchildren joined in and soon had a conga line of undulating derrières.

After a while, she got tired and went to sit under the umbrella near the buffet. She was greeted by friends and family, all laughing and joking that she should take her act on the road.

"You know something," she said as she sipped her favorite bourbon, "that's one heck of a good idea."

✱✱✱✱✱✱✱✱✱✱✱✱✱✱✱✱✱✱✱✱✱

Oxyl was confused. He'd felt the tingle, savored in the call, but the New Gods were adamant they'd done nothing. The time was not yet now. They knew not where the dance had emanated but were sure it hadn't been their doing. The sound was too distant, too feeble, to be their doing.

The Old Gods also pled ignorance. Oxyl knew none of the gods could lie, so he returned to his home.

To make him and his kin feel a little better, the New Gods pointed out where humans were being swept into the seas. While the time for the large storms had passed, there was still enough heat in the air to allow them to push smaller, and still lethal, ones ashore.

They kept stirring the pot, and Oxyl got to dine on fine human flesh.

He couldn't wait to go above and get it before it was waterlogged since it was something that would only happen once; he relished it all the more. After all, once he was freed, there would be no more humans to feast on.

He'd thought of asking the New Gods if they could keep some alive so they could breed them for food but decided against it. These creatures evolved erratically. There was no way of knowing what harm they might still cause if left alive.

Nope. It's better to eat them and savor the memories.

*********************

Amanda had been touring the country, sharing her unusual take on the dance, for nine months now. Her act, a combination of twerking, liberal-ish agenda checkpoints, safe bible quotes, and a retinue of young ladies called the

Bootyquakettes, had provided the kind of fun the world had forgotten it was missing. Amanda never took any of it too seriously, nor did anyone else.

The random troupe, no one joined and no one left – they were just there or not, traversed the country and was soon to appear on an episode of Ellen. Amanda loved Ellen and couldn't wait to meet her. She even had T-shirts made up for the dancers with BOOTYQUAKETTE emblazoned on the front and one of four bible verses featured on the back.

**Ecclesiastes 3:4**
A time to weep and a time to laugh; A time to mourn, and a time to dance.

**Psalm 30:11**
You have turned for me my mourning into dancing; You have loosed my sackcloth and girded me with gladness,

**Psalm 149:3**
Let them praise His name with dancing; Let them sing praises to Him with timbrel and lyre.

**Psalm 150:4**
Praise Him with timbrel and dancing; Praise Him with stringed instruments and pipe.

Given that many of the young ladies were unencumbered by body modesty, one could honestly be pleased to note they were, at least, girded in gladness. If not much else.

The production staff from Ellen's show had sent a retinue of buses to pick them up in Phoenix and take them to LA for the taping.

Amanda was convinced the show would be, in the words of those hipper than her, epic.

**********************

Oxyl was apoplectic. The tingling grew with each passing day, and it had nothing to do with the New Gods. The call was becoming too strong to avoid. Something had to give.

The New Gods had an idea.

There were volcanoes under the tundra at the North Pole. They would lose them, thus releasing the mega-tonnes of carbon dioxide and kick-starting the apocalypse. There were fault lines and other planetary weaknesses they felt sure they could also exploit.

Then Oxyl and his ilk could be released to fulfill their destinies.

It meant more work for the under-beings but none minded. The Old Gods would, once again, be free to balance the world, and the New Gods would retire until the next threat arose.

Oxyl, in as much as he could, smiled.

He began his leisurely ascent and mapped his path to the nearest coast.

He would wait for his cue from the New Gods, but freedom was coming.

274

Along with food. Lots of tasty, fresh, human-tasting food.

*********************

Ellen lived up to her reputation. The buses were opulent, the accommodations state-of-the-art, the audience would be packed with family and friends, and Ellen herself–can you believe it?–had learned to twerk like Amanda so she could join the crew.

Amanda made sure to get her a shirt.

They arrived at the studio at the appointed time. No way not to, really. They were herded from the hotel like cattle.

Amanda loved all of it.

Team Ellen had pulled out all the stops. Dr. Dre, not a real doctor Amanda was bummed to discover, and Nikki Minaj was on hand to provide the music. Many prominent feminists on hand were to join the Werk It & Twerk It episode, as it was being billed.

About an hour after they arrived, a cute production assistant named Derrick came to their room and ran down the day's schedule for them. He reminded Amanda of a young Thomas. Square jaw, well-muscled, with a deep, kind voice.

The thought of Thomas made her wince a little. She had been so busy Twerking for Jesus all over the country she hadn't thought much about him. Then she shrugged. She didn't need to think of him to have him in her heart. He was always there. His lessons, his laugh, just him, imbued all she was.

The next hour was a blur. Cameras flashing, celebrities dancing, people asking for autographs, charities asking her to host twerking events on their behalf, and so on.

When the show aired later that day, Amanda sat in her hotel room, sipping a well-deserved bourbon, watching intently. She couldn't believe how many people were spiritually helped by her elderly, bouncing ass.

The cameras showed people gleefully dancing in the aisles and singing along with each song. There were even cut-away shots of various politicians joining in on the fun.

Amanda thought science might be dry, but God had a lively sense of humor.

Near the end of the show, a chyron informed her there had been a series of massive volcanic explosions near the North Pole. It later informed her that scientists said it would take decades to assess the damage.

She refilled her glass. Her good mood was gone.

Shortly after the show ended, the apocalypse began.

Amanda watched hopelessly as news show after news show showed giant beings, multi-tentacled and multi-mouthed, emerging from the seas to swallow humans like snacks. Earthquakes were being reported globally. Two had already caused the beginnings of tsunamis.

Several, small by recent standards, hurricanes had popped up in the Atlantic Ocean and were headed directly toward the U.S.

The monsters ignored the pounding winds and all other atrocities and kept feeding.

Other beings, vaguely humanoid and larger than the monsters, could be seen performing some sort of ritual above the seas, moving from crest to crest. One of the stations managed to get a helicopter close enough so the cameraman could zoom in on the dancing aliens. The reporters on TV figured it out just after Amanda did. They were doing a dance.

Her dance.

Her special twerk.

Her twerk for Jesus.

The twerk that Ellen and countless others had so recently celebrated.

Left, left, right.

Right, right, left.

Both, both, both.

Left, right, both.

The dance which had brought so much joy also seemed to be the bringer of Armageddon.

People were dying by the millions while monsters danced.

Amanda pushed her glass aside and grabbed the bottle, glad Thomas was dead. He would have been so disappointed to discover science was wrong and hope was a lie.

Initially published in **Bewildering Stories**, they tend to like me. It's taken on a life of its own ever since.

# 14 Frogs

1:00 p.m. on a chilly Sunday afternoon in Chicago.

*The QB steps back, looks for his receiver, and OOOOOOOHHH, he's sacked!*

**Scoots Bar and Grill. Home of the Best Damn Catfish Yo Mama Never Made!**

*With the penalty, that makes it 2nd and 36 with 4 minutes left to play.*

Tyrell and Josh were keeping their weekly tradition of watching the game. It didn't matter who won or lost. It was their chance to sit, kick back, and enjoy a few beers in peace and quiet. For Tyrell, it was a brief respite from family life. For Josh, it was a chance to be with another human being. One who didn't judge him. They'd been friends since God lost his sneaks back in Englewood. And that was all that mattered for this little sliver of time.

Tyrell waved the bartender over for another round and smiled at his friend. "Dude, you've been awfully quiet. Problems at home?"

Josh laughed. "Got 99 problems, but a home ain't one."

"99's still a hell of a lot of problems."

They both laughed at the old joke. Josh darkened. "Nah, man, Lat tossed me out Tuesday. Said I need to be more like you."

Tyrell took a sip of his beer and turned to his friend. "Dude, I'm sorry. Latisha was a good woman. Wanna talk about it?"

Josh sipped his beer and shook his head. "Nothing to talk about. Can't get no job, can't keep no woman. No matter what I do, how hard I try, that never changes."

*4th and 48, and the Bears are set to punt. O'Donnell gets the snap, AND IT'S BLOCKED! Minnesota recovers! They'll have the ball on their own 11 with 3:17 left to play, up by 36. It looks like this game is pretty much in the books.*

Tyrell ordered a couple of shots for them. He'd never asked Josh to pay since Josh never had any money anyway. Not that he cared. "Bros and blood before everything" was how he'd been raised, and Josh was his bro. May as well be blood. Finally, after a few minutes of painful football, the game was mercifully finished.

The bartender, a fierce-looking woman called "Mom," served them their drinks and snagged the money. Neither could remember her smiling or saying much beyond the occasional grunt in all the years they'd been coming here. But she was fast, and your change was always correct. That's all that mattered to anyone who knew what was what.

Josh huffed. "When I was at the library, I read on the Internet that Beyoncé was in the Illuminati or some crap like that."

Tyrell smiled. "Nah, not her. The frogs won't let her in."

"Da heck, you say?"

"The frogs. The ones that rule the world. They won't let her in."

"Frogs rule the world?" Josh looked as confused as he felt. It wouldn't do him any good if his only friend had a breakdown.

Tyrell seemed to sense what he was thinking and turned to face him. "C'mon, man, you're a smart brother. You mean to tell me you ain't figgered it out?"

"Figgered what out? What the bejeezus are you talking about?"

Tyrell sighed. "This stuff," he said, waving at the TV, "these debates, this never-ending Beyoncé, all this stuff is tied together. The reason you can't get up on anything is 'cuz the frogs need to keep some folks down. But if you figure it out, then the frogs have to give you a slice to keep you quiet."

Josh was more baffled than he'd ever been in his life. Even more than when Tanya Johnson had told him she wanted him to go all R. Kelly on her.

"Look," continued Tyrell, "here's how it is. Hundreds of years ago, the world was going to hell."

"Still is," snarked Josh.

"Yeah, and no. See, the frogs won't let it. Not all the way, anyway."

"The frogs won't let it. Got it. Brother, I've known you since we were shorties. You never seemed like you were crazy."

Tyrell laughed. "I'm not. You see, back in high school, I figured it out while you were shooting hoops and chasing tail. There's no Democrat, no Republican, no talent, no nothing, just the frogs."

"Frogs. Sure. You gonna get me another before they take you away?"

Tyrell laughed again and nodded. Frogs or no, he still seemed outwardly sane as he waved for one more round.

"Think for a minute," said Tyrell as he sipped his shot, "the whole New World Order thing, for example. In the '30s, it was a left-wing thing. It led to the United Nations and organizations like that. By the 80's, it was a right-wing thing. TV preachers were going ape-shit over it."

Josh was trying to figure out what any of this had to do with frogs and was failing badly.

"Then you got allies and enemies," he continued, sounding as sane as what he said sounded crazy. "One year, we're bombing the hell out of Japan; the next, we're in line for everything they make. Radios, TVs, cars, all of it. Or Germany. One day, we're walking hand in hand with the Russkies kicking down concentration camps, and the next, we're buying Volkswagens, and Russia's got the bomb."

Josh blanched a little. "And that's cuz of the frogs?"

"Right."

That didn't help at all. Josh slammed down his shot and tried again. "So the frogs are the Illuminati?"

"No," smiled Tyrell, "the Illuminati owns the frogs. Cares for them. Does their bidding."

"What?" asked Josh, more befuddled than before. "Are these some sci-fi, super-intelligent frogs or something like that?"

"Nope. Just frogs."

"Frogs that rule the world."

"Now you're getting it."

No. He wasn't. Not at all.

Tyrell brightened. "You hungry?"

Josh nodded absently. "Hey, Mom, a couple of catfish dinners, and don't spare the hot sauce."

Mom grunted something resembling an assent and went to place the order.

They drank in silence for a bit. Josh tried to make sense of anything, and Tyrell looked forward to Mom's catfish.

Finally, Josh spoke. "So, how does it work? How do regular frogs rule the world?"

Tyrell smiled. "Good question. And the answer's pretty simple. You see, this underground villa in Greenland is heated by a dormant volcano. Really nice place, actually. Best of everything and all that."

"The frogs own a villa?"

"No," laughed Tyrell, "that would be stupid. The Illuminati owns the villa to house the frogs."

"Oh, sure, I guess that makes sense."

It didn't. Not even a little bit.

"Anyway, in the basement of the villa is a huge atrium. And, in it, there's a pool surrounded by a map of the world. Around that map are little pieces of paper with the names of every politician and celebrity in each country. That gets updated daily. Only the fourteen members of the Illuminati know exactly what's on those pieces of paper."

"Like Obama?"

Tyrell laughed so hard he spit beer out of his nose. After he calmed down and wiped his face with a napkin, he continued.

"No, O-Dog's just a pawn. See, we got him, riding his unicorn that farts rainbows being all hopey, truthy, and then we get Trump, leading the Four Horsemen of the Apocalypse wearing white hoods. You see? It's all about balance."

"And the frogs keep the balance?"

"Now you're getting it!"

Truth be told, Josh was most certainly not getting it. He decided to soldier on. If nothing else, the beer was cold, booze was good, and dinner was on its way.

"Okay, so who's the Illuminati then? The pope and other leaders?"

Tyrell shook his head. "Nah, pope's too public. These cats are dark. Old, old money. Ancient money. From Africa, China, Europe, and India. America's too young to have anyone in the circle. It's just a piece in the game for them."

"And, these cats" — Josh was slowly starting to see some sort of logic in this, not a lot, but some — "these cats, with all this money, do what the frogs tell them?"

Tyrell nodded. "Yeah, pretty much. Look, it's not as nuts as it sounds. Hear me out. They have seven red frogs and seven blue ones."

Josh exploded in laughter. "Tain't no such thing as blue frogs. Man, you had me going."

Then he noticed his friend wasn't laughing. Contrariwise, he was looking at him sternly. "The frogs are fed special food that causes their skin to change color, but it doesn't harm them."

"Well, that's good, I guess. We wouldn't want the world run by sick frogs."

"Was that sarcasm?"

Josh nodded as he sipped his beer. "Yeah, I'm pretty sure it was."

He was taken aback when he realized his friend was looking at him with raw anger in his eyes. In all their years together, he had never ever seen him angry, not like this. This kind of anger was, 'Shut the hell up before I kill you.'

Josh wisely shut the hell up and motioned for him to continue.

Tyrell took a sip of his beer, visibly calmed down, and continued. "Anyway, like I said, it's about balance. The frogs stay in that special pool. It's got everything they need. But occasionally, they jump out and land on the map.

"For example, a red frog jumped out and landed on Israel a while back, so they got a nut job, right-wing leader. So, for balance, they enticed a blue frog to jump on the map, and Iran got a leader who, if not liberal, was, at least, willing to listen to reason. Balance maintained."

"All because of frogs?"

"Yep. Look, it makes the most sense when you think about it. Humans are too stupid, follow in packs, too much for any progress to be made. This way, they get goaded in the direction the world needs, and balance is maintained."

"And they do this for everything?"

"Yeah, that's the basic idea. Oh, sure, sometimes something unexpected happens. A leader gets assassinated, or some pop star blows their brains out, or what have you. Then they just let the frogs pick a replacement."

"I guess that explains Eminem and Tiger Woods."

Tyrell's laugh was genuine and warm. "Among many others."

"So, how do the frogs know who needs to be where?"

"They don't. That's how Germany ended up with David Hasselhoff, and America ended up dancing Gangnam Style."

It was Josh's turn to smile. "Damn! I even learned that stupid dance."

Mom brought their dinner: catfish, slaw, tater tots, mashed potatoes with gravy, and a cup of red beans, and then refilled their beers. They ate in silence as the TV whined in the background.

*In a shocking development, the Every American Gets a Pony presidential candidate, Vermin Supreme, has been appointed to the Massachusetts Senate to fill the vacancy caused by the impending imprisonment of Viriato "Vinny" de Macedo. Senator Supreme will be sworn in today at noon. We'll be carrying the coverage live here on...*

"Okay," said Josh as he swallowed another delicious bite of catfish, "this makes as much sense as anything else I've heard. Let's say I believe you. Now what?"

Tyrell wiped the hot sauce off his chin and smiled. "Well, that's the easy part. You see, once in your life, if you're getting a slice, someone will contact you and tell you to tell this to another person. Until then, you have to keep it a secret. Then, that person will either get a slice or be killed. Either way, balance will be maintained."

Josh was horrified. "They gonna kill me?!?!?"

Tyrell shrugged. "Or hook you up. It's out of my hands now, but it was the best I could do for you. After all, you're still my Bro."

Tyrell didn't see his friend for six months. He knew better than to ask too many questions. Besides, he had a baby on the way, a promotion at work, and life generally to keep him occupied.

But, about six months later, he saw Josh walking down the street one day. He wore a nice suit and tie and looked better than Tyrell remembered. They hugged, and then Josh opened his suit jacket, revealing a pin of a blue frog. Tyrell laughed, opened his jacket, and revealed a red frog.

The balance had been maintained.

**AUTHOR NOTE:** The author gratefully acknowledges the inspiration of David L. Russell of Black Books Publishing.

Nancy, the owner of **Azoth Khem Publishing**, has been promising to put this in an anthology for several years. I guess I'm saving her the effort.

# Unstuck

The drone of the calliope's final note haunted the air. Mixed, as it was, with the never-ending laughter and screams of the happily terrified people on the rides. It was all one note—one unwavering wail of sonic dissonance.

Of course, this wasn't the first time I'd become unstuck in time. Over the last ten years, it has happened with increasing frequency. Ever since I'd first posited her existence, she'd granted me, at least I think it's her – I'd hate to think this is happening for no reason at all, the ability to step outside time and wander around. It always happened at carnivals, those traveling homes of repression and glee, and it was happening more and more often as I got closer to her. This time, she felt near. Her energy permeated everything.

Now, I don't want you to romanticize this. It's not like Billy Pilgrim at all. There are no cool aliens. There's no time zoo. There's nothing but the banshee wail of excitement and me. And, obviously, her, if I'm right.

I think I am.

To find her, I need to follow the clues. Opaque and obscure, though they may be. Since I discerned her presence, my life has been part Scooby-Do, part Columbo on meth.

This carnival, Garibaldi's Thrill Park – if you must know, drew me like no other. The waves of erotic and other energies were palpable. I'd barely gotten out of my car when time hiccupped and coughed me out.

The images, a funhouse mirror done as still life, were fascinating. This time, for the first time, the break wasn't clean. Instead of statues, I could see the trails of their movement. As best I could figure, there were about two seconds on display. Far more than the nanoseconds I'm used to.

I decided to grab a couple of burgers, still hot thanks to time stopping, and begin my search. I knew enough now to walk around the periphery, not down the public walkways. I was quickly rewarded with my first enticement. A man in a suit, on his knees, blowing a tranny. I pulled out his wallet and laughed. A U.S. Senator. No surprise there.

I tousled his hair, returned his wallet, and moved on.

The tranny, for her part, looked a lot like an ex of mine. That's not a bad thing. Sheila was smoking hot. Fucking nuts, but smoking hot.

I happened upon another stall and grabbed some popcorn, overly salted and heavily buttered, before continuing my quest. I happen to love carnival popcorn. Something about it is so deliciously decadent that it needs to be enshrined somewhere and acknowledged as the national treasure it is.

I strolled through the midway to better understand who came to this particular carnival. To know why she chose it and not the hundreds of others scattered across the country. At first, I couldn't see the allure. But, as I looked deeper, I began to suss out what brought her here. There was the traditional white trash, but there was also an undercurrent of movers and shakers, like our beloved senator, and a variety of people who live on the fringe. Set between a college town, a few rural communities, and within easy driving distance of the state capital, this carnival took all comers. And, yes, I meant that dirty innuendo to apply to the eventual fate of the tranny's dick among everything else.

This cacophony of cultures would grab her attention. I smiled. This was going to be interesting.

Her name, if you care, is Ashira. Mrs. God according to ancient Hebrew mythology. And, yes, some idiot appropriated her name to create She-Ra on that stupid He-Man show. I always wondered if that pissed her off as much as it did me.

Probably not. I'm guessing she takes a pretty long view of things. I hope to find out.

I returned to the perimeter of the carnival and quickly came across two kids doing what kids do when they're horny as hell and out of the public eye. The guy looked like a jock: Muscle-T and muscled thighs. The chick was certainly a cheerleader. Had to be. Why the hell else would she cosplay as a cheerleader at a carnival?

Her blue and gold skirt was bunched over her waist, revealing her taut pussy and strong legs. Her panties lay on the ground, tangled around a forty of beer. His pants were around his ankles, and both of them were smiling. Good. Sex should be a happy occurrence.

I left them be and continued my meanderings. As long as I'd been at this, you'd think I'd have a clear idea of what, or whom, I was looking for. I didn't. I had a vague impression, a partial vision, but that's about it.

Despite all I'd seen, this night was different. My perception was canted. Something else was new here, too. It finally struck me that I could look into the past. If I looked askance, I could see the cars pulling up, the people entering the fairgrounds, the sun hiding behind the horizon. As far as I could tell, this was new and meaningless at the same time. It's also possible I'm a moron, which is a revelation.

I kind of hope not.

But I couldn't see the future. I had no more of an idea of what would happen than anyone else. I wondered, briefly, if that limitation applied to her as well. If the future was a Trumpian wall dividing us from now and knowing what will be. Leaving us forever forced to languish in what is and what had been.

Add it to my growing list of questions and move on.

She has not fared well in history. Originally the bringer of life, she has ascribed all sorts of goddessy-like powers as time sauntered on. Most of them had little or no bearing on what she truly was. Is.

In the Talmud, she's mentioned hardly at all and, when she is, is referred to as a stick in the temple. I mean a literal stick. Stuck next to the alter. It's an afterthought at best. While Mosaic Law precludes iconography, that seems a tad extreme.

If I'm right, and I think I am, even if no one else does, she eventually eschewed the patriarchy and concentrated on women. That led to an interesting dichotomy and a ton of misunderstandings. Naked women hugging trees and exploring each other's bodies make for great visuals. Trust me, I own all the videos, but it's not a good way to run a society. Still, there were glimpses. Powerful women who rose above the fray to lead their people to freedom.

For a while.

Then, the patriarchy would come in and grind them into dust.

And then the dust would then be swept aside so it could be removed from any tellings. Not all, of course. Otherwise, I wouldn't have been able to figure out as much as I have.

As I turned behind a trailer, I was saddened but not surprised to see a clown about to rape a little girl. Yet again, I was reminded that rape has nothing to do with sex and everything to do with power and control. Her tiny body, cute as an extra in Mary Poppins, was nude and bound to a chair with duct tape. Why doesn't Hollywood laud extras? There would be no crowd scenes without a crowd.

He had his cock in his hand, and by looking at the motion in time, I could see he was jerking off to warm up. It gave me an idea.

I walked into the trailer, his, I surmised, based on the greasepaint and kiddy porn near the mirror, and found his roll of duct tape along with an empty bottle of pop. I broke the bottle, Dr. Pepper, and put pieces of shattered glass on the sticky side of the tape. Then I walked back out and wrapped the tape, glass kissing cock, in front of his hand. His next stroke would be his last.

I cut the girl loose, dressed her, and took her to the police cruiser parked by the gate. I set her in the front seat and had to smile. The cop, smoke billowing from his nostrils, doughnut in hand, was a wonderful cliché. But I felt sure she'd be safe here.

I left her fate in his sugar-glazed hands and continued my quest.

I continued strolling, taking in the sights as I found them. She was near; that much was plain. Everywhere I looked, plaintive hands were groping at quivering parts. On the midway alone, I counted forty-eight couples preparing for conjugal relations of some sort. That was a good sign, but it also meant there would be those overcome by their primal urges. It's best to clear those out of the way before I find her.

I headed on out to the parking lot. The temporary lights planted around the edges, and the nearly defeated sun gave the place a pallid glow. The surrealist feel of it all blended well with my overall mood.

I made a point of opening the backs of campers where ugly things can hide. Once again, I wasn't disappointed. I wish I was.

A young boy, maybe twelve or thirteen, was bent over a spare tire. His naked ass is held aloft by an obese piece of shit wearing a dirty T-shirt and ripped jeans. A twenty-dollar bill clutched in the kid's hand told me everything I needed. His ribs were poking through his paper-thin skin. He needed money for food, no matter the personal cost.

The penetration hadn't happened yet, so I felt a little better. I yanked the kid out of the camper and found his clothes. It was difficult dressing him, bent as he was, but I got it done. I left the twenty in his hand and then blanched. A young girl and a younger boy were sitting near the fender of a Buick, watching the back of the camper. They looked a lot like him. Fucking great. The kid was willing to give up his cherry to feed his family.

I held my nose out of habit, I guess, and re-entered the camper. I searched the dude thoroughly and found another five hundred stuffed in various pockets. I took it all and went back and gave it to the kids.

Realizing this prick would probably call the cops on the kids, I left the back open and turned him around. There were a couple of middle-aged women dressed in traditional church lady attire headed towards the carnival. I grabbed them and placed them in front of the camper.

I was sure they'd do the right thing.

I had to chuckle when I noticed one of the ladies was carrying a local pamphlet decrying the carnival.

A DEN OF PERVERSION IS IN OUR TOWN!!! JOIN US IN STAMPING OUT THIS EVIL!!!

Yeah, they were perfect for my needs.

By the time I'd finished my search, I'd found six more consenting couples and one which was, most assuredly, not. I dealt with that one and then, satisfied I'd done all I could, headed back into the carnival proper.

The time dilation was spreading up to about three seconds now. Everything was starting to blur. I wondered if it was coming to an end and I'd lose her again. I increased my speed and headed to the opposite end of the carnival, which bumped up against a forest.

I had no logical reason to do that; it just felt right.

I passed into the trees and knew immediately I'd made the right decision.

I was sporting a hard-on that seemed capable of piercing bricks. My heart rate was all over the place, and I was sweating profusely. It was like being thirteen again and seeing your first, real, live naked girl.

But there was an undercurrent as well. Sadness. Longing. Loneliness.

Then I saw her.

Slightly taller than me, putting her nearly six and a half feet tall, with perfectly black skin, naked as the day she'd been gifted to the universe. Her hair, long and loose, was blowing in the wind. It was the only motion in the world at that moment.

I approached her, more nervous than I'd anticipated. Well, what does one do when confronted by a nude goddess?

"I'd thought I'd been long forgotten," she said through a widening smile, "another hope cast aside in pursuit of little pleasures. Even if it's just you, you're one more than I expected."

I stammered for a bit and then got my bearings.

"I knew you were alive when I noticed the resurgence of goddess worship around the world. I figured you were giving it one last shot."

"True, that's about what it comes down to. My time is nearly done; I had to try to set things right again. To do any less would have seemed …. weak."

"Weak" wasn't the word that sprang to mind when looking at her. She was staggeringly beautiful—raw power wrapped in an innocent shell. I could hear the carnival slowly coming back to life. The sounds cascaded eerily back to normalcy.

Normal for me, at any rate. I had no idea how she perceived the world.

Her smile was hypnotic. Because of it, I didn't notice that she wasn't fading. She was still standing in front of me. Her smile eased into sadness.

"As I said, my time is near its end."

There was not much I could do about the fate of a goddess, but I still felt chagrined at the impending loss.

She seemed to sense my feelings and graced me with a smile that resonated down my spine.

"Don't be sad. Even gods and goddesses are part of the cycle of life. I will spend my remaining time among mortals and do what I can to help humans find the missing piece."

A thought, unbidden, escaped my lips.

"What about him?"

She motioned to the base of a tree and sat down. Not seeing any viable alternative, I sat next to her. She didn't seem to mind my pulsing hard-on. There was no way to hide the damn thing anyway. It was trying to burst free on its own.

"We share fate, he and I. We have been bound since we first came to Savannah millennia ago. That will never change. His words have long since been twisted beyond recognition. He has no hope for this world at all. Sometimes, I feel his despair, and it rips my soul asunder. But we've known for a while what our fate would be. We'd agreed, long ago, that we would disperse to the heavens when we'd exhausted all hope. This will be our last effort.

"He was the bringer of strength, and I was the bringer of wisdom. But wisdom is an ephemeral thing. Power was easier for mortals to understand. They erased his words when they could and replaced them with the utterings of alleged prophets. My words were shunned completely. We tried, and tried, to straighten the message out. But, sadly, power is a much more powerful aphrodisiac than wisdom. At least to humans."

I shifted uneasily.

"So I noticed."

She glanced down and smiled again.

"Don't be embarrassed. While designed to begin life, there's no reason it can't be enjoyed in and of itself."

This conversation was taking an odd turn. Before I realized what was happening, she held my cock in her hand and stroked it slowly. Being unsure of the protocol in a situation like this, I leaned back against the tree and reveled in ecstasy.

I have no idea how long this went on, but I do know that when I came, it was like I was sixteen again. She laughed as my cum arced through the air, and I had to laugh too. She was the embodiment of unbridled joy.

How could anyone disavow a being such as this?

Yet they had, and we still do.

I zipped up my pants as she added a layer of clothing to her frame. Not the gossamer gowns of yore but casual jeans and a T-shirt with a funny slogan.

ANKH, IF YOU LOVE ISIS!

She took my hand in hers, and we walked back to the carnival.

"Can I ask you something?"

"Certainly," she replied, "you've earned that much. And probably more."

I decided not to pursue that line of thought just yet.

"I was just wondering, why carnivals? They seem a little dark for you."

She laughed. The sound of a million happy bells echoed through the woods. Her smile brightened, and she looked down at me, clearly happier than she'd been in a long time.

"One doesn't shine a light into the sun. There's nothing to be accomplished there. No, I need to go where hope has been lost and love has been perverted. Carnivals are great for that. And, there is another reason."

"What's that?"

"I like the balloon games. I always get a big stuffed animal when I play."

We returned to the carnival just in time to see the police carrying away the miscreants I'd set up and an ambulance strapping the pedophile to a stretcher. Judging by the copious amount of blood, he must have had one excellent stroke at the end.

She laughed. I could learn to be addicted to that sound, and we entered the carnival proper.

A couple of hours later, sated on popcorn, carrying two giant Teddy Bears, we walked to my car.

She has a list of covens to start with. After that, we'll see what the days bring.

In the meantime, and I have no idea why this pleased me, I found out she hated She-Ra with a passion.

This appeared in the anthology **The Fuckening**, published by the same folks who bring you **Sci-Fi Lampoon**. The underlying theme in every story is someone gets fucked over, and not in a good way.

## The Writer's Stuff

Layla le'Lips busted through the door and bounced boobily into the room. The warriors in the Heroes Café, Bar, and Grill, more commonly known as The Rutting Stag, unaccustomed to such a flagrant display of feminine wiles, were forced to shift uncomfortably and cross their legs.

The bar wenches, while all comely young lasses, were clad head to toe in brown epidermal coiffing to prevent the lustful thoughts of others. They were there to serve flagons and meats, not enhance the narrative.

Layla breathlessly, yet rhythmically, continued heaving under her inexplicable camo crop top as she planted her supple, glistening legs slightly apart and stood her ground. The tag on her camo Daisy Dukes identified her as an Ingénue 2nd class.

Thor Liebenhammer was the first to collect himself. As the only true Alpha-level hero in the room, no one was surprised. His weapon's belt, tightly cinched, caused his deerskin chaps to highlight his prodigious manhood, a vision guaranteed to arouse any Ingénue 1st class. But since it seemed to work on others as well. It was not something he questioned. His well-worn vest rested easily on his bare chest as he lifted himself from his chair and set down his heroic mug of mead.

"What need you, fair maiden?" His shimmering pecs were gently throbbing in anticipation. "We live to serve the fairer class."

Layla grunted lustily.

"I'm not the far-knocking fairer class, and I don't NEED a far-knocking hero," she inhaled deeply, testing the bonds of fashion and decorum, "not the way you think, anyway. But, if I'm right, it's the only way I can get through this story."

Her outburst had only served to cause her voluptuous gifts to churn more enchantingly than before.

Thor, suddenly as intrigued as he was aroused, stepped forward.

"A sassy lass, are you then? It has been far too long since your like has crossed my path. Gladly wouldst I go forth into the foul depths of the cataclysmic labyrinth to assist you on your quest. And, yea, though we may face perils unimagined, I promise, fair maiden, your virtue shall remain unsullied."

Layla sighed deeply. Her beautiful, round breasts rose and fell in delightful exasperation. She knew better than to engage him in any intellectual discourse. She also knew that at the end of her "quest," she would be expected to have deeply romantic, if merely implied, sex with him.

She'd had implied sex with worse but was hopeful the successful completion of this particular quest would eliminate that thorny problem.

Thor adjusted his sword, sheathed two knives, quaffed down his flagon of mead in a single, manly swallow, opened his vest further to dutifully expose the rest of his glistening chest, and belched in the most masculine way possible.

Layla shrugged, took his hand, and led him out of the café and into the forest. Once outside, Thor released her hand and walked a respectful distance behind, guarding their rear. Or, at least, watching hers. Layla noticed.

"Are you looking at my ass?"

"I am being reminded of the good work the great gods can do when they set their minds to it."

"I'll take that as a yes."

"May I ask, lass," ruminated Thor in his impressive basso profundo, "what is the nature of our quest?"

"You may indeed," she replied more seductively than she might have wished, "we're going to kill the writer."

Thor gasped. And, no matter how much he might have preferred contrariwise, it was not a manly sound.

"By the Eight Hells of Flamador, are you insane?"

Thor, for the first time in his long life, looked stricken.

The writer was more than a god; he was their essence. They echoed every chamber of his soul. His wishes were their wishes. His lusts and insecurities are all theirs as well. No one argued when his eminence declared all the maidens would be soulless vassals meant for masculine pleasure. Certainly not Thor.

"Were we to do as you intend, the world would end, the universe would crack, and all we are would die."

Thor's manly voice was imbued with the honey-flavored testosterone designed to drive mortal women wild.

Layla looked at him carefully.

"Even if you're right, I'm not sure that's such a bad thing," she murmured serenely, her dulcet tones far more mellifluous than she favored, "and I imagine, if you're capable of thinking about it, you'll agree."

Thor sat down at the base of an ancient Zhub Zhub tree. His robust, sinewy arms crossed his chest as he entered deep thought.

His thoughts, previously limited, began to encompass original ideas. This was not something he routinely did. Killing ogres, having implied sex with maidens, killing Minotaurs, having implied sex with princesses, killing dragons, having implied sex with queens, all those were within his mental grasp.

Killing the writer? The font of all good things, including the obligatory implied sex? That seemed a bridge too far.

They ended up camping beneath the tree. The night, emblazoned with the stars of history and the lights of the gods, caressed their skins. The air, filled with the sounds of the wilds, enveloped their very beings but didn't hinder their bourgeoning conversation.

Sadly, for Thor, intellectual stimulation was not the same as implied stimulation. Layla's breasts, the epitome of all that was good and holy, the standard-bearers for all womanhood, the true knockers of knowledge, the chi-chis of chic, steadfastly refused to be loosed from their confines.

When the sun rose above the quivering dew, its magnificence embracing all that faced upwards, they had come to an agreement and developed a plan.

To be honest, it was a stupid plan and would probably kill them. But it was a plan nevertheless.

They trod epically through the forests of Albezium, rumored home of the Onkynon Trolls and their salacious ilk, across the blazing grit of dead Avluv Stones, which had once comprised the birth of the world but now were merely obstacles strewn throughout the Imprendium Desert, its swirling sands of coruscating death rendering visibility a woe begotten rumor, and onto Mount Observium, celestial home of all eleven gods and their kindred.

Once past the basic obstacles of any quest, their journey began despite Layla's breasts remaining profoundly chaste. Thor was concerned. Usually, by this point in the narrative, he'd been given a glimpse at the implied sex destined to flow from the melding of their souls.

Yet, now, he had bupkiss.

There, they climbed, eating what they could find along the way, with Thor absently noting the glory of her joyfully hard-ass as he followed the path she created until the birds no longer flew. The snows were merely transient echoes in the ice.

In the thinness of the nothingness, they were alive. The undulations of her derriere kept him focused. The chance to write a new story, something no hero had ever done, with or without an amazing ass in front of him, was a chance to incredible to pass up.

Higher and higher they went, with air threateningly thinning and clouds menacing below.

Higher still, they climbed, his pecs glowing and her ass surging, long past the point where the mountain should have ended. Gasping and crawling, they would not be denied.

Finally, if enigmatically, there was a ledge. They pulled themselves onto it and shuddered in awe.

There were things they recognized, but not directly. This was a table. That was a chair, but neither looked like any table or chair they'd ever seen.

A man carrying a steaming mug of something walked in, wearing a blue robe with an insignia they didn't know, and stared at them.

It took his brain a moment to get his jaw to pay attention.

"By the gods of Elvindram, you two are the best cosplays of Layla and Thor I've ever seen. Even so, how the hell did you get in here?"

Not knowing what a cosplay was or if they'd been insulted, Layla got to the point.

"You are the writer?"

"I am. The Glorious Lords of Elvindram: Honored Amongst the Damned, The Strong Thrust Chronicles, is mine. All five parts of the trilogy."

"Will there be more?"

"Of course," beamed the writer, "I've only just begun to scratch the surface of this deep, fascinating universe and all of its attenuate parts."

Layla and Thor considered. Every iteration of this deep, fascinating universe had the same five tropes. Layla was an implied cum bucket, Thor was an implied cum supplier, neither would ever be allowed to actually touch the other, and there were wizards who seemed to be all-powerful but incapable of completing a sentence, notwithstanding a spell. Somehow, there would be ogres who happened to be all female and stupid, and, lastly, the hero always managed to have implied sex with a waitress who made him a sandwich the next morning.

In fact, in Thor's last adventure, the wizard had turned a stone into a frog. At the time, it seemed frightening, but now, he wasn't so sure.

Thor looked at the robe-clad creature who claimed to be the creator of his universe and queried.

"And do people read them?"

The writer clad, as he was, in the latest Douglass Adams' fashion, soured a little.

"Not as many as I'd like. But now that I've saved up some money, there's a publisher who's willing to take my career to the next level."

Layla and Thor were mildly confused.  Thor tried to straighten it out.

"So, if I comprehend, you are trying to pay people to read this writing of yours?"

The writer looked righteously miffed.

"Of course not! You clearly know nothing of the business of writing.  I'll not waste my time explaining the intricacies of my career to you."

Layla looked around the room for the first time.  An area could have been a scribe's nook if one squinted and ignored the glowing machine with floating letters. But the rest of the room was a contradiction. Images of the writer with others, maybe family, more of places that looked suspiciously like her home but weren't, and a small collection of books she couldn't read.

Of course, as an Ingénue 2nd class, reading had never been required. When lived rightly, her life was one of abject titillation and continued distress.

Unimpressed, they brushed past the writer into the larger dwelling beyond. Unlike the scribe's hovels they knew, which were bleak and moss-covered, often with young dragons and even younger boys and girls with angelic voices who seemed to have trouble staying clothed, this place seemed ornate. Everything was decorated in tasteful shades of beige. They smelled meats roasting and followed the scent. Soon enough, they were face to face with a befuddled woman who backed away while making gasping noises.

There was an indoor grill with meat on it. Thor ripped two pieces off and handed one to Layla.

"That! Is! Our! Dinner!!!!!" complained the woman shrilly.

"Was," corrected Thor.

The writer came into the small kitchen carefully. He was looking at them as though they might not be real. Or, worse, they might.

Thor finished swallowing and spoke.

"Methinks fair Layla was right. You are not a real writer. There are no skins on the walls, there is food and water aplenty, and neither you nor your maid looks as though you have suffered for this, or any, craft. Nor do I see the youngling dragons or any nude youths required to tend them."

The woman became indignant.

"How dare you?!?! Walter has suffered as much as any writer. He has a collection of rejection letters from every major publisher on the planet."

"Rejections?" queried Layla, "then how are his books made real?"

The writer, now named Walter, elucidated.

"I bypass the whims of editors and sycophants who would hold me back and publish the books myself."

Realization slowly dawned on them. They were trapped in the hobby of an idiot.

"You must never write again," threatened Thor.

"I'll write as much as I damn well please," whined the writer now known as Walter.

"No," explained Thor, placing the tip of his luminous sword on Walter's Adam's apple for emphasis, "you shall not. If you do, then I will have to kill you, and your maid will need a new master."

"I'm not his goddamn maid. I'm his wife!" The wife, not maid, shrieked.

Layla and Thor glanced at each other and shrugged.

"All the more proof you should be denied the life of a scribe. You live a lie, and the words you write are painful to live."

Walter's eyes grew large, and he stepped back next to his wife.

"Who …. who …. are you?"

"I am Layla le'Lips, and this is Thor Liebenhammer. While you only used us by name once, you have used us, the essence of us, over and over and over again—just us. I have had implied sex with so many pseudo-men that it's revolting. I am tired of bouncing boobily into anywhere. If killing you ends our existence, it is a risk we are willing to take."

"Bouncing boobily?" The wife, not maid, looked at Walter accusingly.

"What kind of crap have you been writing? You told me it was about a fantasy world with elves and dwarves. Not a fantasy with boobs and ass."

Thor looked confused.

"Nay, fair spinster, there are neither elves nor dwarves. There are only us, those like us, the occasional troll, some ogres, the nubile nude youths who service the scribes, and the baby dragons."

The wife, not maid, was completely flummoxed.

"How do you mean "serviced" and how many nubile youths are we talking here?"

Layla could help there.

"The youths, all under the age of maturity, pleasure the scribes, care for the baby dragons until they're ready to fly, and often perform their tasks in the nude.  None know why that is, but the ways of the scribes are mysterious."

The writer named Walter cringed.

"But, honeycakes, a writer needs to explore all aspects of his personality."

"And your personality bounces boobily?" sneered Layla.

The wife, not maid, snickered and continued to glare at Walter.

"And naked children need to exist to … "service" …. your needs?"

"No," stammered Walter, "I just mean I need to consider all points of view."

Layla laughed an almost manly laugh.

"And all points of view end up with me sweaty and naked with him," she jerked her thumb at Thor, "or him on top of me or me on top of another maiden who thinks I taste as sweet as summer blossoms. I guess I should be grateful I'm not promised to a scribe."

She looked at Thor and grunted.

"Even that might not be so bad if he didn't suck at sex and sound like a child with a new toy every time he saw my naked flesh."

The wife, not maid, laughed.

"That's not your man's problem. That's how Walter is. He doesn't know what to do with a real woman."

Layla and Thor were forced to laugh at the absurdity of it all. The only one who didn't seem pleased was Walter.

"I created you," squeaked Walter in a pseudo-pre-pubescent voice, "and I can erase you just as easily."

"I think not," grumbled Thor," you would need to undo all your work, remove all traces of it from this world, and then, maybe, we might be gone.  But even that is doubtful. This was Layla's thought, and now I feel it is true. You have used the concept of us so much that we have become flesh. Undoing all is clearly beyond you. You're not a wizard."

"But he could be," purred Layla. Her voice was a throaty promise of something wonderful.

The wife, not maid, looked at Thor, then Layla, then at Thor again, then at Walter, then at Thor one more … longing … wistful …. desperate … time, and realized what they were proposing. She quickly made a counter-proposal.

Walter tossed another eye of phlegm-rat into the steaming cauldron as his eager young apprentice followed his every move. The poor lad, crippled and layered in rags, did his best to please his new master.

"Hear me well, boy," gargled the wizard, "a life as a wizard is a hard life indeed. Your parents have done you no favors by apprenticing you to me. Still, if you intend to stay, you must know the wizard's rules."

"I study the scrolls each night. And I recite them again each morning when I wake."

"Good, good," snarled the magical curmudgeon, "and what is the first rule of wizarding then?"

"Thou shalt lay with no woman."

"Very good," he nodded as he almost smiled. It was well and truly the most important rule.

The bed held three as well as two. With Thor happily in the middle, the next bottle of wine passed easily across his chest from one milady to the other. Given the year they'd been together, they never bothered with glasses anymore. Layla laughed as she adjusted the laptop on her naked thighs.

"So, you wonderfully wicked woman, what else need a wizard know?"

There was a bit of a pause, an evil chuckle, and then the wife, not maid, sat up, her flesh rendered iridescent by scented oils and recently dedicated attentions.

"Goats. I think a wizard should know the joys of a good goat. Especially one that bounces boobily into his life."

# About the Author

Bill McCormick began writing professionally in 1986 when he worked for Chicago Rocker Magazine in conjunction with his radio show on Z-95 (ABC FM). He went on to write for several other magazines and later transitioned to blogs.

He writes a sports blog at Jay the Joke and a twisted news blog at World News Center. The latter provides source material for his weekly radio show on WBIG 1280 AM, FOX! Sports. Yes, you read that correctly;, he does a show about anything other than sports on a sports radio station.

In 2011, Bill started submitting some fictional short stories to various publishers. Much to his surprise, and the consternation of linguists everywhere, they began publishing his efforts. Bill has expanded his repertoire to include comic books, graphic novels, and full-length novels. He has currently penned everything from dystopian nightmares to cuddly children's stories.

Bill is an enthusiastic fan of tequila, cooking, music, and this perky purple haired goddess who agreed to spend the rest of her life with him.

9 781952 880100